HER FUGITIVE HEART

HER FUGITIVE HEART

THE RAVI PI SERIES

ADI TANTIMEDH

LEOPOLDO & CO
—
ATRIA
New York London Toronto Sydney New Delhi

LEOPOLDO
& CO
ATRIA

An Imprint of Simon & Schuster, Inc.
1230 Avenue of the Americas
New York, NY 10020

First Leopoldo & Co/Atria Paperback edition April 2019

LEOPOLDO & CO/ATRIA PAPERBACK and colophon are trademarks of
Simon & Schuster, Inc.

For information about special discounts for bulk purchases, please contact
Simon & Schuster Special Sales at 1-866-506-1949 or business@simonandschuster.com.

The Simon & Schuster Speakers Bureau can bring authors to your live event. For more informa-tion, or to book an event, contact the Simon & Schuster Speakers Bureau at 1-866-248-3049 or visit our website at www.simonspeakers.com.

Manufactured in the United States of America

10 9 8 7 6 5 4 3 2 1

Library of Congress Cataloging-in-Publication Data

Names: Tantimedh, Adi, author.
Title: Her fugitive heart / Adi Tantimedh.
Description: First Leopoldo & Co. / Atria Paperback edition. | New York :
Leopoldo & Co / Atria, 2019. | Series: The Ravi Pi series.
Identifiers: LCCN 2018024914 (print) | LCCN 2018026048 (ebook) | ISBN 9781501130656 (ebook) | ISBN 9781501130632 (paperback) | ISBN 9781501130656 (ebook)
Subjects: LCSH: Private investigators—Fiction. | GSAFD: Mystery fiction. | Suspense fiction.
Classification: LCC PS3620.A6955 (ebook) | LCC PS3620.A6955 H464 2019 (print) |
DDC 813/.6—dc23
LC record available at https://lccn.loc.gov/2018024914

ISBN 978-1-5011-3063-2
ISBN 978-1-5011-3065-6 (ebook)

To my sister Orathai, who always does the right thing through thick and thin.

*I*f you're reading this, I might be dead.

Well, hopefully not. I don't mean to be melodramatic, but you never know. This is the third book I'm about to fill. That much has happened in the last three years. This one is about how everything finally went to shit.

Julia is checking this. Sometimes she writes some of it, fills in the gaps I left out.

So. Where to start?

Oh yes.

I could still see gods. They weren't going away. They were a part of me and they always showed up to watch whatever I'd gotten myself into and comment on it.

I was still working at Golden Sentinels Private Investigations and Security Agency. My colleagues were a bunch of brilliant, dangerous fuckups with nowhere else to go. My annus horribilis could be attributed almost entirely to them. Or rather, what our boss Roger Golden had us getting up to.

Yes, "annus horribilis." The poncy Latin term for "shit year," and there's no other description for what I just had. You can thank the Queen for introducing it into common use. Julia and everyone at the firm have said it put me in a dark mood for months, but I don't know how else to react to nearly getting murdered for no good reason by a bunch of idiots. If you can think of a better way to react and go about one's life after that kind of unnecessary trauma, I will make you my life coach.

This made both Julia and me decide it was more necessary than ever to have a record of everything we'd been doing in our job as investigators at the firm. We consulted with a lawyer and everything. Actually, we consulted with my friend David Okri, my old mate from university who got me this job at the firm in the first place, and he wouldn't stop nodding and saying "Absolutely! Record everything Roger made you do!" before recommending another lawyer to keep on retainer to avoid conflict of interest since he was Golden Sentinel's legal counsel. Then he told us he was getting a lawyer himself for when the shit hits the fan, not "if" but "when." It says something when your lawyer decides he needs a lawyer. Thanks, Roger.

Don't get me wrong. My colleagues and I were a fairly tight team. There were Ken and Clive, the ex-coppers and old-school bruisers, though their tendency to drop bodies and then try to hide them really bit me in the arse this past year. Mark Oldham, the melancholy genius investigator who was self-medicating his existential despair with all manner of psychoactive substances, both natural and man-made, added to my troubles. Benjamin Lee and his obsession with mischief and surveillance both nearly got me killed and saved my skin. Olivia Wong, our resident hacker and cybersecurity expert, was the only one who didn't land me in any shit, though she had plenty of her own shit to deal with. She's a banking heiress whose tycoon dad blacklisted her from the banking industry for hacking into the family business's security system years ago to prove it was insecure. Then of course there was our resident American, Marcie Holder, bringing in contract work from the CIA that always put us within a hairsbreadth of total fucking doom.

And did Roger, our boss, care? Did he hell. We came to realize that everything he did, everything he had us doing was to further his agenda of getting more money and power. Even Cheryl Hughes, who founded Golden Sentinels with him, was starting to get fed up with him and his various plots. This was already a tense year going in. David was certainly bearing all the stress from that.

The goddess Kali is sitting on the sofa and laughing at me right now. My patron goddess, not my choice, and I'm stuck with her. The other gods tend to follow when something happening to me interests them and they show up to be a Greek chorus to my predicaments. Shiva is always not far behind. He's the head of them all, so of course he comes along.

Oh, and I married Julia. That was a drama and a half. We'd come a long way since we first met. She was part of a case I was investigating, and became my girlfriend, then she became the case because of her sex addiction. Next thing I knew, Roger had hired her as an investigator because her English Rose looks gave her cover for getting into places and asking people questions, and for being the perfect honey trap. That made me worry because having a *sex addict pose as a femme fatale was like locking an alcoholic in a brewery, but she actually avoided sleeping with any of her marks because she had substituted the dangerous thrill-seeking stuff for sex. She saved emotional intimacy and actual sex for me. What a pair we made, a sex addict with a literature degree and a former religious scholar who hallucinated gods. When we decided to tie the knot, we told our parents, and Julia's parents immediately took the reins to plan the wedding. My parents were actually relieved that it fell to her parents to deal with the wedding ceremony, so no need for us to have a big fuck-off Indian wedding, since none of us wanted to spend over twenty grand and invite more than a hundred relatives over from India. We made my mother promise she was not going to borrow money for the wedding gifts since that was what had put me in the service of Mrs. Dhewan. Mrs. Dhewan was the neighborhood Asian housewife/mafia boss who had me doing the odd job for her and her mostly benign gang. Even so, planning the wedding was its own drama with Julia's mother doing it. At least getting married was the one good thing out of this fucked up year.*

Julia is telling me I'm rambling on and we should really get back to writing down what went down in the past year, so that's what I will now do.

No, the gods didn't put me up to this. The gods don't force me to do anything, yet I seem to end up doing whatever they want anyway, or whatever they find most amusing. It's all win-win for them, one big funny reality TV show they're bingeing on in real time. If I get killed, I don't think they'll even be sorry. They'll probably just go find some other poor bastard to follow. I'm just another puppet playing out a cosmic joke that's my life.

Julia is telling me I'm getting morbid again. Mental illness is no fun. Julia doesn't believe I'm mentally ill. She agrees with Mark, who thinks the gods are really here, that they're really some kind of consciousness from someplace else trying to communicate with us and I'm the conduit. My father says I might be a shaman. What good are shamans in the modern day with all that noise from the media and the Internet and no one will really believe you, eh? Honestly.

All right, all right. Sorry, Julia. Let's get on with it.

So, onwards and upwards.

I really hope I'm still alive as you read this . . .

FACE ON, FACE OFF, KARMA

ONE

We'd settled into a groove at Golden Sentinels Private Investigations.

The usual cases clearing up messes for celebrities and rich clients. The uptick in revenge porn had actually been very lucrative for us, since we were getting more and more female clients whose exes had posted intimate photos and videos of them out of spite. Ken and Clive were very happy because it gave them an excuse to go after awful bastards and beat the shit out of them.

"This is Ravi." Marcie Holder brought the client to me. "He'll be coordinating the team on your case."

Bella Hasterley (I've changed her name because we're supposed to protect our clients' privacy) was that rare TV star and model that did not have on her phone any naked selfies or videos of her having sex with her boyfriend, which was a minor miracle for celebrities in this day and age. She also had two-factor authentication and additional PINs that had kept her phone and social media accounts from getting hacked. I might not have been a fan of her movies or TV roles, but I could at least respect her security consciousness. Given the number of celebrity clients who came to us because their photos and videos had been stolen and shared, Bella was a rare case. Yet she had discovered a video posted online of her having loud, noisy, messy, violent sex. One of her fans on social media told her about it. As she pointed out when Marcie brought her to Golden Sentinels, she never filmed herself having sex or allowed any of her boyfriends to do it, so where the hell did this video come from?

She showed us the video, posted on free porn sites on the Internet. That was her, eyes blinking, face contorting, mouth moving and uttering the sounds on the video. But her body in the video had tattoos she didn't have.

"It's AI mapping," Olivia said.

This was the new form of revenge porn that was going to bring in even more lucrative business for us. It used a computer program to graft someone's face onto a porn video. The program was released to open source tech forums that let anyone with a bit of coding know-how study the face of a person from the videos they appeared in and map that face into any other video. What the script kiddie punters liked to do was take their favorite celebrities' faces and put them onto the bodies of porn stars fucking in videos. This wasn't a simple bit of Photoshop cutting and pasting, but a more sophisticated product that allowed the face grafted into the video to turn and change expressions naturally over the original face. You needed lots of preexisting videos of the face you wanted in order to have the AI map it from as many angles and movements as possible. After the face was grafted into the new video, there was still a lot of fixing needed to make the transition look seamless. It was tedious work that only the truly dedicated or obsessed would bother with, and there were plenty of those buggers out there for this stuff. Only an experienced coder could make the face look better than a grotesque distorting blob out of a Francis Bacon painting, though it was still far from perfect. If you couldn't tell if it was real, there were already programs and AIs out there that detected any alterations in videos.

I wasn't any kind of hacker or expert in that sort of thing. Roger had put me on this because I was a pretty face for the female client to feel comfortable with. He encouraged me to flirt with such clients, but I refused. For some clients, merely smiling and saying something reassuring was already considered flirtation. The whole office looked like a womb-like tech start-up here in Farringdon, designed with the best feng shui principles, the brightest colors and components, to make visitors feel as comfortable as possible. I was one of those components. Roger had said that I worked well as the face of an investigation like this one since I would present a façade of normality, because everyone else working on it was mad as a bag of hammers. Marcie would use her experience as a PR agent—this case had come via her contacts in the business, after all—to play best friend to the client. Marcie and I were basically there to hold Bella's hand while Benjamin and Olivia set to work, with Ken and Clive standing by in case they were needed for old-school footwork. Mark was off helping the Mexican ambassador on a personal matter since he was on retainer. They were probably off somewhere sharing a spliff together. Julia was spending the afternoon at her weekly group therapy. Cheryl sat at her desk, quietly keeping an eye on everything to keep it from spinning out of control.

Basically, I was the investigator wrangler here.

"My tits look better than that!" Bella said. "And this girl has way more cellulite than me! It's an insult that whoever made this couldn't even pick a better body substitute!"

Then Olivia and Benjamin broke the video down into its component code and looked over it, which is painstaking work to those of us not used to scanning lines of numbers and symbols.

"See that watermark in the video code?" Benjamin said. "It's in a lot of these fake celeb sex vids lately. It's the work of one bloke. Like an artist signin' his paintings."

Of course Benjamin had seen enough porn videos to recognize individual watermark codes. He'd probably catalogued them all by now. And not just for work.

TWO

It was a piece of piss for Olivia to just trace the ISP of the account that posted the video, then get the email addresses linked to that ISP so we could review them and find where he—for it was usually a "he"—got the video from. Then Olivia traced the source of the video to another email address, then another; the video passed between dozens of collectors. We also looked on the Dark Web and found the email address for a coder who created fake porn videos for hire, and whose videos bore the watermark Benjamin recognized. He advertised that he used the new algorithm to create those fake porn videos using the faces of celebrities and offered to put anyone's face on a porn video for commission. We then reviewed his email correspondence to cross-reference the email addresses of his customers. Unsurprisingly, Olivia found with the coder Bella's ex-boyfriend's emails where they negotiated the fee for the fake video. The coder programmed the AI to study Bella's face from footage of her various television shows, talk show appearances, and spots on the red carpet at premieres. Then the coder had the AI map her face from those videos and graft it onto the face of the porn actress in the sex video. We presented the trail to our client, in case she wished to take this to the police.

"I knew it was him!" Bella said. "Spiteful git with a steroid problem and cocaine habit! Failed wannabe reality TV show contestant!"

She could bring formal charges against him since this fell under UK revenge porn laws, harassment laws, and altered image laws. David would later get together with Bella's lawyer to go through the ins and outs of the laws and what was prosecutable and help them draft their briefs. One more service for Cheryl to put on Bella's bill. Whether the ex could be successfully prosecuted was another issue, though. Marcie, who was friends with Bella's PR people, advised them on the best statements they could make to the press.

"Talk about it as being like sexual assault and how a woman's right to control her privacy and sexuality now has to include her right to control her own images," Marcie said. It was all about optics these days, often quite literally. We were in the business of helping our clients control their narratives, after all.

Bella's lawyer could send injunctions to all the websites that hosted the video to have them taken down, so within a day, copies of the video disappeared from all the known streaming sites. We explained to Bella that anything posted on the Internet was forever, so while her lawyers could continue to make websites take the video down, it was never going to completely disappear from the Internet. It would still be shared on forums and pirate download sites, but no longer in the mainstream, a digital collector's item amongst Internet arseholes. We had driven the video underground. This would not be the last time we did this for a client this year.

We accomplished all this in less than three days without even needing to leave the office. No footwork, no knocking on doors, no making phone calls. All done online. This was what a lot of investigation work consisted of nowadays.

When we presented Bella with our findings, she was surprisingly calm as she said she still wanted her ex to pay in some way. That was Ken and Clive's cue, which they jumped at happily. They took it upon themselves to drive out to visit him. I should add that this was not officially part of the service we provided at Golden Sentinels. This was something Ken and Clive volunteered to do. Everyone needed a hobby, and this was theirs.

When they came back to the office the next day, they were in an awfully good mood.

"Arsehole said he was just being funny," Clive said.

"So we told him we were being funny, too, when we knocked his teeth out and smashed up his computer gear," Ken said.

Bella's ex wasn't going to report his assault to the police since he was beaten up for posting revenge porn, which was already against the law. Ken and Clive shared a hearty laugh over that. Little chance of them getting arrested because they still had mates in the police force, who often turned a blind eye to what they got up to at this firm. Marcie smiled at them indulgently. I often wondered what went through her mind. I always suspected she harbored a bit of bloodlust under all that superficial friendliness of hers. Bella's ex would try to sell his story about getting beaten up to the tabloids, but since he wasn't famous without her, and didn't have anything new about her to sell, they didn't bite. And anyway, the story would be that he was beaten up for posting a fake porn video of her, which just made him look like another newly toothless dickhead not even interesting enough for the tabloids. I'm not naming him here because he doesn't deserve any attention. We didn't have to tell Bella about the extra perk Ken and Clive performed for her as part of the Golden Sentinels package. She could guess perfectly well on her own. She was slightly horrified but didn't lose sleep over it.

Olivia decided as a bonus, and to put in some coding practice, to muck about with the face-mapping program. She found the original source code for the face-swapping algorithm—it was easy enough to find it on sites like PasteBin and GitHub—and rewrote it slightly with a bit of malware embedded in it. She proceeded to post it in all the usual places it could be found, with the claim that this was an update to patch out some bugs and make the swapped faces in the videos run more smoothly. She also spoofed the email address of a friend of the enterprising programmer, a fellow script kiddie, and sent him the new code saying it was a patch. The worm the code unleashed would bury itself in the computers of whoever downloaded it, install a program at the root, and delete the entire drive. We went on the Dark Web as a follow-up and saw that the friend's email and solicitation had been removed. We saw posts on the face-mapping fake video forums that he had to shut down his business because he got an extremely nasty worm that wrecked his entire computer setup. There were many panicked posts about Olivia's corrupt code messing up people's computers, warning users not to download the program. Even if anyone tried to go back and remove Olivia's malware, it would take them ages to unpick the code and rewrite it, which would require lots more testing to remove new bugs and glitches that came about, turning it into a full-time job. Probably too much hassle. Digital scorched earth.

This was poisoning of the well, karmic payback for anyone who touched it. Nobody who used this program had good intentions, ever.

And Olivia did this simply because she was bored. She indulged in an epic bout of digital social engineering to pass the time. Even though I didn't actually do anything other than talk the client through what was done, once again I'd unleashed chaos upon the world. I didn't do any of this or tell the others to do it, but I was party to all of it. Kali applauded behind my shoulder.

There would be other programs that mapped faces into videos to create fake videos of things that never happened, of course. The cat was well out of the bag. We were going to have our hands full with clients coming to us for help to prove these videos were fake, not just porn videos but also videos showing them doing things they never did, intended to fit them up. Politicians were getting done with their faces manipulated into inflammatory speeches they never made. They would come running to Roger in a panic, begging him to help prove it was bollocks. Roger was more than happy to lend a hand, of course.

"More business!" Roger said, rubbing his hands. "More favors done and owed! More friends in high places!"

More of our New Normal.

Bagalamukhi, goddess of deception and truth, danced around us whenever we got a case involving faked videos. She wore bright, vibrant colors in her designer clothes, and laughed in delight, reveling in the Internet feeding her more power than ever. She would stand over Benjamin and Olivia's shoulders as they worked away at their computers deciphering fake videos.

That this was considered normal and tame at Golden Sentinels spoke volumes about how far we'd come since I first started there. In the next few months, I would come to wish the insanity we dealt with in the rest of the year were *this* normal.

THE ENGLISH COUNTRY MANOR MYSTERY

ONE

"**D**o you ever wonder if we might be in the End Times, Ravi?" Mark Oldham asked.

"That's not really something I think about," I said.

"Look around us. It feels like we're all teetering on the edge of disaster. Economy's in the toilet. People going batshit in the streets at random. Politicians selling everyone out, even though they hire *us* to clean their dirty laundry and find dirt on their opponents . . . What do your gods say about that?"

"The gods don't tell me anything," I said. "And I don't make it a point to ask them."

"You really should talk to them, Ravi," Mark said. "Get closer to them."

"Don't start," I groaned. "They only make things more cryptic and confusing. And that makes me even more paranoid than I already am."

"So what do you do with them, then?"

"It's more like what I *don't* do."

"Well, that's already your default mode, mate."

"Mark, my main priority is to not piss them off. Anyone with half a brain knows not to piss off the gods. It never ends well."

"Fair enough." He shrugged and took another drag on his spliff before passing it to me.

"And I'm an atheist," I said. "They're just in my head."

"I like the way you parse that contradiction," he said.

Contradictions certainly defined my life. I wanted to be a good bloke, but my job was to do lots of bad things. I wanted a quiet life, but I was always diving face-first into chaos. As a good Hindu boy, I was expected to marry a nice girl, yet my wife-to-be was an adrenaline junkie and barely recovering sex addict in the deceptive guise of a blond English Rose. I'm an atheist, yet my head was filled with gods who wouldn't leave me alone. I was afraid I was going mad, yet I often found myself in situations where I felt like the sanest man in the room.

Story of my life.

Where Mark and I were, you wouldn't think the world was in chaos or falling apart. We were in the garden of a ten-acre estate owned by Stephanie Beam, widow of the late rock star Alfie Beam, who had bought this mansion and its very large garden in bucolic Sussex, half an hour away from Brighton. It was very much the picture of England's Green and Pleasant Land, far away from the woes of the present. Walking around this place, you could make yourself believe there were no council estates in London burning down, no amateur bombs going off in the Tube, no cars careening into crowds in tourist spots, no hypocritical government teetering on the brink of collapse, no surprise hurricanes sweeping through the British Isles, no American presidents with a screw loose threatening nuclear war. If Roger had had his way, he would have moved into this estate and turned it into his personal theme park for Fantasy England, entertaining foreign guests for business deals.

And dancing along the garden with cocktails in their hands and Bluetooth headsets in their ears were the gods, dressed in expensive designer evening wear as if they always belonged here. They were waiting for the guests to arrive and the show to begin. Lord Shiva was leading the reveries. Lakshmi, goddess of wealth and abundance, was the most at home here in her golden evening gown. Ganesha looked perfectly natural with his elephant head and tuxedo. They looked ready to star in a Noel Coward play. Bagalamukhi was drinking a cocktail and having a laugh with Louise Fowler.

That's right, Louise, Julia's late sister who died years ago before she could complete transition to a woman. It was because of her death that I had met Julia, on the first case I was the primary investigator on at Golden Sentinels a few years ago. Louise was a popular model and media personality who managed to keep secret that she was transgender all the way to the grave. Julia and their parents made sure of that. And now she was back. I saw her standing with my gods one morning in our kitchen when Julia and I were having breakfast, and realized she was here to stay. She wasn't a ghost. I didn't see ghosts, only gods. She was so popular when she passed away that you could say she had become a god. I got over my initial surprise to suss out that she was Julia's god, after all, so why wouldn't she be around Julia? Louise the god was the best, idealized version of her: she was fully transitioned. Her tits were gorgeous, her hair was perfect, her makeup was flawless, and she wore the latest fashions with panache, as befitted a supermodel. She seemed to sense when I was getting particularly anxious, and while the gods laughed, she would smile kindly, offer a reassuring wink, and say something funny to break the tension. That was what Julia said Louise was like. She had a talent for putting people at ease, making them feel welcome. Perhaps I conjured her as a counterpart to the gods. Sometimes I could swear Julia could see her, too. She seemed to behave as if she knew Louise was there, but I didn't ask her about it, because I didn't want to think about what it meant if other people could see my gods. It would mean they were not just my gods. They were *the* gods. What if it was Julia's desire to have her late sister and best friend near her that summoned Louise into my sight? Whenever Julia and I worked a case together and went out to interview witnesses, Louise would come along and stand next to us like a partner, unlike the gods who stood to the side and watched like a touring audience.

But I'm getting ahead of myself. I've been rambling a lot lately when I try to get my thoughts and memories of the past year down on paper. How, you might ask, did we end up getting the run of a large country mansion? This was something our boss Roger had been planning for a long time and was finally putting into play.

"**R**ight, children," Roger had said at the office weeks ago. "I'm going to need you all on for this. I'm going to be throwing a weekend get-together with some friends new and old."

"What do you need us there for?" I asked.

"All my plans, children," Roger beamed. "All the plans I've been laying for over three years, all the friends I've been makin'—"

"All the arse you've been kissing," Cheryl muttered.

"It's all coming together," Roger said, ignoring her. "I'm throwing a little get-together, a little party for our clients, former clients, people I've been doing favors for in the last five years, to bring them all together for a weekend of hobnobbing."

"To what end?" I asked.

"I have a business proposal and I'm looking for partners."

"Partners with lots of dosh," Olivia said.

"Very good! Can I get through my announcement without you children interrupting? Daddy's talking."

Ken and Clive snorted from their chairs, and aside from that, everyone clammed up.

"I'm going to butter up these VIPs with a very pleasant gathering at a mansion out in Sussex, the whole English Manor Experience, if you like. We'll have a butler, staff, a gourmet chef cookin' 'em a proper nosh-up. I've done a deal with Madame Felicity to bring in some of her girls—"

"The supermodel-looking ones?" Benjamin asked, eyes lighting up.

"If you like, yes," Roger said. "To entertain the gentlemen I'll be hosting, to soften 'em up, as it were, for the business pitch I'm going to make."

Madame Felicity's call girls were so expensive that none of us could ever expect to be able to afford them. Working in proximity to them was going to be strictly "look, don't touch" that weekend. They were reserved for the guests.

"And what business pitch is that?" Julia asked.

Roger glanced over at David Okri. David shook his head. Then he saw me see him shake his head and looked away sheepishly. If I was a suspicious man, my Dodgy Business Detector would have been pinging, but I was strictly in neutral no-judgment mode.

"Let's just say we're expanding into something much bigger," Roger said, smiling that chancer's smile of his. "Something I've spent years puttin' together. They buy in, partner up with me, we launch the plan, and we could be on top of the world."

Cheryl really hated that smile. She had been putting up with it for thirty years. I wondered if at one point she might have been charmed by it.

"You're not paying for Madame Felicity's girls, are you, boss?" Mark asked.

"Stone me, no!" Roger said. "Never spend your own dosh if you can help it. Didn't I teach you all that from Day One? No, no, the girls' fees are paid by my guests. They reserved their services, you might say. This is a rare opportunity for them to spend time with these top girls since Madame Felicity has them otherwise booked up for the rest of the year."

"Call girls as the price for admission," Cheryl said with a hint of disdain.

"To these rich bastards, those girls are well worth it," Ken said.

"This doesn't sound like an investigations case," I said. "What do you need us for? Providing security? Surely these guests would have their own people and bodyguards?"

"Good question, Ravi!" Roger said, warming into Teacher Mode.

I recognized that from back when I taught secondary school in North London, that thrill when my students started to give a shit enough to ask questions rather than just heckle. "I want you lot there to provide security for the manor and keep an eye on the guests."

"Here we go." Benjamin Lee grinned. "You mean you want us to bug them."

"Right you are!" Roger cried. "Full whack."

"Luvly-jubbly!" Benjamin rubbed his hands.

As the firm's techie and surveillance expert, he lived for using the latest bugs, drones, and whatever recording devices, some of which he built himself, to gather people's secrets, the more embarrassing the better, as long as he got to cause mischief.

Marcie had been curiously silent through all this, listening intently.

"So we're not cleaning dirty laundry, then," Olivia said. "We're *gathering* dirty laundry on prospective clients."

"Not clients," Roger said. "Business partners."

"They're investing in Golden Sentinels?" Marcie Holder perked up.

"Not this firm per se," Roger said. "It's a new company that's going to be like a sister company to this one."

"Another private investigation agency?" Mark said. "I thought you said Golden Sentinels was supposed to be your flagship business."

"Not a private investigation firm," Roger said. "Something else altogether that's going to open a lot of new doors for us."

I noticed Cheryl didn't look particularly pleased about any of this cheery talk, and David was unusually nervous as well. He betrayed his poker face by pursing his lips every few seconds, a sign I'd recognized since uni that he was nervous.

"You know what the deal is, right?" I said to David.

"David has been instrumental in helping me write the business plan for this new venture," Roger said. "We needed to get every term, every clause, every bit of legality right."

"Bloody better," Cheryl said, still glowering.

"So come that weekend, I want you all to set up shop in Beam Manor and get the place ready. You can coordinate with the staff; they're already expecting you and they're fully prepared to help in what you need to do."

"And they're all right with the stuff that's going to go on there?" Mark asked.

"They've seen all kinds of mad shit when Alfie Beam was alive," Roger said. "His rock star parties were off the charts. Alfie had orgies, yoga and meditation weekends with his guru, druidic ceremonies to welcome the solstice, you name it. This will be a doddle compared to all that."

"I'm not going," Olivia said.

"Ah yes," Roger said. "Your parents flying in from Hong Kong that weekend."

"Sorry, Roger," Olivia said, barely glancing up from her computer. "Confucian rules. I have to go be a good daughter."

"Of course," Roger said, not batting an eyelash. "The Wongs want to spend time with their only darling daughter. Who am I to stand in the way of that? Give your old dad my regards."

If any of the rest of us tried to beg off this assignment, that might be a firing offense, but not Olivia. Being his goddaughter had its privileges.

"I'm sure everyone will be fine without me," she said. "I've set up the listening network like you asked. You should be able to log in and use it to keep tabs on the guests and record them when you need it. I can run interference from London if you need me, otherwise I'm stuck taking Mum to Harrods while Dad visits his mistress in Bayswater. And I'll be having a serious chin-wag with Dad."

"About what?" Benjamin asked.

"He's expanding his investment portfolio here in London, and I might point him towards some properties."

"I thought he blacklisted you from the banking business," Mark said. "Do I detect a bit of thawing in his disposition?"

"He's been hinting," Olivia said, "that if I get back in his good books, he might think about lifting the ban on me working in the financial world. I suspect my mother put him up to it."

"Are you thinking about leaving this place and finally going into the proper world of banking?" I asked.

"Let's see what my dad has to say first," she said. "Anyway, I'll have my phone and computer, so I can provide any backup and intel you might need from my end."

"And this venture has nothing to do with me," Cheryl said. "Someone has to keep an eye on Golden Sentinels business while you're all away. You lot had better watch your Ps and Qs. Stay out of trouble."

"Yes, Mother," Mark said.

"I want you lot to set up shop in the manor," Roger said. "Ken and Clive provide the security. Benjamin, you're on tech and surveillance detail, manning the computers. Ravi, Julia, Mark, Marcie, you all are my team; you show the guests around, play host, keep them out of trouble, or if they get into trouble, keep it from getting out of hand."

"Out of hand in what way?" I asked.

"These are rich and powerful men with particular tastes," Roger said. "Use your imagination."

"I'd rather not," I said.

"It's probably much worse than you imagine anyway," Mark said.

"Whatever happens, Benjamin will record everything," Roger said.

"So we're staying in the manor?" Benjamin asked.

"You'll be in the servants' quarters," Olivia said. "Not the big guest rooms, and you won't get a valet to hold your underwear for you in the morning."

"Very *Upstairs, Downstairs*," Mark said.

"Only with more call girls and voyeurism," Benjamin said.

"I want to re-create Sodom and Gomorrah in an English garden," Roger said. "And make sure we have video of it!"

I glanced over at the gods. They were all lounging on Roger's expensive sofa, watching us intently like the audience at a preview. Kali licked her lips with her long tongue. Ganesha laughed a snorting laugh. Shiva smiled like a Cheshire cat. Lakshmi was helping herself to Roger's gin. She would be right at home at the manor, the goddess of wealth and abundance in her element. No way were the gods going to sleep in the servants' quarters. They were going to have the best rooms, and no one was going to notice them, since they were in my head.

"This is fairly typical of the parties I went to when I was alive," Louise said. "Piece of piss."

"Perhaps we'll see a reenactment of a section of the Mahabarata," Lord Shiva mused.

"In modern dress?" Louise Fowler said. "It could be an allegory for the times."

"If you like," Ganesha said.

This was getting awfully meta. My gods were now discussing literature with Julia's goddess. My mind must really be wandering to start seeing fan fiction about gods. Even my insanity was reacting to the boredom of this assignment.

"David will get you files on all the guests," Roger said. "Familiarize yourselves with them. You'll know what to look for when they show their fancies."

I sensed a wheeze coming, what we called a big social engineering hack, for that weekend. At the back of my mind, I started to think that we might be the bad guys here. There were no good guys that weekend, but after I read through the guest list later on, I knew that there were even worse guys than us that we would have to pretend to cater to but really to get the goods on. That still didn't make me feel any better. The gods loved to watch me squirm.

"Have fun being in service, darlings," Olivia said. "Hope it doesn't turn into a whodunit."

THREE

Come that Friday, we were off down the motorway in the company BMWs. Julia sat next to me as I drove, Mark and Benjamin in the back. Ken and Clive drove Roger and David in the other car, ahead of us.

Olivia phoned us when we were on the road. I put her on speaker.

"Sorry I couldn't be with you, darlings," she said, "but I already have my hands full back here."

"You're just happy you don't have to be out here getting your hands dirty with us," Benjamin said from the backseat.

"I'm not exactly having fun entertaining my parents here in London," Olivia said. "My dad's using me to keep Mum distracted."

"I wish I had rich parents to keep me from doing surveillance on dodgy tycoons," Mark said.

"Say hello to the combat butler for me," she said.

"The what?" I said.

But she'd already hung up.

We met Wittingsley, the mansion's butler, when we arrived. Later, I had read the file on him that Olivia sent to my phone, and I understood what she was talking about.

"Oy oy," Benjamin said. "Behold the monolith that walks like a man!"

Julia shushed him.

Wittingsley greeted us as we drove up to the service entrance of Beam Manor. He was a big fella. Bloody hell, he was large. And looming. In a butler's uniform.

"Reckon Ken and Clive can take him?" Benjamin whispered.

Julia nudged him to shut up.

But the clash of titans that Benjamin hoped to see was not to be. The moment Ken and Clive clapped eyes on Wittingsley, they shook his hand warmly.

"Awright, Tel?" Ken said.

"Service treatin' you well, then?" Clive said, smiling.

Turns out they knew Wittingsley from way back. Clive knew him when they were in the army together. Of course they did. Large, violent peas in a pod.

Terrence Wittingsley was not just any butler, but none of them were just any butler these days. Butlers are not just servants in tuxedos who serve dinner and receive packages. They're an institution that goes back centuries and a source of fascination to Anglophiles from abroad. There was something about the formalism, the strict etiquette and the ritualized nature, of their jobs that non-British Anglophiles liked to make a fetish of, and it wasn't just the idea of a uniformed servant as a status symbol for wealth and history. Any of us British punters would find the fuss foreigners made out of butlers a bit weird and classist. Senior butlers weren't just servants. They ran the household like the manager of a company—coordinating the staff, managing the household budget, overseeing the supplies and upkeep of the manor—and they were very well paid for that. When I was teaching secondary school, I once had to explain to my students that to be in service was a very particular institution that was unique to Britain. Butlers were specially and rigorously trained at accredited academies.

Wittingsley, in particular, was also an army veteran, who had served in Afghanistan, so he was trained in tactics, weapons, and unarmed combat before he came back to the UK and ended up becoming a butler. He was hired by Alfie Beam when Beam had made enough off his records and rock concerts to buy a mansion in Sussex. This was back in the days when being a rock-and-roll star was a bigger deal, before social media and online piracy decimated the music industry. Alfie and his wife Stephanie had been well acquainted with Wittingsley long before they got rich, and they knew he could be trusted to keep all their secrets. And Alfie had enough secrets to fill a whole wing of this mansion. Wittingsley knew the full details of Alfie and Stephanie's finances, their drug dealers, the girls and guys they had affairs with; he probably knew where all the bodies were buried. To serve Alfie and Stephanie Beam and clean up after them for their rock-and-roll lifestyle would have needed the skills and fortitude of a combat butler.

Wittingsley was a *literal* major domo. He commanded a whole staff of housekeepers, valets, footmen, junior butlers, and maids at Beam Manor.

And according to his file, he was not to be fucked with. Apparently, he'd foiled at least one attempt to kidnap the Beams' son when he was little. Wittingsley put the would-be abductor in the hospital, and the poor sod never walked right again.

"Imagine that," Mark said. "The butler's the bloody Batman!"

Wittingsley showed us to our rooms in the lower floors, near the kitchen and the pantry. We were the help, so we got the servants' quarters. Even so, these were very nice rooms, better than any bedsit you would be paying a fortune in rent for in London these days.

"We're on a minimal staff at the moment," Wittingsley said. "While Mrs. Beam is away, not much needs to be done other than the usual upkeep. Pretty soon, we'll all be gone."

"How do you mean?" Julia asked.

"Mrs. Beam is talking about putting the mansion up for sale. Now that her husband is gone, she's been spending more and more time in Spain and is thinking about moving there permanently. She won't be needing my services anymore."

"Will you miss all this?" Julia asked.

"It hasn't been the same since Mr. Beam passed away," Wittingsley said. "The house has taken on a melancholy air. Might do the missus good to start fresh abroad. She's got at least one gentleman friend to keep her company over there."

"Wittingsley, mate," Benjamin said. "Care to show me the guest rooms? I'm gonna give 'em a once-over."

And with that, Wittingsley left us to it while he led Benjamin to bug the rooms.

"If we know our Tel, he's not gonna have to worry about money for a while," Ken said.

"How much do you reckon he's got saved up?" Clive asked.

"More than enough," Ken said. "Since he doesn't gamble. The bigger issue is what's he gonna do with himself. Man needs a mission, that one."

"How did Roger blag this place anyway?" I asked.

"He knew Alfie Beam back in the eighties," Mark said. "Helped cover up the messy parts of Alfie's overdose when that old rocker finally karked it, helped with the funeral arrangements, made sure Steph got the money and assets and kept them away from Alfie's thieving manager. Roger's been close with Steph ever since."

"Think he shagged her?"

"Roger likes us to think he did," Mark said. "But Olivia heard from Cheryl that it never happened, much as Roger might have liked to. And he wasn't married yet at the time."

"I'm sure Cheryl would have had something to say about that," I said.

"Like cut his bollocks off, you mean?" Mark grinned.

"He'd have been lucky if that was all she did."

FOUR

We took a tour of the mansion and the rooms to get the lay of the land. We were going to be moving all over the place all weekend, so it wouldn't do to get lost. Wittingsley told us that Roger had sorted out what parts of the mansion would be off-limits to the guests so we could keep their wanderings around the mansion within a designated area. Those off-limits parts were where we and the staff could hide out away from the guests. Benjamin directed us to hide webcams and microphones all over the guests' rooms so Roger could record them. When that was done, we all went out to the garden to share a spliff. Marcie savored the strain Mark had brought, one that generated a calming buzz. She had been rather tense over the past year, for obvious reasons.

"'Ere, Marcie," Benjamin would keep baiting her, "how are you lot operating now that your president is a fucking moron and the whole world thinks that?"

Much of the apocalyptic chaos we'd been feeling in the air this past year was down to the American president, who was probably the worst ever in history. He seemed to stumble through all aspects of politics and diplomacy like a demented bull in a china shop, committing faux pas after faux pas, insulting America's allies, including Britain, and even slagging off his own intelligence services. I read in the papers that morale in the CIA was at an all-time low. Benjamin knew exactly what buttons he was pushing when he reminded Marcie of all this.

Marcie knew not to react or show weakness, but I could see her cheeks grow red and feel that heat rising from her. She would just smile and look up from her carton of yogurt and say, "Ahh, we just do what we always do."

Benjamin would bait her at least once a day, every day, his South London sneer varying in thickness, and her answer and smile would be the same, with her smile varying in tightness.

There had been a tense, rather apocalyptic atmosphere not just in the office, but in the world in general as well, in the past year, a feeling that things might go completely pear-shaped at any moment. That it might be something inevitable or something that came out of left field didn't make any of it better. We were living in a time when the world felt unmoored, and Benjamin, of course, found it all a great laugh. His mischief-making was not without insight, which made it all the more galling for Marcie. As a CIA agent whose cover was a PR specialist and private investigator, Marcie Holder was supposed to be one of those people in the shadows who knew what was what, or at least pretended to as they scrambled to play one-upmanship with the intelligence agencies of every other government out there, including the UK's. That she was using Golden Sentinels Private Investigation and Security Agency meant we were her assets, part of her network, and on the firing line of whatever horrible shit might come next.

I remember Marcie telling me that for decades the CIA were often at odds with the president of the United States in varying degrees, and they would just do whatever the hell they wanted in secret anyway. This was virtually standard procedure. If he really pissed them off, they would do little things to fuck with him, subtly going against him or undermining him, sometimes without him even knowing it. That explained all the off-the-books ops and subcontractors they used to ensure deniability. They would find ways to circumvent review, oversight, create workarounds and apparatus for deniability. Subcontractors like Golden Sentinels, for example. While Roger formed the firm with Cheryl, Marcie was his controller, and much of the firm's coffers were bankrolled from jobs Marcie brought him. That made us her assets, whether we liked it or not.

We were part of that apparatus. Golden Sentinels Investigations and Security was one of the many independent contractors the Company employed to get information for them so that they could deny to the president and the Senate Intelligence Committee that they were doing anything untoward. Mark and I wondered if we would be used in an op they might pull against the president. That would mean we could end up pissing off the US government, and it would be naïve to expect Marcie or her bosses to lift a finger to protect us if we got rumbled for doing what they paid us to do. Ever since the Company had entered what could now be considered open warfare with their own president, we had the feeling we were falling deeper into the rabbit hole of possible doom. I was seeing the gods a lot, which would suggest we weren't being paranoid.

I suppose we should have been relieved that the job this weekend was one from Roger himself and not Marcie. Still, she was showing an inordinate amount of interest in it, which was worrying. She said that given her background in public relations, this weekend was a nice diversion from the political shit going on in the Company.

"All these bigwigs," she said. "Good to keep track of."

"Like who you might turn?" I asked. "Sources of information, possible assets?"

"You never know," she said.

"So you don't know everyone Roger invited?" I asked.

"He didn't show me the list," she said. "Like he didn't want me to know."

"As his controller, do you feel the need to know all the dodgy dealings he gets up to?"

Marcie shrugged. "As long as he doesn't do anything to compromise our plans," she said (by "our" she meant the CIA, and by default, US interests), "he can do whatever he likes. And anyway, I've met some of these guests before. A lot of them are former clients. I just didn't expect Roger would invite nearly all of them. It'll be interesting to find out just what kind of business proposal he's pitching to them."

"What play do you reckon Roger's going for?" I asked. "Money or power?"

Marcie winked at me. I was the pupil impressing the teacher. She liked that I had sussed it out.

"He's looking for investors," she said. "But investors in what? That's what I really want to know."

"So Marcie," Mark said. "How *is* the war with your own president going?"

"Naaah, we're not at war with the president," Marcie said, a bit too breezily, and laughed, a bit too quickly and too long. "I'll say it again: the intelligence agencies are not at war with the president."

We watched her walk off to mingle and make introductions.

"They're totally at war with the president," Mark said.

"We are in deep shit," I said.

FIVE

Wittingsley had the staff line up and greet the guests as they arrived in their limousines. Very posh, very old-school to have the butler and household staff formally greet the guests as if they were the aristocracy. All part of Roger's ploy to make them feel really special, and they expected nothing less. He was giving them their fantasy of living a grand aristocratic weekend. Judging from their files, these were wide-boy types, self-made men who didn't inherit their money. The closest they got to the Establishment was to donate money to the Tory Party. Roger must have been offering them something ridiculously grand.

By late afternoon on Saturday, the party was kicking off proper and the gods were very present here this weekend. It kicked off with a drinks reception in the garden, all very *Midsummer Night's Dream*.

We had acquainted ourselves with the guests' profiles in the form of dossiers Roger had us read the week before, in preparation for the party.

"The better to anticipate their needs," Roger said. "And the chinks in their armor."

"Quite an international coterie of rich bastards," Mark said.

There were three Britons—Julian Reeves, Marcus Hastington, and Stewart Hartley—all prominent donors to the Conservative Party. We decided to just call them "The Tories" to keep things simple. Of course they requested the specialist services of Madame Felicity's highly in-demand dominatrix Mistress Tania and her assistants, with all their expenses and equipment charges paid in advance. There was Jürgen Kleiner, a German venture capitalist who had made his fortune in investing in rare minerals, oil, and other resources, as well as some arms companies. There was Jüst DeBeer and his three brothers, South Africans who owned a telecoms company in Johannesburg.

"All middle-aged, right-wing white blokes, total net worth a few tens of millions of pounds," Mark said. "Must be a hell of a business plan."

"And Laird Collins?" I said. "Interzone? What's Roger planning? Some kind of joint venture? Interzone means guns and mercenaries. None of this smells good."

As the help, we hung on the fringes to watch. The gods were romping. They were frolicking. They were whooping it up in this garden, weaving in and out between the guests and the staff like they belonged here. I didn't like that. It never bode well for me. Lord Shiva was leading a dance down the path in the distance. Lakshmi was here, in her element amidst this wealth and abundance. Kali wagged her tongue and whirled in anticipation of the coming chaos this weekend could throw up. Ganesha with his elephant's head and sage eyes swayed and jigged. They were all dressed in their best finery since this was a proper party. They were in for a right do, and they expected that I would deliver it to them. How I was supposed to do that, I had no idea. That was what made it fun for them. I was going to put on a show.

I wonder if I'll ever not be unnerved by the sight of Lord Shiva in Armani or Kali in Versace.

Our phones pinged. Benjamin had texted us all a video of the head of the neo-Nazi party of Ukraine dropping dead of a heart attack in the middle of a speech.

"Well," Mark said. "That's unusually gratifying."

"How does he find these links?" I asked.

"He has a feed that looks out for them," Mark said.

"WiFi in the basement's really good," Benjamin said on the Bluetooth.

"Roger's asked me to stay close to the Tories in case they say anything interesting," Julia said. "They've taken a shine to me."

"Of course," Mark said. "They want an English Rose."

"More specifically," Julia said, "they want me to sit and watch Mistress Tania abuse and humiliate them. They even offered to pay me."

"Should we tell them that before Julia started working for us, she was drugging and raping a Tory MP on a regular basis?" Benjamin asked, perfectly rhetorically.

"That might only turn them on even more," Julia said. "And pay me even more."

"Don't worry," Marcie said. "Cheryl's issued all the ladies with these anti-pervert flamethrowers."

Wittingsley had furnished the girls with what looked like a small, longer-than-normal metal tube that I thought was a lipstick, until Marcie flicked the switch and a pink jet flame shot out the end.

"Bloody hell," I said. "Where did these come from?"

"I convinced Cheryl to let me order some from China," Benjamin said. "These are big over there."

"These look like giant versions of my butane cigarette lighter," Mark said.

"Ahh, Chinese pragmatism," Benjamin said. " 'Let's just set the rapists on fire.' "

"See, Ravi?" Julia said. "I feel safer already."

Beside her, Louise nodded in approval.

Out of the corner of my eye, I saw the two figures approaching that I was most dreading: Laird Collins, head of Interzone, the private military contractor we kept having to deal with in our work. And where Collins went, Ariel Morgenstern was never far behind.

Collins walked towards me with that charmer's smile, Ariel behind him in an elegant black business suit. I'd already learned how to spot the bulge of her holster under her jacket.

"Ravi." Collins offered his hand, which I shook with extreme distaste that I hid as best I could.

"I'm surprised you're here," I said. "Doesn't Interzone already have contracts worth tens of millions more than Golden Sentinels'?"

"Your boss has presented us with an interesting proposal," Collins said. "One that's intriguing enough for me to think about."

"Does this involve Roger using your people for whatever it is he has planned?"

"Why else would we be here?" Ariel said. "Well, I'm always happy for an excuse to come to England."

I winced.

"When we have a moment," Collins said, "I'd like to talk to you about your opportunities at Interzone. We might be able to finally entice you."

"I'm fine where I am, Mr. Collins," I said.

"The world is changing faster than ever," Collins said. "You'll want to be on the winning side when the time comes. Your insight from God can be very useful to me."

"What do you mean?" I must have blinked and showed weakness.

"Don't your visions tell you anything?" Collins asked.

"The gods never tell me anything interesting that I haven't already thought myself," I said. "That's how it's always been."

"You're selling yourself short," Collins said. "Prophets don't get a lot of honor or credit these days."

"I'm not a prophet."

"You're a shaman," Collins said. "That means you serve as an intermediary between humans and God."

"Is working with Roger part of your plan to bring on the Apocalypse and the Second Coming, then?" I asked.

"All my decisions are for that end," Collins said, smiling. "We'll talk again. My offer to join Interzone is still open."

With that, Collins went off to mingle with the guests. Unfortunately, Ariel didn't join him. She lingered with me.

"So you and Julia are tying the knot," she said, smiling. "Is it going to be an Indian wedding?"

"Her parents are planning it," I said. "It's actually going to be an English wedding."

"Oooo! All the women are going to wear fancy hats! I like fancy hats. They make good targets. That is going to be so much fun!"

Ariel went off to rejoin Collins.

I tried to catch Julia's eye, but she was busy talking to the Tories, whose interest in her was too leering to be strictly business. I suddenly wondered if Julia had invited Ariel to the wedding and my blood ran cold. Surely Julia wouldn't do that, would she?

Would she?

I noticed that Mark, Ken, and Clive were all watching me with weird smiles on their faces, just what I needed. I saw Julia watching me also. Our eyes met and I couldn't read her expression.

SIX

In the past two years, Roger had shown me a thickening file of what Interzone and Laird Collins had been up to on his jobs. That Collins was a born-again Christian who believed everything he did, everyone he killed, was God's work and part of his mission to bring about Armageddon, the Second Coming of Christ, and the Rapture, which made him the most dangerous and insidious creature I'd ever met. Roger had obviously asked Marcie to get him the Interzone information using the excuse that since Golden Sentinels was also an independent contractor for the CIA's outsourced jobs and it was in all our interest not to step on each other's toes should we end up pursuing the same contracts on opposing sides, which was precisely what had happened when I had my first run-in with Interzone two years ago.

"I'm amazed you haven't stopped poking at the hornet's nest with a stick even after you knew what they were capable of," Cheryl had said before we left London.

"Somehow, I just can't help it," I said.

"Do the gods make you do it?" Mark asked.

"It's all me," I said. "I just hate the fuckers."

The gods certainly loved watching me do it. It was as if Kali was especially delighted every time I insulted Laird Collins to his face. It wasn't even as if I believed the gods would protect me from the day Collins might decide he'd had enough of me and it was time for Ariel or his faithful soldier Jarrod to shoot me in the head and dump me in a ditch somewhere. No, they didn't compel me to continue to despise Interzone and its band of Rakshasas, demons in human form, it was my own middle-class upbringing and morality. They really offended me on a fundamental human level. They were the embodiment of chaos and murderous indifference as far as I was concerned. Kali actually once told me she enjoyed them because they were catalysts for rebirth. I suppose what she meant was that the people they killed were released back into the cycle of reincarnation. It couldn't be a coincidence that Ariel had a tattoo of Kali on her arm. Ariel certainly didn't think so. She believed it was fate, kismet, that we would be in each other's life. And Julia was there to serve as, what, a witness? Julia believed she was there to protect me from Ariel.

Julia and I getting married didn't faze Ariel even one bit. She had thought it was marvelous when we emailed her the news. She didn't think it would put a damper on getting to have sex with either or both of us, even though we hadn't seen her since we left Los Angeles last year. Julia just had to do her own poking of the bear by texting Ariel a photo of the engagement ring I gave her. I don't think I'll ever understand the way women taunt each other while pretending to be friends. I hoped Ariel would be far, far away, probably in some war zone in the Middle East, by the time we had the wedding.

Roger's other ulterior motive for compiling a file on Collins and Interzone was to look for any leverage he could use against them in the future. He had always vowed he would bring down Collins, and if it took over thirty years, so be it. His revenge would be cold and sweet. Whatever happened between the two of them back in the 1980s, it was personal for Roger, even if Collins seemed to regard it all with utter indifference. I wondered how the hell Roger could possibly get back at Collins. After all, Golden Sentinels was peanuts compared to the behemoth that was Interzone. We were a bunch of small franchised firms of private investigators. There were far bigger and more upmarket international firms out there. That Golden Sentinels had gotten as far as it had was down to Roger's dog-and-pony show and Cheryl's business savvy. Interzone was in a whole other league—their contracts were worth tens of millions, providing entire regimes with military might and firepower, a small side trade in arms-dealing with the CIA's tacit approval, since they could pass the list of their clients back to the Company so they could keep track of them for, you guessed it, leverage. According to the file Roger had put together, the rumors that Interzone was involved in human rights violations, the killing of civilians in the Middle East, and even targeted assassinations were all horrifyingly true. Collins had even ordered his own employees killed when they threatened to sue or blow the whistle on the company's activities. I was quite sure Ariel might have pulled the trigger on more than one of those occasions. If Collins felt like it, he could have Roger knocked off at any time. That he felt Roger was too far beneath him to be worth the bother only inflamed Roger's hatred of him even further.

And yet here he was breaking bread with Collins in this country mansion, laughing it up as it were. What a sight to behold. I had a vague flash of panic that Roger might throw me as a bone to Collins to show how chummy they were getting, but Roger privately reassured me that this was never going to happen.

"He wants you so badly?" Roger said. "That's exactly why he's not gettin' you, old son. Rest assured. The more he doesn't get to have you and your secrets, the more torture it is for the bastard. And that's good enough for me."

Would it surprise you if I said this didn't particularly put me at ease one bit?

It must be a bloody big deal if Roger was willing to shake Collins's hand and work with him. The only thing that could possibly bring them both together was money, and lots of it. Lots and lots and lots of it. And not just money. Power. It had to be power, since that was what both Roger and Collins were drawn to. The type of power that put them on the board as major pieces, not just pawns to be moved. That was what Roger always wanted: to be a big fish swaggering about in front of the hoi polloi.

Now that I thought about it, no wonder Cheryl refused to be a part of this weekend. Her disapproval of Roger's decisions had been growing over the last three years, possibly even before I started working for the firm. If there was one thing I'd learned in my time at Golden Sentinels, it was to trust Cheryl's judgment on everything. That she reacted to whatever Roger had planned for this weekend with utter disgust the likes of which I hadn't seen before—and we'd had plenty of occasions when Cheryl expressed her disgust at Roger's actions—didn't bode well for us. But what could we do? We were employees and Roger had ordered us to work this weekend doing what we did best—keeping tabs on people, taking photos, recording video and audio, and waiting for whatever silly buggers they got up to, since Roger liked having leverage. He said these weren't clients we were recording. They were friends and future business partners.

"If I pull this off," Roger said, "we're in for the top, lads!"

The gods laughed and applauded when Roger declared this to us. It was the type of approving laughter and applause that was anticipating something horrible to happen. I could tell. The gods were reveling in Roger's hubris, which meant a huge fall was coming. I just hoped Roger wasn't going to drag the rest of us down with him. And I wasn't expecting the gods to protect me.

"The gods giving you shit?" Marcie said, seeing my face.

I shrugged.

"I suppose it's good that you all can take my psychosis in stride," I said.

"Chill, dude," Marcie said. "You're not psychotic. A little neurotic, maybe. That's about it."

That caught me up short.

"You know," I said, "for a British person, that might actually be *worse*."

"You are our witness and our soldier," Lord Shiva whispered to me. "Have at it, my son."

"Do us proud, my precious boy!" Kali said.

SEVEN

The afternoon ended with Roger leading the guests on a tour of Alfie Beam's mansion, showing them the living room where Alfie's guitar, gold records, and assorted memorabilia were on display. Madame Felicity's girls paired up with their assigned clients and clung to their arms to bolster the guests' sense of privilege and male pride. Roger had been a personal friend of Alfie's and was able to sweeten his narration with a lot of anecdotes the official biographies never brought up, mostly stories involving drugs, groupies, orgies, and Alfie's forays into occult rituals when he and Stephanie went through their mystical phase. Roger kept the guests' rapt attention as he regaled them with his depiction of the mansion as part of Alfie Beam's myth, a myth they were going to be a part of when they had their own party later in the evening.

"So these guys are all Alfie Beam fans," Marcie whispered, amused. "I should have guessed Roger might have sold a party here as part of the package."

"Except for Collins," Ken whispered.

"Yeah," Clive whispered. "Fucker couldn't give a toss about one of our greatest glam rockers. He was a national treasure, Alfie was, God rest his soul. Collins is just here for the money and the power, probably see how he can fuck the boss over."

"This bloody dick-swinging contest will be the death of them both," Ken whispered. "Mark my words."

"Roger really has a touch of the used car salesman about him in his gab, doesn't he?" I whispered as we watched from the back of the room.

"That's what he probably would have ended up doing if he didn't become a private eye," Mark whispered back. "Family business."

Then came the big dinner, which took place in the grand dining room. Roger and the guests ate the lavish five-course dinner cooked by a celebrity chef client who owed him a favor. The girls sat with the guests as their trophies at the table.

We weren't part of dinner, so we stood outside the dining room while Roger had the door locked. He didn't want us inside to hear what they might be saying while Wittingsley served the food in the most formal manner imaginable. Wittingsley told us that we would be getting the same meal in the kitchen once this was over.

"Benjamin, you're taping the audio inside as well, right?" I asked.

"Of course I am, but Roger's not really talking about anything in his business plan. It's mostly small talk and things like 'As you read from the prospectus I sent you' and 'We are in this together.'"

"That's it?"

"He's just makin' small talk. David's just standin' there looking like he's shittin' bricks," Benjamin said.

"What about Collins?" I asked.

"He's just sitting there not sayin' a word. Ariel's lookin' over the room like she's sizing up everyone to see which ones she would want to shoot first."

"Well," I said, "that's her default mode."

"I didn't see any prospectus or business proposals lying around," Mark said. "Whatever it is, Roger must have already pitched them before today."

"And less than a dozen investment partners in this venture," Marcie said. "Which means one, these guys are putting a fortune into Roger's plan, and two, Roger's keeping the circle small so there's less chance of anyone leaking details about it. These guys all have plenty of skeletons to hide. This business venture is probably going to become another big pile of skeletons."

We all felt the same tension. If Roger was keeping this thing a secret from us, how bad could it possibly be? And how bad could it get if it blew up in his face and bit us in the arse?

"If Roger's getting into bed with Interzone, that's it. I quit," I said.

"Calm down, Ravi," Julia said.

"I'm serious. I don't care. I'll go work in a McDonald's if I have to. I'm out."

"If McDonald's will have you," Marcie smiled.

"Yeah," Benjamin chuckled on the Bluetooth. "You'll be lucky if you can find a job at McDonald's these days."

"Ha bloody ha," I said.

"You're not going to get much trying to eavesdrop outside the door, chaps," Benjamin said. "I'm gettin' everything from the camera feeds and I'm already bored out of me face."

"I'm not going to force you to quit with me," I said to Julia.

"Of course I'll come with you," she said. "We have some money put away that should tide us over for a little while."

"So Roger didn't invite these guys here to pitch them his plan," Marcie said. "They've already bought in. This weekend is a party to celebrate the partnership. Roger's too cheap to pay Madame Felicity's girls out of his own pocket. He must have used some of the funds from their buy-in to get them a weekend with the most exclusive girls in London as a sweetener for the deal."

"Probably claim it off taxes, too," Clive snorted.

"And he has us here to see what kind of dirty laundry we can pick up on his partners," I said. "Which means it's the kind of deal where Roger needs to have blackmail as an insurance policy."

"Typical Roger," Mark said.

"Oy oy," Benjamin said. "Ariel's excused herself and comin' out."

The doors opened and Ariel made straight for me.

"Man, it's boring in there," she said, and took my arm. "Mind if I borrow him for a minute, Julia?"

She didn't wait for Julia's reply before she dragged me around the corner of the hallway.

"Just what is the business venture Roger's been on about anyway?" I asked. "That even your boss wants in on?"

"Roger didn't tell you?" Ariel said. "Guess you're not supposed to know. Way above your pay grade, babe."

I glanced up at Benjamin's webcam, hidden on the chandelier. He would be at his terminal now watching Ariel molest me and recording it all, which was ironic since I was the one who'd put that camera there in the first place earlier that day.

"Wanna find a room?" Ariel said, pushing herself close and rubbing against me. I could feel her heat through the silk blouse and expensive black pantsuit. "One more for the road while you're still a free man. Julia can join in if she can sneak away from those pasty-faced assholes."

"We're done with that stuff," I said, thinking of the best excuse. "I'm not doing the open relationship thing anymore. I'm taking my marriage seriously."

"Is Julia really going to go along with that?" Ariel asked, her voice full of innuendo. "Can she actually resist fucking other people?"

"Of course she can. She's been in recovery for over two years now. She's taking it as seriously as I do. That's the whole point of getting married. We're making a serious commitment."

"We really should be committing together, all three of us."

"Ariel, we really can't do that anymore."

"I get it," she said. "No means no, so you keep saying it like you believe it."

"Why do you want to have sex with me so much anyway?" I asked.

"You seriously have to ask?" She raised an eyebrow. "You didn't object when we first met."

"That was before I discovered you were a murderous sociopath," I said.

"Come on, that only turned you on even more. You have a type, Ravi. You like dangerous chicks."

"That's not true."

"You really think Julia is less dangerous than I am just because she doesn't carry a gun?" Ariel said. "She and I recognized each other the moment we met. You went from me to her without missing a beat and we can totally see why. You just won't admit it."

"I really don't know what you see in me," I said. "I would have thought you'd find some 'roided-up soldier with tattoos and piercings and be bonking his brains out all the time while discussing gods and spirituality."

"What makes you think I haven't?" she asked. "Too many of those guys have PTSD."

"So what am I?" I asked. "Your relief?"

"Oh, Ravi, you really don't understand women, do you?" She chuckled. "You're the only one with the gods I like. Specifically, the goddess I like."

That would be Kali. Who stood over us with a cocktail in her hand wagging her tongue.

Ariel kissed me deeply, only breaking off when her phone buzzed.

"Dinner's over. They're coming out. Guess we ought to head back." She sighed.

We walked back in time to see the door to the dining room open and the guests streaming out, each with one of Madame Felicity's girls on his arm. The Tories nodded to Julia, gesturing at her to join them.

"That's my cue, lads," she said and went off.

Ariel winked at me and went off to join Collins.

"Don't worry," she said to me. "I'm not fucking him. I'm here as his bodyguard."

"Our job's done for now. I reckon we can just skive off for the night," Benjamin said on the Bluetooth.

"It's not as if we're saving lives," Mark said.

"Not this weekend, anyway," I said.

"Let's go eat some of that posh nosh," Ken said.

"Yeah, I want to see what the fuss over the lobster is about," Clive said.

We made our way to the kitchen, where Wittingsley had the staff lay out our meals, the same fancy spread the guests had, only with the sense that these were the leftovers. Not that we were going to complain about a free dinner cooked by a five-star Michelin chef. The kitchen was nearly as big as the Golden Sentinels office back in London.

Dinner was fairly uneventful. The food was fancy, though we thought it overrated.

"Not much better than a curry from the local pub," Ken said.

Mark took out a Baggie of magic mushrooms and waved it.

"I'm going to partake in some visions tonight, kids," he declared.

"Is that such a good idea?" I asked.

"What else is there to do? It's a lovely evening, conditions are perfect for a good trip. You're all as bored as I am. Care to join me?"

"No thanks." We all declined.

"I'm really beat," Marcie said. "I'm just going to bed."

"Wittingsley?" Mark asked.

"I'm on duty all through the night, sir," Wittingsley said. "You never know what the guests will need."

"Well, I'll be in the garden all night if anyone changes their mind," Mark said.

The rest of us retired to our rooms. I was glad I managed to avoid running into Laird Collins or Ariel.

EIGHT

I was on the verge of dozing off when I heard the shouting from outside my room.

It was after three in the morning.

I stepped outside my room and followed the noise to the hall. I thought that was Cheryl's anti-pervert flamethrower going off and one of the girls had set someone's crotch on fire.

Rudra, god of thunder and retribution, was bellowing and puffing out his chest in the hallway.

Kleiner was looking at him, frozen in terror. He caught my eye and pointed at Rudra.

At first I thought I was dreaming. Why was this man seeing one of my gods? He saw on my face that I could see what he was seeing.

A familiar tune began to play in the air, gathering steam. I recognized it immediately. It was Richard Wagner's "Ride of the Valkyries."

Behind me, I heard the galloping of hooves.

I turned around and saw a large, muscular blond woman in armor and a horned helmet, her sword drawn, riding on a winged steed.

Kleiner started to tear off his clothes, screamed, and ran off.

Rudra began to laugh. He clapped his hands with joy.

Then he was gone.

The music faded as Kleiner receded farther and farther away.

And I was alone in the silent hallway.

I went back to my room to grab my phone and put on my Bluetooth earpiece. Then I headed for the guest quarters.

When I got there, I saw the South Africans rolling naked on the carpet in the hallway, laughing and crying while Lakshmi towered over them, smiling, gold dust drifting off her clothes. They looked like they were losing their minds at the sight of the goddess who was the sheer embodiment of wealth. Then she turned her back on them and walked away, a fine golden mist trailing in her wake, and the men leapt to their feet and ran after her in blind worship.

"Benjamin, you there?"

"What's . . . up . . . mate . . . ?"

"Why are you huffing and puffing?"

"Push-ups. Keepin' meself active so I don't sit on my arse all night watching these screens and nod off."

"I need you to check the screens. Things have gone seriously pear-shaped."

"What's happened?"

"The guests are all going doolally."

"You what?"

"Just look! They're all freaking out in various ways! I think they're hallucinating."

I left out the bit about them specifically hallucinating *my* gods. And a Valkyrie.

"Oh, fuck me! That's a lot of naked men freakin' all over this manor."

"Tell me," I said.

"South African bloke is rollin' around on his bed. The bird wot's with him is trying to talk him down. She's got it under control. I'd swear she's done this before. She's literally fucking him into submission. Guess Madame Felicity's girls really have special skills."

"Who else?"

"German bloke—"

"Kleiner."

"He's havin' a right old time, tearin' off his clothes, ran into his room, whoops, he's run out of his room."

"Shit. Where are Ken and Clive?"

"Checking on the South Africans in the East Wing hallway."

"What are they doing?" I asked.

"They're just dancing around in a circle, look like they're havin' a grand old time."

"I'm close by. I'll check on them first."

It took me three minutes to get to the East Wing. DeBeer's partners were there all right, dancing with Lakshmi. She reveled in their worship and adoration. She was what they loved, wealth and abundance. The girls who paired with them gathered behind them in attendance like nymphs, ready to catch them if they lost it completely.

"Ken? Clive? Where are you?" I asked on the Bluetooth.

"Lookin' for Kleiner," Ken said. "DeBeer and his mates aren't in any danger, so we're going for Kleiner."

"Gentlemen," I said to the South Africans. "It's late. The goddess Lakshmi has granted you her blessing. Time to turn in."

They reluctantly stopped dancing, but smiled at Lakshmi as they broke off. Madame Felicity's girls escorted them back to their rooms and made sure they went in and shut the doors.

"The girls are puttin' 'em to bed. Looks like they're gonna have it off," Benjamin said.

"Benjamin, if they get out of bed and act up again, tell me."

"You got it, mate."

"Hang on," I said. "Is it just the guests who are tripping? What about everyone else?"

"Madame Felicity's girls are all fine. They're either stayin' out of the guests' way or trying to talk 'em down. Some of 'em are even having sex with the clients, or letting the clients watch 'em have sex. That seems to be keepin' those blokes under control."

"What about Roger? Where is he now?"

"Huh. He's fast asleep in his bed. Hear him snorin'?" Benjamin said. "Maybe we should tell him what's happenin'."

"What's the point?" I said. "Roger would just get angry and tell us to do exactly what we're doing right now. Better to do without him shouting in our ears."

"Fair enough."

"All right, that's one less person to worry about," I said. "What about the others?"

"Let's see," Benjamin said. "Ken and Clive are on the ball. They're further in the east wing chasin' down Kleiner. He's runnin' around stark-bollock-naked and gibberin'. He should be passin' you around the corner about . . . now."

The strains of Wagner's "Ride of the Valkyries" grew louder the closer I got to the corner.

Sure enough, Kleiner ran towards me.

"*Die Walküre!*" he was screaming. "*Nein! Nein! Ich bin nicht bereit!*"

He was looking over his shoulder at the Valkyrie in her furs and armor, on horseback with her sword drawn, bearing down on him. She was howling her battle cry, her arms massive, her horse breathing fire and brimstone out of its nostrils—

Kleiner plowed right into me, sent us both arse over tit.

I rolled on top of his back and sat on him to pin him down until Ken and Clive caught up.

"Ravi! What the bloody hell's goin' on!" Ken cried.

"Someone's drugged the guests," I said.

The Valkyrie sneered something that I assumed was a swear word in German, turned her horse around, and trotted off down the hall.

"What's this one on, then?" Clive asked as he and Ken pulled Kleiner to this feet.

"Looks like Mark's magic mushrooms," I said.

"Do what?" Ken said.

"Mark didn't do this. Someone must have taken them off him and doused the guests."

Kleiner was calmer now, but still muttering, "*Ich bin nicht bereit.*"

"I think that's German for 'I'm not ready,'" Clive said.

"In his mind he's being chased by a harbinger of death," I said.

"He should be so lucky," Ken said before he and Clive disappeared around the corner with Kleiner. "We'll give 'em a sedative from the first aid kit. He'll sleep it off like a baby."

"Do you know where the music's coming from?" I asked.

"What music?" Clive asked.

"Never mind," I said.

"Come on then," Ken said to Kleiner. "Off to bed with you."

I went back to talking to Benjamin.

"Can you confirm if it's only the guests who are wigging out?"

"Looks that way. Julia's safe, by the way. She's fully clothed in the Tories' room. Mistress Tania and her assistants are tyin' 'em up and gettin' 'em under control."

"Thanks, Benjamin. What about everyone else?"

"David was workin' on his laptop in his room, then turned in. Marcie's out like a light, catchin' her beauty sleep."

"Marcie's asleep? That's unusual. I thought she'd be up looking for us, asking questions, and exchanging gossip."

"I can only tell you what I'm seein', mate."

"Where's Mark?"

"He's out in the garden, trippin' out like he said he was going to do. Havin' a grand old time from the looks of it."

NINE

I found Mark sitting on a stone bench conferring with Lord Ganesha. Ganesha was nuzzling Mark's head with his trunk.

"Ravi!" Mark said. "Ganesha is my new best mate, man!"

"You can see him, too?"

"Is this what it's like for you all the time?"

"More or less, except I don't experience slowed time or pretty lights, which I assume you are from the 'shrooms?"

"Pretty!" Mark said.

"Mark, we have a problem. Someone's drugged the guests. They're all tripping like you are."

Mark and Ganesha both looked at me quizzically.

"I have to ask you this. Did you douse the guests?"

"Of course not, mate. That goes against my ethics as a psychonaut. I do this because I want to discover things. You have to be prepared for this or it can be traumatic. You don't douse people if they don't want it. Nobody should get forced to go on a vision quest."

"But didn't Roger ask you to supply the party with drugs?"

"Mainly cocaine. Rich folk like these buggers aren't into magic mushrooms," Mark said. "They're more into cocaine and poppers. They come for the sex and the fun. The last thing they want is to discover new insights about themselves."

"You did bring an awful lot of mushrooms," I said.

"That was in case any of you lot wanted to go spirit-walking with me if things got boring."

"Do you still have the rest of the 'shrooms?"

Mark reached into his pocket, looked puzzled.

"That's odd," he said. "The Baggie's gone."

"Somebody picked your pocket?"

"Must have done," Mark said. "I never leave my product lying around. Must have happened after I took my dose."

"Mark, I think someone's trying to sabotage Roger's weekend here."

"An inside job? Seriously?"

"Unless it's a bloody ninja who's been hiding from us all along, it has to be someone here," I said. "It's mainly been the guests who were drugged. The rest of us, the girls, the help, we're sober. Aside from you, and you did it to yourself on purpose."

"It's targeted, so it's not for shits and giggles," Mark said. "Who do you think would want to do that?"

"Someone who has it in for Roger," I said. "Must be."

"But Roger's offering a business deal to the lot of them that stands to make 'em a shit load of money. Who would have incentive to mess with his plans?"

"What about Interzone?" I said. "Roger and Collins hate each other's guts. Maybe Collins thinks he can cut Roger out and take over the deal himself, whatever it is."

"That might not be bad for us, though," Mark said.

"Might get Roger and us off the hook, yes," I said. "Here's another question. If Collins and Ariel wanted to sow chaos, why just douse the guests? Why not douse everyone? Us, the girls, the staff, so everyone's off their face and freaking out?"

"Perhaps because there would be too many variables?" Mark said. "Someone could get hurt or worse. Collins's strategy is controlled chaos. To leave enough of the people here compos mentis is a tactic to leave witnesses, and maybe someone to frame."

"I suppose it's just as well there aren't more guests," I said.

"That's another thing," Mark said. "Roger handpicked these prospective investors or partners. DeBeer is in telecom in South Africa, so this could involve infrastructure. Kleiner is in minerals and resources, so that's probably what they're all interested in for the return on investment in Roger's plan. Interzone is muscle, so they're providing protection. The Tories have access to government ministers, so the government might be in on this. He must have made the pitch through the guests to get some kind of approval, so this business plan could go to the higher reaches of the government, but it's all hush-hush."

"So it's all about this bloody business plan," I said. "And Roger wouldn't show it to us."

I had to give it to Mark. Even when completely off his face on powerful hallucinogens and nuzzling a god with an elephant's head, his intellect was sharp as ever. Perhaps more so.

"It's not even on the computer at the office," Benjamin said through the Bluetooth. "Olivia and I never got to see it either. What the fuck's he keepin' from us? And why? So we can plead innocence?"

"This business plan is sounding worse and worse the more we think about it," I said. "And if Interzone wants to nick it off Roger, that could make things even worse, even if we're off the hook."

Mark was already bored and turning his attention back to Ganesha.

"I get it now, Ravi," he said.

"Get what?" I asked.

"You don't need drugs to see gods. You've never stopped being on a vision quest. This must be what it feels like to be a shaman."

"I'm not a bloody shaman!"

"You don't choose the role, mate. It chooses you."

"Benjamin," I said on the Bluetooth. "Can you check where the hell Collins is? We have to find him."

I left Mark hanging out in the garden with Ganesha and went back in the house.

Wittingsley was staggering along the hall, leaning on the wall for support.

"Ah. Mr. Singh. You've caught me at a bad time."

"What happened?"

"I think I may have been drugged. Everything's a bit strange. Time's slowing down, space is distorting a bit."

"I think someone's drugged the guests."

"So I heard. Mr. Lee told me on the intercom."

"What happened to your leg?"

"I came across Mr. Collins a moment ago. He was having a rather bad time of it. Seems he was terrified. I tried to calm him down and take the gun off him but he kicked me in my leg and dislocated my ankle."

"Christ, you shouldn't be on your feet."

"I've reset it myself, but the swelling could take some time to go down. I have a first aid kit in the kitchen. If you could be so kind as to lend me a hand?"

I helped him get to the kitchen.

"Where's the rest of the staff?" I asked.

"They're all asleep in their chambers."

"And none of this racket has woken them up?"

"Evidently not. The walls are quite thick here."

Wittingsley took off his shoe and began to wrap his ankle with a bandage from the first aid kit. Batman was out of action for the night.

"You better stay here," I said. "I'm going to track Collins down."

"Mr. Singh, be warned. Mr. Collins has a gun."

"That's just brilliant," I said.

TEN

I knocked on the door to the Tories' room.

Julia answered, still in her blouse and skirt.

"Everything all right?" I asked.

"All quiet on the Western Front—and back," she said with a smile.

She opened the door to let me see. Mistress Tania and her two partners, all in leather corsets, holding cat-o'-nine-tails, stood next to the bed while the Tories were trussed up naked like hogs, blindfolds, ball gags, and earplugs keeping them in a form of sensory deprivation. They were moaning quietly and, I could have sworn, rather enjoying this. Those were moans of pleasure, not suffering.

"All right?" Mistress Tania said.

"Good thing you came with a full arsenal of equipment," I said.

"Have a bit of faith, love," she said. "We're all professionals here."

"Sorry I doubted you."

I filled Julia in on what was happening.

"Now, none of you feel strange, like you've been drugged?" I asked.

"Right as rain," Mistress Tania said. Her assistants giggled and gave me the thumbs-up.

"I might be having a bit of a contact high," Julia said. "But that's all."

"Sounds like your addiction talking," I said.

"I have it under control," she said. "None of them wanted to have sex with me, so no worries there."

"You might have to bring this up in group therapy," I said.

Julia looked at me in mild annoyance.

"Wait, why did Kleiner see a Valkyrie?" she asked.

"I don't know. Maybe he's obsessed with death and Wagner."

Since Julia and Mistress Tania already had things well under control here, I told them to lock the door and keep the Tories safe. Three more guests safely tucked away, now I only had to find the most dangerous one.

ELEVEN

Collins was stumbling around the hall waving his pistol. Benjamin helpfully told me on the Bluetooth that it was a Glock 9mm semiautomatic.

"Ravi? Is that you? I never thought it would be like this," he stammered.

I approached him slowly, my palms out, conscious of the gun in his hand.

"Mr. Collins, give me the gun. You don't want to be shooting at anything tonight."

"I'm not relinquishing my weapon!" he screamed.

Great. He was completely off his rocker.

But wait, if he'd been doused, too, that would mean it wasn't him who drugged the guests. He didn't strike me as someone who would drug himself with a psychoactive hallucinogen to throw suspicion off. That meant the saboteur was someone else.

"I see you now!" Collins cried, pointing his gun at Lord Shiva and Kali, who both stood in front of him, smiling with drinks in their hands.

"You see the gods?" I blurted out in surprise before I could stop myself.

"The arms, the blue skin . . ." he said. "Her black skin . . ."

Shit. He was definitely seeing my gods.

"Mr. Collins, you never want to point a gun at gods," I said.

He quickly lowered his arm.

"I'm sorry! I meant no disrespect!" he cried.

"None taken," Lord Shiva said, his voice surprisingly debonair.

"I have so many things to ask you," Collins said.

Shiva and Kali just burst out laughing.

"Don't mock me!" Collins screamed. "I serve a greater power! A greater cause! You will talk to me!"

"Silly, foolish little man," Kali said, licking her lips with her frighteningly long tongue. "You do not presume to make demands of the gods."

They laughed again, even more mocking now.

Collins began to shake. Sweat was flooding off him. He was having a really bad trip. This was definitely not anything he'd signed on for. He couldn't have been behind the dousing. He would never agree to an experience like this. Losing control was his greatest fear.

"How do you know we have any answers for you?" Shiva said, smiling.

"You must! You're gods!"

I slowly moved closer to Collins, hoping to take the gun off him.

"What if the gods aren't in control?" I said. "What if they were never in control? Suppose they're witnesses to time as much as we are. They can just see the threads that we can't?"

"Are you saying everything is preordained?" Collins asked, blinking. "That we have no free will?"

"Free will is an illusion," Lord Shiva said, and took a sip of his cocktail.

Collins looked at him, stricken, then turned back to me.

"He was talking in your voice!" Collins cried.

"I didn't say anything," I said.

"I knew it! You and the gods are in on it together!"

"No, we're not!" I said. "I'm trying my damnedest to ignore them!"

"Yet you still manage to do what needs to be done," Lord Shiva said, winking at me.

"You really are the instrument of the gods!" Collins cried.

"The gods don't control what I do!' I said. "Listen to me! I think the gods are as helpless as we are in the wheel of time! There is no real order in the universe! There's a randomness that's just cause and effect! That's all there is to it!"

"Is that what the gods tell you?" Collins asked.

"I don't talk to the gods about metaphysics because they only exist in our heads," I said.

"Yet you and I are both seeing them now!" Collins said. "That is what I've wanted! To commune with the gods!"

"For what?" I asked. "I tried the enlightenment route when I was doing my PhD in religious studies. It didn't work for me. What little faith I had instilled in me as a child didn't hold up by the time I became a teenager. I tried to stick at it because my father wanted it, and every day in university calling myself a religious scholar just put more and more pressure on me until I had a nervous breakdown and quit. That's what religion's done for me. It took years for my father to forgive me for dropping the studies. That just proved to me again that there's no order to anything. There's only us and what we do, and what happens after we do it."

Collins was sweating and twitching profusely. He was having a much more externalized version of the crisis I had when I was twenty-five, and it looked like he was having it even worse.

"But I have such plans!" he said.

That only made Lord Shiva and Kali laugh uproariously again. Shiva in his tuxedo and Kali in her designer cocktail dress, her multiple arms adorned in gold and jewelry. This was their late-night dinner theater. It occurred to me the gods were treating this evening as one of those country house murder mystery weekends where the guests could wander around the mansion following whichever actor or plotline took their fancy. Of course laid-back Ganesha would just hang with Mark in the garden. Of course Lakshmi was at home in this palace of wealth. Of course Bagalamukhi would happily wander the place from one group to another and then go back to hang out with Benjamin, at home with all this deception and duplicity. The gods could pick and choose their fun on this weekend in the country. Of course Shiva and Kali would follow Laird Collins and fuck with him for a laugh. His ridiculous ambitions for bringing about Armageddon and the Rapture must have looked very amusing to them. And while I thought I was just doing my job and earning my salary, I was their unwitting tour guide through this whole weekend. Stuck in the middle again.

"Mr. Collins," I said. "You might want to put that gun down."

He looked at the Glock in his hand, astonished, as if he'd just remembered he was holding it.

"The Wheel of Time," he muttered.

"Sorry?" I blinked.

"If everything is predestined, that means everything that's going to happen was supposed to happen," Collins was thinking out loud.

I didn't like where this was going.

I especially didn't like how intently Shiva and Kali were watching us.

"And if the gods don't intervene or influence," Collins said, "they won't stop me from shooting you right now."

He pointed the gun at my head.

Shit.

It occurred to me that I probably shouldn't have been talking to him like I had been and winding him up. I could have just lied my arse off and told him whatever the fuck he wanted to hear to calm him down, but I probably just hated him and his arrogance so much, that arrogance that he used to justify all the people whose lives he destroyed and deaths he caused in the name of lucrative contracts and a ludicrous Grand Plan. For all the social engineering I did on the job, the little white lies, the false identities I adopted to get the truth on my cases, I couldn't lie to the likes of Collins or Roger or my colleagues, because we were all in the same club. Lying to our own never worked. I was thinking all this possibly as a way to keep from panicking at the prospect that I was about to get my brains blown out by a religious zealot. I felt oddly detached about everything unfolding before me.

What if all this was truly predestined? Was I fated to get my head blown off in a country mansion by some nutter off his face on drugs in an idiotically bad scenario straight out of the *Daily Mail*?

Collins was hyperventilating. I could see all the sweat drenching his face as he tried to focus and aim the gun at my head.

"Maybe this is the final test," Collins stammered. "God has been testing me. Maybe if I shoot you, your gods go away, and it'll just be my God."

"What if you're wrong?" I said.

"Oooo-er!" Shiva cooed.

"What if you kill me and this continues?" I continued. "Let's say my gods are not just mine. They're actually here. If I'm their chosen shaman, do you think they'll be happy if you kill me? What if they decide to visit their wrath on you?"

"My God is the one true God!"

"Yeah, and what if he's fucking with you as much as mine are?" I said. "There is no order to anything! It's all just random! It's all just us and what we do!"

"I have faith!" he cried.

"Where is your God in all this?" I said. "Shouldn't you be seeing Him tonight as well as mine?"

Confusion and shock crossed his face. He turned and looked around. Even then I didn't think it was a good idea to run or dodge. We were in a large hallway with nowhere for me to take cover behind. I had thought about rushing forward and at least grabbing his gun arm and turn it upwards away from me, when Kali appeared behind Collins and stuck a syringe in his neck.

He turned around to face her in surprise before his eyes rolled back in his head and he collapsed in a heap. His gun was transferred to Kali's hand—no, Ariel's hand.

As time slowed down and I waited for my life to flash before my eyes, my senses must have played a trick on me to see Ariel as Kali. Kali was standing ten feet away with Shiva, watching. They applauded. The look in Kali's eyes indicated she knew what I was thinking. She enjoyed my apprehension.

"Babe, talk about cutting it close," Ariel said, smiling. "Admit it, you really do like living on the edge."

TWELVE

After she had secured Collins's gun, put on the safety, and tucked it in her jacket, Ariel and I carried the unconscious man back to his room. I took his shoulders, Ariel took his feet. Bloody hell, he was heavy.

"I think he's broken," I said.

"Poor Laird," Ariel said. "He wouldn't stop talking about how much he envied you. He wanted to touch God."

"That's never a good idea," I said.

"He just found out the hard way," she said.

"How did you find me anyway?" I asked.

"I was looking for him," she said. "And I knew he would go off looking for you."

"With a gun. Was he always planning on shooting me? Did he think he could take over my gods after he got rid of me?"

"I never thought he was going to take it *that* literally," Ariel said. "We always figured he'd hire you away from Golden Sentinels and treat you like the company shaman. He'd probably have given you an office and consulted you on a daily basis."

"All that bollocks about Armageddon," I said. "I can't believe he picked Interzone's contracts in countries he believed he could bring about the Apocalypse. How many tens of millions of dollars in contracts did he get just to sow perpetual war?"

"Actually," Ariel said. "The board of directors has been raising a lot of questions about that lately. They think we might have lost out on some major contracts because of Laird's Armageddon agenda."

"Armageddon agenda. Catchy name for a plan to end the world," I said.

"We're not the only PMC with that kind of plan, you know," Ariel said.

"Somehow I don't find that reassuring," I said. "Do you believe in all that, Ariel?"

"Not really. I'm on my own spiritual journey. Kali's my gal."

"So you keep saying."

"I don't believe in ending the world, if that's what you mean," she said. "I've read enough of the Bible, then Buddhist scriptures, Sufism, the Koran, the Bhagavad Gita, the Ramayana, and I don't believe in a final end. I think things just keep going. It's not a single race with a finishing line, it's a cycle."

"You don't have any religious agenda when you shoot people," I said.

"Nope, but it's still fun."

"That's where you lose me."

"Yeah, yeah, you're more comfortable marrying Julia 'cause she doesn't like to shoot people. Hey, Kali likes me."

"Don't start."

I groaned. Out of the corner of my eye, Shiva and Kali walked behind us, listening intently and sipping their drinks.

"How do you know I don't have a relationship with Kali and she doesn't point me in your direction?" Ariel said. "If you ask me, Laird here totally missed a trick. Instead of serving gods, why can't we be gods?"

"That's just bloody insane," I said. "Why would anyone want to be a god? It's narcissism and egotism. And how the hell would you do that in the real world? You're not a god just because you might shoot people and have the power of life and death over them. That's where you fail, Ariel."

"Chill, Ravi," she said with a laugh. "Being a god is way too much responsibility. I'm just messing with you."

We got to Collins's room and put him to bed.

"Hey, he's out for the next six hours," Ariel said, lying back in the bed next to Collins. "Wanna fool around?"

"Good night, Ariel."

I left, collected Julia from the Tories' room, and we retired to ours for the evening.

THIRTEEN

The guests left on Sunday morning. We watched their people guide them into their cars, but not before they shook Roger's hand. They all looked refreshed and in a good mood. They complimented Roger for the presentation and the general do. None of them brought up tripping their faces off and running around in terror the night before. The gods were gone. The show was over. They didn't need to see the help dismantle the set. Everything felt grayer, like the world was having a hangover. The comedown from a Midsummer Night's Dream was always anticlimactic.

After the guests had gone, Wittingsley handed all the girls a nice, thick envelope for their night's work.

"Courtesy of Mr. Golden," he said. "For a job well done."

"Might as well be combat pay," Mistress Tania said. She was out of her dominatrix gear and wore a denim jacket and jeans. Gone were all the expensive dresses as Madame Felicity's girls were finally off the clock.

The girls were very happy with their bonuses, a tip to them outside of the fees Roger had already paid to Madame Felicity. They piled into the two vans and headed back to London, back to their lives when they weren't moonlighting as call girls.

As for our lot, Ken and Clive were their usual surly selves, as if this was just another job. Benjamin was slightly bleary-eyed from staying up most of the night, until everyone was safely to bed, but nothing that two cans of his favorite energy drink at breakfast wouldn't sort out in short order. Mark was in a very good mood because he'd gotten to experience something he'd wanted for a long time. He finally met my gods. Julia was perfectly chipper. Only Marcie was not happy. I'd never seen her so genuinely nonplussed before. She sussed out when she woke up that someone had drugged her so she fell asleep and missed all the night's excitement. Someone had made sure of that. She would spend the next two days at the office grilling me at every spare moment for every single detail I had about what happened the night before. She was actually going to play detective on her own. I'd never seen her want to go after someone before, and I wouldn't want to be her target again.

We went through the mansion, took down Benjamin's webcams, packed our overnight bags, and put it all in the boot of the cars. Benjamin inventoried the cameras and microphones and put them back in their cases along with the screens he'd brought to watch the footage on. We made one last round of the mansion and the grounds to clean up and make sure we left no trace of us behind. The staff had woken up none the wiser to the night's events and were cleaning up whatever mess had been made, which was surprisingly minimal. Soon after we left, the furniture would be covered up and the mansion shut down for the season. The estate agents would come around shortly to assess the place for sale. Some foreign oligarch was probably going to end up buying it in the end. The memorabilia that commemorated Alfie Beam's career would be auctioned off at Christie's after their appraisers catalogued it all, which would fetch Stephanie another nice earner for her retirement to Marbella.

I found Roger standing in the garden. He lit a cigar and took a long, luxurious, almost sexual drag on it.

"Alfie would have had a laugh over what happened last night," he said.

"You planned it all along," I said.

"Of course I did. Nothing left to chance. Good result, Ravi," he said.

"How the hell do you measure that?"

"The weekend was a roaring success! The guests all had a marvelous time. They all said they were going into business with me. Even Interzone."

"After Laird Collins threw a complete wobbly and nearly shot me in the head," I said.

"Chin up, old son. That was well in hand. I told Ariel to keep an eye on him and have a sedative ready. You were safe as houses."

"Easy for you to say," I said. "Wait, Ariel was in on it with you?"

"I've had a dialogue with her in the last few months," Roger said in that tone he used when he was enjoying being evasive.

"To turn on her boss? Are they planning a mutiny at Interzone?"

"There have been rumblings," Roger said. "I was open to fanning those flames."

"Except we all could still end up getting burnt," I said. "I'm still trying to wrap my head around the games within games you're playing."

"Ravi, Laird Collins pointed a gun at my head back in 1989 and he was stone-cold-bloody-sober at the time. I did not conduct myself with half the calm and dignity you did, I'm ashamed to say. I had to throw away the trousers I wore that day. He would have pulled the trigger, too, if Cheryl hadn't talked him out of it."

"Was I bait that you laid out for Collins?" I said. "Just so you could have history repeat itself last night with me, for a different outcome?"

"Nerves of steel, Ravi," Roger said. "That's what you got."

"To be honest, I think I was too bemused to be terrified. It was so absurd it didn't occur to me to shit my pants."

"Collins would have pulled the trigger and killed me that day in 1989," Roger said. "And he didn't have to. I just happened to have a piece of evidence he was assigned to get back, and I would have gotten a payout big enough to be life-changing if I'd kept it. Cheryl saved my life by giving it to him. That was when I vowed I would get back at the fucker, no matter how long it takes. Not because he won that day, not because he humiliated me, but because he was perfectly fine with murdering me without a second thought, all for the sake of power."

"Power that you fancy getting a piece of," I said.

"I don't kill people," Roger said. "That's the difference between him and me."

"You gambled with my life," I said, still so calm that I surprised myself. "If he'd killed me last night, you would have just had Wittingsley and Ken and Clive cover it up and carried on your business plan."

"Come on, Ravi, didn't you at least feel a bit of gratification at seeing that bastard taken down several pegs? After all his pompous self-righteousness and belief in the Rapture and the Apocalypse, a bit of magic mushrooms and he pisses his pants in abject terror. I waited more than twenty years to see that. Well worth it, and it's on video!"

I had watched earlier as Ariel and Jarrod helped a rather wobbly Collins into his car for the trip to the airport. He was ashen, diminished, as if he'd been through the wringer with the gods, which you could say he literally had been the night before. I didn't feel good about seeing one of the most dangerous men in the world humiliated.

"What's this business proposition you've been pitching anyway, that you need to drug your investors to have blackmail material on them for?"

"Better you don't know, my son," Roger said, smiling.

"Because it might be incriminating?"

"I wouldn't have asked you lot to put in the extra work if this wasn't important. You'll know when it comes to fruition and we're covered in clover."

"David must know if he's the one having to write the contracts. Just how dodgy is this business deal that's made him so nervous?"

"David has a touch of moral and ethical scruples like you," Roger said. "You're a mensch. I'm not."

"At the rate you're going, we ought to get danger money," I said.

"I haven't forgotten you lot," Roger said. "When you go into the office on Monday, Cheryl will be giving you all a nice little bonus for this weekend. I asked her to put in an extra for you and Julia, something for the wedding, eh?"

That was the Roger Cheryl had warned us about in private. He would put you in harm's way, push you in the deep end and leave you to struggle your way out, throw you under the bus for his agenda, then make it up to you with a speech with his silver tongue and extra money. He genuinely didn't see why you would be upset about any of it. In his eyes, the money should be compensation enough. Money was the great equalizer. He might not actually be capable of guilt or remorse at all. That was the mindset of a chancer. I could imagine now why Cheryl regretted falling in love with him and eventually fell out of love, but perhaps after it was too late.

"Ready to go?" Julia asked.

"One last thing," I said.

FOURTEEN

Julia and I caught up with Wittingsley as he limped back towards the mansion, nursing his ankle.

"Ow! Bugger!" He winced and cursed at the pain.

"You orchestrated the drugging of the guests, didn't you?" I said.

"It would appear you have me bang to rights, sir," he said.

"You're the only one who could have had the guests so precisely doped up and avoided having the staff or us drugged. You made sure the staff had a simple sedative in their food and drink so they'd sleep through the pandemonium. Especially our Marcie."

"No witnesses outside those of us in the know," Julia said. "So Roger could have total deniability."

"Mr. Golden paid me handsomely to get it done properly, sir, but I couldn't have done it myself since I had to organize the staff for the whole weekend. A senior butler's job is to delegate."

"When you were briefing Madame Felicity's girls, you didn't just give them the lay of the land. You instructed them to douse the guests' drinks and food. That's how only the guests started tripping their brains out once they were with the girls. They were all targeted."

"It's actually from an old American playbook," Wittingsley said. "When the CIA were testing LSD on unsuspecting civilians in the early sixties, they used brothels they happened to control. They got the ladies there to slip the mickey into their clients' drinks and observed them through two-way mirrors in the bedrooms. The hapless gentlemen didn't know what was happening to them, and they were never going to report it to the police. The spies had perfect cover and deniability."

Bloody spies and their games again. Games Roger was happy to play.

"And all those women have gone back home to London and their lives, scattered to the wind," Julia said. "For them, it's probably another night on the job, catering to the kinks of their clients, and for a higher rate than usual."

"Quite," Wittingsley said. "Thank you for the help, miss. My ankle's been a bit weak since I shattered it back in Iraq. I should get on with closing the mansion down, dismissing the staff, and packing up."

"You mean doing a runner," Julia said.

"Quite right, miss."

"I really ought to turn you in," I said. "After the mess you caused."

"None of the guests are likely to press charges, sir. This is how some people do business. Your Mr. Golden paid me twenty thousand pounds for my services this weekend, including making sure the guests had a suitable dosage of mushrooms. If I were to be interviewed, I might have to tell the police about that."

"Ravi, he was doing what Roger wanted," Julia said.

"If I may ask, sir," Wittingsley said, "how did you deduce that I was the one behind the drugging?"

"When I ran into you in the hall," I said, "you said you were having a bad trip like everyone else, but I realized you were faking it to throw the scent off. Everyone who was tripping was seeing the same things, sort of a shared hallucination, don't ask me why or how. You weren't seeing or reacting to what they were seeing. You were just acting like you were tripping on acid and experiencing slowed time, instead of seeing odd visions. The guests were all off their tits."

"Ah," Wittingsley said. "I should have consulted with Mr. Oldham for more details on how to fake tripping."

"So what's next for you?" I asked.

"Well, I'm out of a job once this mansion is sold. Off to the wild blue yonder with me."

"I expect someone will always need a butler-bodyguard," I said.

"Some of those people are not necessarily the type of employer one is proud to serve," he said. "But there are a few interesting offers on the horizon."

"You mean you're in the job as much for the crack of it as paying the bills," I said.

"I imagine you're the same, sir."

"I'm stuck in this job because I'm sort of trapped in it," I said. "I can't really escape."

"That's what you like to tell yourself, sir," Wittingsley said. "In my experience, if a man really wants out, he will find a way. Neither of us truly wants it."

I left Wittingsley to his own devices and walked back to the car. The sky was getting dark by the time we got back to London. So was my mood. "I can't believe the guests were all smiles when they left," I said. "Doesn't that strike you as incongruous after the night's events? Did they even remember any of it?"

"It's not something they're likely to forget," Julia said. "The Tories were well chuffed. They had a great time losing control like that. Yes, they cried and moaned and hallucinated God knows what, but Mistress Tania had them well under control. Since they were tied up and blindfolded, they couldn't do themselves any harm. She's talked people through head trips before. Took good care of them."

"Thank Christ for that," I said.

"You might hate to admit it," Julia said, "but Roger might have judged all the guests perfectly. I think he knew how they would react to the drugs."

"If he did, that means he knew who was going to have a bad trip," I said. "It means he knew that Laird Collins would not enjoy losing control and going completely round the bend . . ."

"Ravi? What's wrong?"

"It means that was why Roger wanted me there." I had a sinking feeling in my stomach. "So that I would talk to Collins about the gods and that would completely fuck with Collins's worldview. I was the bait and the weapon, Roger's revenge against Collins."

"Are you upset that Roger used you for the very reason he's always kept you around?" Julia asked.

"I'm offended that Roger used me and the gods to mash Collins's head into paste," I said, seething. "That's not how you use gods. You should never use gods to get revenge at all. It's hubris. The gods will make you pay for that. And if Roger's pissed off the gods, that puts me in the middle. Again."

Julia went quiet as it sank in. I didn't know if she believed the gods were there. She tended to act as if they were. She especially took comfort in the notion that Louise was there.

"Bloody hell, so the butler did it, after all," Benjamin said. "The oldest but least used cliché ever."

Mark laughed.

"I'm sure old Roger knew about the whole irony of it all," he said. "It's just like him to fuck with convention like that."

"When he called Willingsley a 'combat butler,' I thought he was joking," I said. "Now I know what a combat butler does. He could have told us instead of having me chasing down who spiked the food."

"And made us accessories and conspirators?" Mark said. "Imagine how much shit we'd be in if this even ended up in court. No, you provided Roger with his deniability."

"Oh, right," I said. That actually hadn't occurred to me in this instance. "So Roger keeping us in the dark was, in his own way, keeping our arses covered as well."

"It's not from the kindness of his heart, I can tell you," Mark said. "He wants to keep Golden Sentinels as his primary business, as a backup. I heard him talking to Cheryl about that."

"This doesn't leave us clean," I said. "We're still implicated in whatever he gets up to, by association alone. He's taking a fucking big gamble here."

"Roger's gotta be Roger," Mark said. "Always gotta chance it."

"And he might land us in the shit in the process," I said.

Louise was riding in the car with us, beaming from the backseat between Mark and Benjamin as we headed back to London.

Both Louise and Julia looked happy.

Louise settled into the backseat and sipped on her cocktail.

THE PEAR-SHAPED
ANTITERROR CAPER

ONE

"Deep shit" had been my prevailing mood for more than a month, ever since this case. I had not been in the best of moods. It's hard to maintain a sunny disposition when you were nearly beheaded in a terror video. The gods hadn't been much help. They thought it was a great laugh, especially the bit where I was rescued and the clusterfuck that followed.

But I'm getting ahead of myself.

Julia has suggested I talk about the case that had put me in a dark mood. I don't really want to talk about it, but I might as well do it now to get it over with, and out of my system. I've tried to write about this several times, but mostly it was just writing "fuck" a lot. It was that unpleasant. I promised Julia I would pull my finger out and get on with it.

Before things went off the rails, we went to Sunday dinner as usual with my parents. Anji and Vivek brought baby Daya so Mum and Dad could coo over her and not talk about Julia's and my wedding ceremony. The gods milled around us at the dinner table. Louise was in a Holly Golightly dress, her hair in a Hepburn bun.

I wondered if the gods had their own ongoing soap opera when I wasn't looking, aside from reenacting the Mahabharata and the Bhagavad Gita, of course. Perhaps that was why they liked to show up and watch my life. Now they had a new god in their midst, Louise, who wasn't even from the same culture. Now that I thought about it, it sounded more like a sitcom.

In case you were wondering why I never talked about what my sister and her husband do for a living, it's because she specifically asked me not to. On pain of death. Mind you, Vivek would have been utterly chuffed if I'd mentioned what he did, since he thinks everything I do is glamorous and grand. I haven't told them or my parents about the hairier situations I get into as an investigator, and that is how I plan to keep it. They would be horrified and my parents might drop dead from the shock. Rest assured, Anji and Vivek work in perfectly normal, totally legal middle-class white-collar professions that never require the services of the likes of me, and that is how we all like it.

My parents were getting on well, or normally, anyway. Mum was helping out at the local food bank giving out provisions to the people who needed it. Mrs. Dhewan, who owned the food bank and was Mum's friend, was also the local gangster who ran her own little kingdom in my parents' part of town.

The dominating topic, of course, was my impending wedding to Julia. Her parents had insisted on being in charge of the wedding, much to my relief. More specifically, Julia's mother was planning it all, and my mother had been spending a lot of time with her. The result: two Bridezilla mums. They'd been arguing for weeks now about everything from the flower arrangements, to the color schemes, the style of the hats, the gift lists, the seating arrangements. My parents were actually quite delighted that I was going to have an English wedding. Julia and I were going to be married in a church. There was going to be a reception with speeches and dancing, only much plainer and more anodyne than you would expect from a Hindu wedding. The church was booked, the hotel was booked for the reception afterwards. The gift list had to be planned. This was virtually a full-time job. Which our mothers took charge of. Which became the next big source of stress for everyone.

Two words: Bridezilla mums.

This had to be an absolutely perfect wedding, of course, but our mothers' ideas of what constituted that were not 100 percent in synch. Julia's mother was very Church of England. Mum kept trying to introduce elements of Hindu custom into it. I suspected one of the relatives back in

India had put the idea in her head in one of their phone conversations. Some of the other relatives were actually thrilled to be attending an English wedding, a fun reason to fly over from India for the first time since my sister's wedding more than a year ago.

"Did you go over to see that woman?" my father asked.

"Of course I did, Dad. It would have been disrespectful not to," I said.

Dad was referring to Mrs. Dhewan. Julia and I had stopped by to say hello on our way to dinner with my parents.

"Wonderful, Ravi!" she said. "And what a lovely girl Julia is! The two of you work very well together!"

We had helped her out with some bits of bother with her businesses a few months ago, tracked down some dodgy suppliers of Bollywood DVDs who owed her some merchandise after they did a runner and left her video rental business in the lurch. Since that was what kept that local Asian community up to date on the latest movies, it would not do. So we got Olivia to do a search and hacked the supplier's website, shutting it down with a DDoS attack that paralyzed their business until they agreed to supply Mrs. Dhewan again. Not everything with her needed to be a gang war, fortunately.

"If you need any help with the catering or supplies for your wedding, you'll let Auntie know, won't you?" Mrs. Dhewan said and beamed.

Of course, we invited her to the wedding. My father harrumphed when I told him.

"That's all the boxes ticked," I told Julia as we drove home. "Now we can just try to get through this without our mums driving everyone mad."

I knew it wasn't exactly going to be easy, but we'd done our part. Any stress that arose after this wouldn't be our fault. It was just as well, really, considering what was to come.

TWO

"**G**ather round, children," Roger said. "We have a High Priority assignment with a very large bonus in it."

"Yeah?" Benjamin said from his workstation, perking up.

"This is a Very Special Missing Persons case," Roger said, in his usual patrician manner, with its insistent hint of condescension. "There's a certain gentleman who needs to be found, and quickly."

"So why is he so important?" I asked.

"He wants to come in from the cold, to the West, which would be quite a coup. He possesses invaluable information on a whole number of things."

"This sounds like a spy swap," I said, my skepticism rising. The gods, though, were perking up as much as Benjamin was.

"I'm just painting a pretty picture, Ravi. You don't want to hear another boring story like too many other cases."

"Do you have a name for this guy?"

Roger left a dramatic pause.

"Hassan al-Hassah."

Ken and Clive nearly fell off their chairs.

Benjamin nearly spat out his espresso.

Olivia didn't even look up from her computer.

Julia was as surprised as I was.

I looked at Marcie.

"Did you bring this to Roger?" I asked.

She smiled and winked at me.

"Hang on," Mark said. "How did this job land at our door?"

Marcie stood up, one of those rare instances where she took over the floor from Roger, which was not good.

"Al-Hassah disappeared in heavy shelling in Basra six months ago," she said. "Everyone thought he was dead, but there was no DNA evidence. Rumors and disinformation ran wild. More than a week ago, al-Hassah made contact with our guys in Istanbul through back channels and provided proof of life, then negotiated his surrender to us. Not even the British intelligence services know about this, and we intend to keep it that way until the right time. The CIA agreed to let al-Hassah sneak into London and turn himself in to the US. Don't ask how he got here. He has his ways. As for why, well, he was Oxford-educated and he's actually kind of fond of England, for all his anti-West rhetoric."

"Hang on," Clive said. "Why wouldn't you lot let MI5 or MI6 know about this?"

"No offense, Clive," Marcie said. "But your intelligence agencies don't inspire a lot of confidence in us."

"I take your point," Clive said.

"And anyway, he's ours fair and square."

"The CIA were the ones who originally trained him, after all," Mark said. "How do we know he wasn't working for you lot all along and this was really him coming in from the cold?"

"You don't," Marcie said, her smile tight. "The Company asked for proof after proof to determine that he was in fact al-Hassah, since we'd heard about his doubles roaming around the Middle East for years. Once we were satisfied, we spent a fortune ensuring his safe passage from Pakistan to Germany before he finally arrived in London."

"So what went wrong, then?" Mark asked.

"There was a rendezvous set," Marcie said. "And he didn't show up."

"Oopsie," Benjamin said.

Ken and Clive glared at him.

"Since we trained him originally—by 'we,' I mean the CIA—since that was way before my time," Marcie said, "there are certain parties on our side that would love to see al-Hassah dead before he can sing. He knows a lot of our dirty little secrets in the Middle East, considering he was one of the biggest dirty little secrets. To some of my guys, he's a lot less embarrassing to have dead than alive."

"Given his nostalgia for England," Cheryl said, "he probably thought Britain was a bit more civilized a place to give himself up in."

"So when was he supposed to hand himself over to you?" I asked.

"This morning," Marcie said. "Our people had an agreed meeting time at his hotel, where he would formally hand himself over along with a computer containing the files he had on his entire organization. Our people went to his hotel in Mayfair and found him absent, the bed wasn't even slept in. The hotel staff told them he left the previous evening on his own and hadn't been back since."

"Maybe he had cold feet," I said. "Or he was going to double-cross you, or he was snatched."

"He could have decided to give himself up to the MI5," Mark said.

"We haven't ruled anything out," Marcie said.

"And you're sure the British didn't know he was coming?"

"We were very careful about leaks," Marcie said.

"So why come to us?" I had to ask. "Surely you've got every American agent in London and their au pair combing the city for him right now."

"Here's the thing, guys," Marcie said. "We're fucking desperate. We don't have a clue where he could have gone. The trail's completely cold. My station chief said to use all resources available, so I'm dipping into the discretionary fund to hire Golden Sentinels to help find this guy. We're reaching out to every independent contractor on our books here."

"So you're the client?" I said.

"My company is," Marcie said.

"Once again we're the running dogs of American hegemony," Mark said.

"How are we even qualified to track down one of the world's most wanted terrorists?" I said. "We're private investigators, not spies or special ops."

"Don't sell yourself short, old son," Roger said. "Some of you lot might know someone who knows someone. Ken, Clive, I know you have your old network of informers from your days as coppers. Mark, you know all sorts of people in the shadows. Olivia, I'm sure you can turn up something on the Internet. Someone somewhere knows something. Just make your inquiries."

"This feels well out of our comfort zone," I said.

"Oh, maybe I buried the lead," Marcie said. "Or did you guys already know that al-Hassah has a $20 million bounty on his head, courtesy of the US government?"

Well, that was us told.

"Now, I know twenty million is a figure that makes the brain go doolally and the knees go weak," Roger said. "Greed is a natural human impulse, but I'll thank you not to go all *Treasure of the Sierra Madre* on us. We're all in this together. This will be an agency effort, which means if any of you find the bugger, it has to be properly reported to our client and paperwork needs to be filed. That means you report to me, Cheryl, and Marcie together. Marcie will be our liaison with her station chief at the US Embassy. Proof of identity has to be verified before any talk of the reward will even be brought up."

"With proof of identity," Marcie said, "we're talking DNA evidence, dental records, on top of visual confirmation. We don't want to end up with a double. And he may have gotten cosmetic surgery in the last few years."

"If we get a result and it pays out, the fees will go to the agency coffers and be part of your salaries as usual, but the reward will be doled out as a bonus, equally, to everyone here," Roger said.

I thought I sensed a couple of sighs of disappointment from Ken and Clive, Benjamin, even Mark. Mark surprised me a bit there. I never thought he cared much about money.

"Forget about being the one who gets to the finish line first," Cheryl said. "You find out anything, share with the rest of us. We're all in this together."

"And even if it's split, we all still get a few million each," Roger said. "Nothing to sniff at, eh?"

"Now, off you go. Chop-chop," Cheryl said, clapping her hands.

THREE

The moment Roger and Cheryl finished, Ken and Clive got up and walked out. If there was anyone who could get any information from the streets, it was them.

As we settled back to our desks, I noted that the gods were looking very chuffed. They were anticipating a good show. Kali was munching popcorn. Lord Shiva was opening a large bag of crisps and sharing it with Lord Vishnu. Bagalamukhi was slurping on a jumbo-sized cup of Coke. This was going to be bad. I sensed maximum chaos ahead.

"What do the gods say?" Julia asked.

"They're giving us the thumbs-up, which can't be good."

"Maybe there's a lesson to be learned," she said.

"I'm sure there is, and I suspect we won't come out of this one looking very good," I said. "No matter how much we get paid."

She had that odd look in her eyes.

"Don't tell me you're excited about the money, too?" I said.

"Not really, more for the crack of it," she said.

"We really have to talk about your addiction to risky behavior," I said.

"I haven't started yet, Ravi." She looked coy, which meant she was relishing the prospect of doing some really crazy things for this case.

"Julia, we're probably the least dangerous people out looking for this guy. That means there are far worse people in town searching high and low for him, and we do not want to run into them."

"I know." She shrugged, but the relish didn't leave her eyes or her lips.

It was probably just as well that David was out of town meeting whoever it was Roger had sent him to deal with concerning some paperwork on whatever Roger's Grand Business Venture was, which he still wouldn't tell us anything about. David would probably have freaked out over the prospect of us dealing with a terrorist.

Benjamin was shaking his leg, full of nervous energy.

"Are you already spending that reward money?" I asked.

"Got my eye on parts to build a quantum computer," he said. "It'll be a modest one, but still powerful enough to link up to the big ones at MIT and even a couple of secret labs abroad. I can talk Olivia into writing some code with me to create a program to determine if we're livin' in a computer simulation or not."

"And what would you do with that if you succeed?"

"Ravi, mate, if you can work out the code that controls Reality, it means you'll have found the cheat code as well. Think about it. This is a shitty world we're in. Wouldn't you like to rewrite Reality to make things a bit better?"

"I'm not sure your version of 'better' is that good for the rest of us, darling," Olivia said, not even looking up from her computer. "Knowing you, it'll be full of hentai porn and role-playing video games."

"Ahh, you love it, really," Benjamin leered. "I could make your tits bigger totally naturally, without any surgery or artificial ingredients."

"Fuck. Right. Off," she said, giving him the finger, still without looking up.

I glanced at Olivia, who hadn't batted an eyelash at Roger's announcement.

"You don't seem as excited about the reward as everyone else is."

"It's just money." She shrugged again.

"That sounds a bit blasé," I said.

"Please," she scoffed, "I grew up around greater sums than twenty million moving in and out of the system all the time. I have a healthy respect for money. It doesn't rule me. I know not to let it turn me into an idiot when a large payout is dangled in front of my nose like a carrot. And

I certainly know how to dangle it in front of a gangster or a businessman or a corrupt official to game him into falling into a trap of my making."

I was still processing Olivia's Hong Kong adventure from last year. Every day, I was reminded just how terrifying she was.

"That's a healthy way of looking at it."

"When a sum of money starts going into the tens or hundreds of millions, it becomes abstract. No single person can really wrap their head around those numbers in a practical way, let alone having that much money. It goes beyond paying off one's debts. It becomes something completely Other."

"You seem to have spent a lot of time thinking about it," I said.

"It's an existential requirement in my family. What about you, Ravi? Are you excited about getting a reward for catching the bad terrorist man?" Olivia asked.

"It's blood money," I said. "More than the payment for any of our other cases. I'm not sure I'm comfortable with it."

"But you wouldn't say no to a share of that twenty million, would you?"

"Probably not, but what would I do with it? What do you do with more money than you'll ever need? Pay for an Indian wedding to appease my family after Julia and I have the first English one? Buy my parents a house? They already own their house. Pay off my sister and her husband's mortgage? They wouldn't say no, but it's not something they're having difficulty with. Buy a house or a flat? I don't need a mansion or a penthouse. I'm not going to a casino or buying sports cars or yachts. Give it away to charity and worthy causes? Sure, why not? Invest it so that it moves around in the economy where it gets spent on all kinds of dodgy stuff?"

"I could give you a few pointers there," Olivia said.

"I'm sure you could, and they'll be very sensible choices, but I doubt we'll find him."

"Don't be so sure, darling," she said, and went back to typing whatever code on her computer it was that she found more interesting than what Roger was telling us.

"Children, I'm not expecting you to go running around town

playing James Bond," Roger said, looking up from whatever he was talking to Cheryl about. "This is grown-up stuff. No, I'm just asking you to put out feelers, ask around, use whatever networks of information you have to find this bastard. You are not to approach him or try to nab him on your own."

"Ah, we're just supposed to finger him, then?" Mark asked.

"That's right," Roger said. "There are professionals in town to do the heavy lifting. They'll have to share the bounty with us."

"How do we know they'll even play nice with us?" Benjamin said.

"They have done in the past," Roger said.

"You mean . . . ?" Julia asked.

"Oh Christ, no!" I said.

"Interzone will do the heavy lifting on this one," Marcie said. "The Company contracted them for any extraction and to give you cover."

The gods, watching from the sofa, laughed, as if they had known this was coming.

"We're going to have those dangerous fuckers running around London with guns?" I said. "How is this not going to blow up in our faces?"

"Laird Collins assured us they would work with you guys," Marcie said. "Their liaison and our liaison will be, you know, liaising."

"So Ariel's coming, then?" Julia asked, eyebrow raised.

"They're flying in this afternoon," Marcie said.

"Just what we need when we have a wedding to plan," I said.

"Ah, but think about how much a share of twenty million dollars could help," Roger said. "Consider that your dowry."

"If we even find him," I said.

"I have total confidence in your abilities," Roger grinned. "The lot of you."

"The rest of you can play with this how you want," I said. "I'm out. I have no connections to any sources that could possibly find us a terrorist."

"Fair enough," Cheryl said. "Roger won't hold that against you."

I preferred to worry about whether Julia's and my mum were going to get along as they bickered over the planning of our wedding. If anything, Dad found this rather relaxing, because Mum was focusing her energy and aggression on the wedding and Julia's mum rather than him. He'd been enjoying a lot of peace and quiet at home because of that.

As if on cue, Mum phoned me on my mobile.

"Ravi dear, do you have a moment now?"

"Anything for you, Mum."

"It's just that Brenda and I are having a healthy debate about what you should wear for the wedding."

"I thought I was wearing a tuxedo."

"I've had a bit of inspiration, love. Perhaps you might wear a sherwani instead."

"Ummm . . . I'm not sure. It's a Church of England ceremony."

"Yes, but think about it, Ravi. We're a diverse, multicultural society now, so why not embrace it? Julia can wear a traditional white wedding gown and veil, and you can wear a sherwani and safa—I said 'safa,' Brenda. That's a kind of turban. That's sher-wa-ni, it's a long silk top, usually churidar pants. Gold or brown, Brenda."

"Is Brenda there? How does she feel about it?"

"She hasn't said no. She's actually giving it some thought."

I heard loud protestations in the background.

"I think your mum might be having a fit," I said to Julia.

"Do you have a moment, dear?" Mum said. "We need to get you fitted."

I looked over to Julia.

"I think I have to stop our mums from killing each other."

"Good excuse to get out of the office," Julia said.

"Ah yes," Roger said. "When David comes back, I need him to draft the paperwork for how we might collect the bounty on al-Hassah?"

"That's a bit premature, isn't it, Roger?" I said. "We haven't even started looking for him yet."

"I have faith in my boys and girls." Roger smiled. "Oh, Ravi, you can expect a call from Ariel to coordinate so Interzone and Golden Sentinels don't step on each other's toes."

I winced.

Julia and I left together.

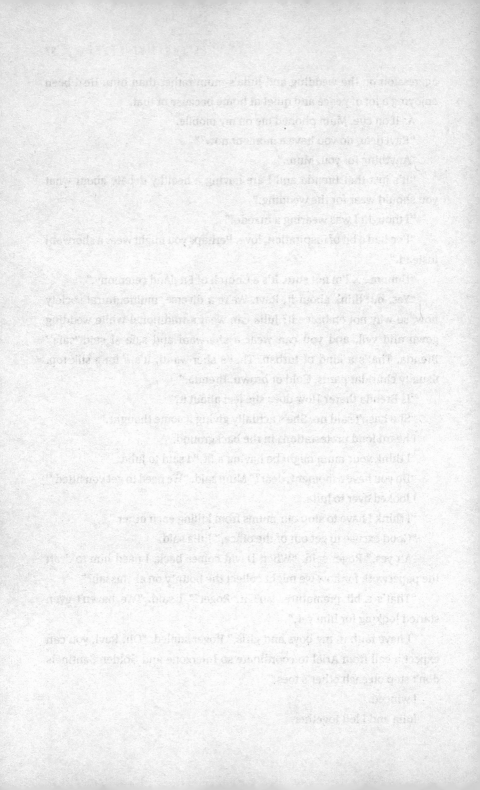

FOUR

We took the Tube down to Oxford Circus and walked to Berwick Street to avoid the car traffic on Oxford Street. Julia's mum and mine were gently debating while the tailor stood politely by the side. The "gentle debate" here was full of increasingly strained passive-aggressiveness, our mothers still smiling as they battled for dominance. Over my wedding attire. Yes, it was all very English indeed.

"If he was a soldier," Mum said, "he would be wearing his dress uniform. As a Hindu, couldn't he wear something from his culture?"

"I suppose he could," Brenda said, very reasonably. "You mean like those lovely turbans that have to be folded elaborately?"

"You're thinking about Sikhs, Brenda," Mum said. "It's Tamil men who wear those. And they usually have very long hair and beards, which my Ravi doesn't. We're Hindu."

"Ah, my apologies," Brenda said, face reddening. "I'm so sorry I can't distinguish between Asian cultures."

"No need, Brenda," Mum said. "You're not expected to be fully informed of all the differences."

And on and on.

"What do you think, Ravi?" Mum said. "Surely you have an opinion on all this."

"I'm perfectly fine with the gray tuxedo and just going old-school," I said.

Mum shot me a sharp look.

"Then again, a bit of color wouldn't go amiss," I added.

My phone rang, which was a relief.

Ariel.

I stepped outside to take the call, leaving Julia to deal with our mums.

"Hey, hon," Ariel said. "Guess we're working together again."

"Is Jarrod with you?" I asked.

"You bet. No way was he going to pass up the chance to get al-Hassah. He had run-ins with his group in Syria. Jarrod would love to pop a cap in al-Hassah's ass, but he'll follow the rules and try to take him alive. We got a full squad with us in London."

"Let's make a deal," I said. "Why don't you lot go ahead and hunt him down? You can have him as far as I'm concerned."

"Aww, don't you want in on the fun, or the twenty million?"

"We're just a bunch of private eyes," I said. "What do we know about finding a terrorist hiding in the city? No, this is entirely your specialty. Have at it."

"Are you okay? You sound a little stressed."

"I'm with my mother and Julia's mother. They're arguing over my tuxedo."

"Oh man, that's rough! Are you sure you don't want to hunt for a mean ol' terrorist with me to take the edge off?"

"No, thank you. Look, I'm just proposing that if I get any information, I'll pass it on to you, since you lot are the ones with the guns and the brutality for going after people like that, and I'm perfectly happy to stay out of your way."

"Come on, you're playing an angle."

"I'm not interested in the reward. It's blood money, and my karma's messed up enough without adding this to it."

"I bet you'll look hot in your tuxedo," Ariel said.

"If I wear a tuxedo. That's still a work in progress between our mums—Look, why are we talking about this? Just do whatever you lot do and find the guy—"

"Don't I get an invite to your wedding?"

Another call. Benjamin.

"I have to take this," I said, and gratefully hung up on her.

"Ravi? Listen, mate, I'm with Ken and Clive. We could use your help with somethin'. Need to pick your brain, if you like."

"What's up?"

"Can you come meet us at Ken and Clive's gaff?"

I walked back into the tailor's.

"Mum, Brenda, we have to go," I said. "But you both have exquisite taste, so I will wear whatever you agree on."

I kissed them each on the cheek and bid my farewells.

"So charming," Brenda said. "Is he like this with all the ladies?"

"Yes," Julia said proudly as she left with me.

FIVE

Clive opened the door to us.

"Thanks for comin', mate," he said.

He looked a bit surprised that Julia was there, but he let us in. Benjamin and Ken were in the living room. Take-out cartons recently emptied of Indian food were on the dinner table.

Ken and Clive's council flat was just off Ladbroke Grove. The place was cramped with old army paraphernalia from Clive's days in the military. Photos of him in uniform. Photos of Ken and Clive in the boxing ring. It might surprise you to know that Ken and Clive's flat was actually sparklingly clean. The CD collection was catalogued by artist in alphabetical order, a lot of seventies glam rock, Led Zeppelin, Marc Bolan, T. Rex, and David Bowie. There were no take-out food cartons on the carpet or unwashed dishes in the sink. The state-of-the-art desktop computer with scanner and broadband connection sat on a desk near the window.

Ken had actually inherited the flat from his late mother, and he considered the place sacred. He told me she only let him have it after he swore to her on her deathbed that he would keep it spic-and-span like she did, and say what you will about him, he kept his promise. There was a picture of her taking up pride of place on the mantelpiece. She looked at least as big as he was, and it wouldn't have surprised me if she'd killed people with her bare hands in her time as well. She looked like Ken, only much more clean-shaven. I found no pictures of his father at all. Maybe he was a Viking god who met his mother and goes around the world leaving large, scary offspring in his wake. I always had the impression Ken was descended from a long line of shitkickers that kept empires running. I imagined his distant ancestor as a very large Celtic psychopath with a very large axe hacking away at Roman invaders and then the family ended up working for whatever regime was in charge of Albion at any given time. Obviously, the "large" and "warrior" genes survived through the ages. Not for his family the glories of rank, promotion, and titles, no. Ken's family provided the A-grade cannon fodder in the armed forces, enthusiastically fighting in wars for King and Country, using patriotism as a cover for the fact that they simply liked to fuck people up.

There was a framed X-ray of Clive's skull up on the wall. It had been taken when he was hit by shrapnel in Afghanistan. The shrapnel had gone into his brain, lodging itself in his pineal gland, and remained there to this day because it was too dangerous to operate. Clive had suffered no brain damage or impairment to any of his higher functions, but a neurologist might have suspected that his propensity for violence was the direct by-product of that bit of shrapnel hanging there in his frontal lobe, where certain emotions were supposed to be, like empathy. Or remorse. There was, however, no explanation for Ken sharing the same tendencies. Somehow, I didn't find this fact particularly reassuring whenever I worked with the two of them.

Clive himself was barely out of his teens when he fought in the Gulf War, and unlike many of his comrades who came back forever traumatized, he merely shrugged and said, "It was awright." I suspect that while his comrades suffered from post-traumatic stress and had nightmares for years, Clive was the one who had provided the nightmares. He applied to join the police force, where he met Ken. They came up together when they were promoted to the detective squad. The two of them were like peas in a pod, two halves of the same violent whole that believed in rough justice beyond the letter of the law. They just enjoyed what they did more than others were comfortable with, like killing and disappearing the worst criminals they couldn't convict, and covering it up. They were so good at it that when they started disappearing certain powerful people who were part of a pedophile ring, their bosses had to frame them for corruption in order to drum them out of the force. They were also a couple, which was unsurprising. After all, the couple that slays together stays together. They didn't hesitate when Roger came a-calling with a job offer.

"There's something we need to pick your brains about, mate," Ken said.

"We have a bit of a problem," Benjamin said.

"So what are you doing home?" I asked. "Can't we go back to the office?"

"We can't talk about this back at the office," Clive said.

"Why not?" I asked.

The gods were all here with us. They piled onto the sofa and watched for my reaction.

"Here's the thing," Benjamin said. "We found al-Hassah."

SIX

"**Y**ou're joking," I said.

"For reals," Benjamin said.

"We found him last night," Clive said.

"Completely by chance," Ken said.

"It was on the case we were on," Benjamin said.

Ken and Clive had accompanied Benjamin on a routine bugging operation in a flat in Earl's Court: the American media tycoon Lucas van Hooten had hired Roger to keep tabs on Vanessa, his dilettante daughter who had come to London as an exchange student and decided to go all Vanessa Redgrave and join the Socialist Workers Party and change the world. Van Hooten owned a right-wing media empire and was concerned that his baby girl was running with the wrong crowd. I was glad Roger hadn't handed this case to me, but he'd been especially nice to me because of my impending wedding, and probably after I threw a strop about nearly getting my head blown off in Alfie Beam's mansion. Benjamin was the one who liked to sneak into people's places to place cameras and microphones in them, so this was business as usual for him. Since this was a high-profile client in a posh part of town, Benjamin asked Ken and Clive to go with him in case they needed to smooth things over with any local coppers that might have come across them. Julia and I were at home fast asleep at the time.

Van Hooten had provided Golden Sentinels with the security code for the building's front door and his daughter's flat's burglar alarm. Benjamin easily picked the lock to her door on his own. Then it was a matter of planting pin-sized webcams all over the place and getting out before she got home from the pub.

Van Hooten owned a twenty-four-hour news channel for which truth was optional and the extolling of the virtues of the Republican Party and the demonization of liberals and people of color was its bread-and-butter. It played a huge part in stirring up Islamophobia and fomenting white America's paranoia about Muslim terrorists, even pushing the paranoid fantasy that entire chunks of the UK and Europe had become Sharia no-go zones even the police didn't dare enter. No wonder Roger didn't give this one to me or Mark. We would have refused.

Benjamin got back to the car to rejoin Ken and Clive, then turned on his laptop to log into the server so he could check the footage from the cameras. The car was nearly at South Kensington when Benjamin yelled "Fucking hell!" and told Ken and Clive to turn back. On screen, who should walk in the front door with Vanessa but Hassan al-Hassah. Or a bloody good lookalike in an Armani suit, brandishing a bottle of wine and a talent for tongue music.

"Fucking hell, it's him!" Clive said.

"No way," Benjamin said. "The world's second most wanted terrorist leader suddenly turns up for a drink with a posh tottie in her flat in the heart of London?"

"Why not? Don't you believe in coincidence?" Ken said.

"Hang on," Benjamin said. "He's a Muslim. They're not supposed to drink booze."

"Yeah, like that's gonna stop 'em," Clive snorted.

Ken and Clive were great believers in the human capacity to yield to temptation. They often watched people do it and stood in judgment, never mind that they gave in to temptation themselves sometimes, usually involving beating the shit out of people they despised.

"Yeah, guess no right-thinkin' man's gonna resist booze and tottie," Benjamin said. "They hardly said a word to each other. But it would've been hard to say much with all the snogging. It certainly didn't look like they were strangers."

Hassan al-Hassah. One of the world's most hated terrorist leaders. He'd had a hand in the planning of almost every major bombing campaign against American and British interests all over the Middle East in the last decade. Americans troops hunted for him in Afghanistan but lost his trail when rumor had it he crossed into Pakistan and hid there under the protection of Pakistani Intelligence. In the meantime, he continued to issue audio and video recordings exhorting true believers to wage Holy War against the West.

"Imagine our surprise when he suddenly showed up in London snoggin' the daughter of the biggest right-wing American media mogul out there!" Benjamin said.

"And you recorded it all?" I asked.

"Too right we did!"

"It took forty-five minutes for their horizontal tango to end," Ken said.

"That was when we three voted we should go for it," Clive said.

"Fuck me," said Ken. "As a postcoital drink, he fixed himself a gin and tonic!

"The bastard's havin' an English drink!"

"Well, he *was* educated at Oxford and Harvard," Benjamin said. "Reckon he developed a taste for the ol' G&T."

"Bastard killed hundreds of innocent people and thinks he can drink our booze . . . !" Clive ranted.

"You know," I said, "there's a possibility it's not him."

"It was fucking him, all right!" Ken said. "Benjamin zoomed in to his face five times and matched it with the online database that law enforcement used!"

"Eighty percent match," Benjamin said. "I even said to Ken and Clive, 'Hold on, let's think about it for a minute. Are we fallin' into one of those 'they all look alike' situations here? It's late, we're tired, and he could be some professor or SWP member she's seeing. He may not be al-Hassah.' And Clive said 'No, *you* think about it, mate! Daddy is one of the biggest media moguls in the world, knows everybody, had business dealings with al-Hassah's family in Saudi Arabia before he declared himself a Jihadist, even went to university with Hassan himself back in the day! Little Vanessa has got a right rebellious streak, what's an even better way to fuck Daddy off than membership in the Socialist Wankers Party? Why, bonk Daddy's old-mate-turned-terrorist-leader, of course! What are the odds, eh? What are the fucking odds?'"

"Okay," I said. "Think about *this*: What if that's just a lookalike?"

That made Ken and Clive pause.

"I told 'em, if we're gonna go all Freudian on the girl," Benjamin said. "Why not try this for size? It doesn't need to be the real McCoy. A stand-in will do just fine."

"It's him," Clive muttered. "I can feel it in me bones."

"If it *is* him, where are his bodyguards? He's an important guy. They're not gonna let him wander around alone."

"They *arrested* his bodyguards in Lahore, remember? Bodyguards said he was dead. These bodyguards weren't supposed to ever stray more than ten feet away from him, and yet they were caught wanderin' about on their own after the drone strike that the Yanks thought done him in. They were obviously meant to make us believe he was dead, throw us off his trail. He could've crossed over into Pakistan, and from there, gone anywhere. It's him. I'm tellin' you."

"Fine," I said. "Maybe it's him, maybe it's not. But your work here is done. Go to Roger, hand over the video links for her daddy to watch her on the Internet, let Roger report Mini al-Hassah to the Yanks, and if he's the real deal, Roger collects the reward and pays us all a bonus. What's the problem?"

They paused and looked down. This was when I could tell the story was about to get worse.

SEVEN

"There was no way we were going to pass up a major opportunity here!" Ken said.

"What are you talking about?" I asked.

"We voted to nab him!" Clive said.

"Right fucking there! Do the world a favor!"

"And you went along with that?" I said to Benjamin.

"Well, yeah," he said. "Seemed like a good idea at the time."

Kali started laughing. Not good.

"Of all the cosmic jokes in the universe," she said, "you had to end up in this one!"

"To be fair," Benjamin said, "I did say we should make sure he was the real McCoy and not a lookalike."

Clive began to talk in a hushed tone, full of restrained rage that indicated the utter seriousness of his intent.

"It's not just about the money this time, all right?" he said. "Ken and me's got mates in the army who were killed by this bastard's people."

"We reckoned we could just capture al-Hassah," Benjamin said, "if that was really him, and turn him in for the twenty-million-dollar reward the US had posted for him. But that wouldn't work. The circumstances behind how we came across him would be hard to explain. Besides, where the hell could we hold him until we handed him over for the reward? It wasn't like we had a bunch of safe houses around town for stashing warm bodies."

"Well, now you have an option," I said. "Tell Roger! He'll sort it out!"

"Er, yeah," Ken said. "There's more."

"You have to hear the rest of it," Clive said.

"What, he got away? Then it's not your problem anymore. Just tell Roger you came across him last night and he'll tell you to follow up on the connection to Vanessa van Hooten," I said.

"You really want to hear the rest of this," Ken said.

"Fine," I said. "Go on."

"All right," Benjamin said. "So. But I want to make it clear that I went along to make sure things didn't go horribly wrong. 'Nah, nah, nothing'll go wrong, it'll be a doddle. You'll see,' Clive and Ken kept sayin'."

"Well, things went horribly wrong," Ken said.

"Of course they did," I said.

"You know," Benjamin said, "London may be the most surveilled city in the world, with the hundreds of cameras stuck on virtually every street corner, but it's still surprisingly easy to disappear someone off the streets if you set your mind to it. At night, the streets are so dimly lit, it's a wonder the city isn't a serial killer's paradise. And the surveillance cameras are only good for catching people in the act *after* the fact. The police aren't going to watch every screen for every hour of the day. They only pour over footage for an incident *after* it's occurred, to see if they can identify the perpetrators, and that's only when they have an idea who they're looking for. If it's a total blank without a previous record, they're lost at sea. Amateurs get caught. We are not amateurs. We knew that we could get away with what we were doin' if it didn't *look* like a suspicious act. That is, assumin' we had to do it at a spot that had a camera pointing at it."

"Yes, Benjamin," I said. "You gave me and Julia that speech when we started working at the firm. You're rambling."

"Sorry," he said. "So then, we waited for al-Hassah to leave the flat and tailed him in the car. It was after two a.m. when he walked out. You know an operation of this type usually takes months to plan, yeah? Months of surveillance and psychological profiling, months of field-testing alternate scenarios and backup plans, months of mapping the target's movements and habits, months of debating over the best method of liquidation, whether by guns, knives, poisons, or faked 'natural causes,' months to choose the best location in which to carry out the mission—"

"Benjamin!"

"Okay! Okay! Here we were with an opportunity brought on totally by sheer dumb luck, an opportunity we would probably never get again if we let it pass, and we were going to have to improvise. We are good at improvising."

"You're preaching to the choir here, Benjamin," I said. "But the more you say that, the more doubtful I'm getting, and I already know you're good at it."

"All right, we watched the street outside the flat to see if there was anyone else watching it. It looked clear. Ken got out of the car and walked across the street to scan the vicinity for any potential hostiles. Clive and I stayed in the car and looked out for any cars that might have pulled up to the building or circled the block more than once. The coast was clear. Could-be al-Hassah really was on his own tonight, which continued to make me doubt it was actually him.

"I started up the car and drove slowly behind Maybe al-Hassah. Ken walked around the corner so that he would end up walkin' towards the man as he came down the street. I had to time my speed for what we were about to pull off.

"Ken shambled up in his suit and tie, looking like some businessman who'd had a bit too much to drink, so our target wouldn't consider him a threat. At least, not till Ken broke into a smile, threw out his arms, and greeted him like an old friend he hadn't seen for a while. Of course, the target was completely taken by surprise, and Ken kept him off-balance by ranting about how long it had been since they last met, how about going for a drink and all that, closing in on him as he did, lookin' like he was about to give the guy a hug. That was when I pulled up alongside them.

"As al-Hassah started to back away from him, Ken delivered a quick punch to his throat, which cut off his air supply and doubled him over, in time for Clive to throw the back door open and for Ken to shove him into the car without any resistance.

"If any cameras caught this, it would've looked like Ken and Clive were meetin' a drunken friend and helping him into a car. Thank fuck I made it a point to use fake license plates so there wouldn't be any way to trace the car if the police ever bothered to. And we were off."

EIGHT

"**S**o we were speedin' off," Benjamin said. "And al-Hassah was asking the usual questions like 'Who are you?' and 'What do you want with me?' before settling into the usual 'I have money' and so on. I watched him via the rearview mirror as I drove. Ken and Clive were practically on top of the guy in the backseat of the car, smiling and laughing like it was all one big joke. I was startin' to get suspicious because he wasn't frightened *enough*. There just wasn't the right amount of fear and panic in his eyes, which is what you would expect if someone were suddenly abducted off the street by two complete strangers, especially if they were large, built like brick shithouses, and bearing down on you like a couple of lions over a gazelle.

"Then Clive said something to him in Arabic that made him freeze. It was a secret code name al-Hassah's network used to refer to him, which Clive knew about when he was in the army. Suddenly, the bastard's mask dropped. The panicked civilian façade fell away and his face became hard and tried to assume an air of authority.

"*Fuck me, it was really him!*

"I'd never been up close to a terrorist mastermind before, and I have to say he didn't look any different or special than anyone else. No buggy, bloodshot eyes, no foaming at the mouth, no furry white cat to stroke provocatively."

"He's not a stereotype anime villain, Benjamin," I said.

"Instead, we had here what looked like a dapper businessman in his fifties with good taste in suits and spoilt young blondes. He was so ordinary it was almost blinding. Imagine my disappointment. Pop culture has a lot to answer for, I can tell you."

"Too right," Clive said.

"Anyway," Benjamin said. "Al-Hassah's demeanor relaxed as he believed he was back in a situation he understood and had some control over. He was a Saudi prince, after all, with all the arrogance and entitlement you would expect, and he looked at Ken and Clive with the same contempt and disdain he would give to any hired help that accidentally spilled a drink on his lap.

" 'You don't know what you are getting into,' said al-Hassah in perfect English. 'For that, I pity you.'

" 'Oh yeah?' said Clive.

" 'You obviously have not been properly briefed,' the bastard said. 'I am to be let free, to go about my business. This is not the time. For the sake of you and your country, I urge you to let me go. It is bigger than both of you.'

"'That's what they all say,' said Ken. 'I got news for you, sunshine. This is the end of the line for you.'

" 'You are making a terrible mistake,' said al-Hassah. 'You are disobeying your orders. If you do anything to me, you will be severely punished.'

" 'Yeah, yeah,' said Ken and Clive, just rollin' their eyes.

"I might have been tempted to say somethin', but I was too busy doin' the drivin' and watchin' to make sure we weren't being tailed. I did wonder about the way he was talkin' to us, and I probably should've asked him a couple of questions, but I was a little preoccupied at the time.

"Meanwhile, Ken and Clive were really gettin' into it."

"Getting into what?" I asked.

" 'You think you're so smart, don't ya? Well, there's no one to help you now,' they were sayin'. 'We can do anything the fuck we want to ya. Nobody knows where you are, nobody knows who you're with. We can keep you alive for days, do you over like all those poor buggers you killed, eh?'

"I saw al-Hassah's eyes in the mirror. He had the kind of panic setting in for people who know they're screwed. That was when he made a lunge for the door. Ken and Clive anticipated this and grabbed him before he opened the door and punched him twice in the face before pullin' out the duct tape. The next ten minutes was mostly the sound of tape ripping as they secured al-Hassah from head to toe, with a tape over his mouth to shut him up and his arms strapped to his side, his knees and ankles together, and the rest of the drive proceeded in silence.

"When we reached the secluded part of the wooded area, I turned the engine off."

NINE

"'Ken, Clive, we need to talk. In private.'

"'Excuse us, we'll be right back,' they said to al-Hassah, who, with his mouth all taped up, was in no position to object.

"We walked out of the car and stood a few feet away. I reminded Ken and Clive that we hadn't quite thought this through, like where we were going to hold the fucker before we turned him in, and how we were going to get the authorities to believe us. Because, you know, it just looked like we'd kidnapped a Middle Eastern man, and it would look like a race-related hate crime. And who the fuck were we supposed to hand him over to anyway?"

"We wasted fuckin' time arguin'," Ken said.

"We were tryin' to tell Benjamin we had it all under control," Clive said. "This was not the first scumbag we kidnapped and disappeared—"

"We don't need to know that!" I said.

"But we had to convince little nervous nelly Benjamin here that Ken and I always have contingencies for doin' this sort of thing, so we could hold him until we sorted out where to take him."

"And just when we got Benjamin calmed down, we turned back to the car to find bloody al-Hassah had managed to jump out," Ken said.

"Somehow," Benjamin said, "al-Hassah, even taped up in the car as he was, must've managed to wriggle his hand over and gotten the door open and was now hopping away in the darkness. Ken and Clive were all 'Shit! Oy! Come back here!'"

"Al-Hassah turned and saw us coming, panicked, and tried to hop faster, which made him lose his balance and fall over," Ken said.

"So there we were," Clive said. "Scramblin' after our quarry, who was rolling horizontally down a steep slope like a runaway log. Most of it was forward momentum and I don't think he was in control, given that his arms and ankles were taped up."

"Ken was callin' 'Bad boy! Bad boy!' like he was a naughty dog runnin' off," Benjamin said.

"How high was that slope anyway?" Clive said.

"Pretty fuckin' high," Ken said. "We got our answer when I tripped, fell into Clive, knocked him over, and the two of us ended up rolling down the hill after al-Hassah."

"We shouldn't have worried so much," Clive said. "Since al-Hassah finally stopped when he crashed into a tree and we crashed into him. The next thing I recalled was a flurry of flailing limps and frenzied strugglin'."

"I was still at the top of the slope," Benjamin said. "So I couldn't see anything down there. All I heard was Ken and Clive effin' and blindin', goin' 'Grab his legs!' 'He's squirmin'!' 'Fuck! He's slippery!' 'He's kickin'!'"

"We had 'im," Ken said.

"Yeah," Clive said. "It was like wrestling with an eel."

"All right," I said. "So you got him. What's the problem?"

Ken and Clive suddenly looked sheepish.

"What?" I said.

"Just tell him," Benjamin said.

"We were just carryin' him back up to the car, yeah?" Clive said.

"It should have been easy," Ken said.

"But he was bloody squirmin'," Clive said. "And he made the three of us go tumblin' down the slope again. Ken and I were strugglin' to keep a hold on 'im. To get a better grip on 'im, I tried to wrap me arms around him and sort of got his neck and head in a chokehold."

"You didn't . . ." I said.

"I didn't bloody do it on purpose," Clive said. "But . . ."

"I heard it at the top of the slope," Benjamin said. "It was that fuckin' loud."

"Just like that," Ken said. "*Snap!*"

"You broke his neck," I said, barely believing the words coming out of my mouth.

"Arms like Clive's around your neck," Benjamin said. "Would have been like twistin' the cap off a beer bottle."

"He was gettin' right on my tits," said Clive.

"You killed him in anger?" I said, keeping my voice as low as possible.

"I was just trying to hold onto 'im," Clive said.

"We sat on top of him for another fifteen minutes," Ken said. "Just to be sure he'd really snuffed it. We listened for the death rattle, which came in due course. There was the usual smell of bowels giving out. Murder is dirty, ugly, poopy business, Ravi. I can tell ya."

"I wandered over to a tree and threw up," Benjamin said. "Then walked back to the car. Ken and Clive carried the body back up and put it in the boot. Then they lit up a fuckin' cigarette like it was postcoital or something."

"Look," Ken said, "it was tirin' work."

"Jesus Christ," I muttered.

"We had to stash the body," Clive said. "We couldn't very well leave it in a clearing or bury it, since there was always a chance of some jogger stumbling on it or a dog digging it up. We have a storage garage in West London not far from our flat, so we drove down there, wrapped al-Hassah in plastic, and stuck him into the freezer."

"This was strictly a short-term measure," Ken said. "Since we knew we would probably need access to it later."

"I took a few hair samples off the head and put them in a small Baggie for the DNA testing and confirmation," Benjamin said.

"'Ere, we saved the fuckin' world and no one knows it was us," Clive said. "Yeah, typical, but I can live with that."

"But in the end, you were there for me, mate. We did it! Come here!" Ken said.

Ken and Clive hugged Benjamin right there.

Kali, Shiva, and Bagalamukhi applauded behind me. I think I was in shock. Julia just sat there, eyes rapt.

"Not to break up this very emotional moment, chaps," I said, "but why are you fucking telling me all this? Why do I need to know?"

"Er, well," Ken said. "We were hopin' you might talk to Marcie for us."

"For what?"

"Do you know how fuckin' scary she can be?" Benjamin said. "Especially if you piss her off?"

"What makes you think she'll be pissed off" I asked.

"The CIA wants al-Hassah alive, remember?" Clive said. "And we fucking killed him."

"This means whatever they wanted from him, whatever intel they can get from debriefing him is lost," Benjamin said.

"She might decide to have us sent to bloody Guantánamo Bay," Ken said.

"Technically," Julia said, "it'll probably be a black site in Romania or something."

"Or just have us bumped off," Clive said.

"Oh, come off it," I said.

"We're not kidding," Benjamin said. "We are up shit creek because we just blew the CIA's plans. They're not very forgiving about that sort of thing."

"Maybe we should buy the first ticket to Mexico or somethin' . . ." Ken said.

"I wouldn't do that," I said. "The Agency has people in Mexico, and besides, it puts you closer to Guantánamo Bay."

"Oh yeah, right. We're fucked, aren't we?" Clive said.

I thought for a moment.

"Okay," I said. "Okay. You're going to have to bluff it out somehow."

"What are you on about?" Ken said.

"Here's the easiest solution: Drag the body out, leave it somewhere, make it look like he died in some accident or mugging or something. Call Roger and tell him you got a tip about the body. Get paid. End of story," I said.

"But what about the reward?" Benjamin said.

"Unless you're able to bring the poor bastard back to life and march him through the doors of the US Embassy, I don't see a lot of other options for collecting it right now," I said.

"What if, you know, we give 'em what he had on 'im at the time?" Ken said.

"Like what? I don't remember him carryin' any computer when we nabbed 'im," Benjamin said.

"Then you'll just have to settle for reporting the body," I said.

"Or retrace his steps and see if he dropped his laptop somewhere," Julia said.

"That's not going to work," Ken said.

"Why not?" I asked.

"There's another problem," Benjamin said.

TEN

I'll let Benjamin tell the rest of the story, since I was already getting a headache:

After Roger made the announcement this morning, we drove the work car back to Ken and Clive's lockup in West London. The place was huge, used to be owned by one of London's crime families through a shell company, but since the family got nicked, the ownership had been tied up in paperwork for the last few years. Ken and Clive knew all about the dodgy paperwork and swung it so they came to pretty much own the place under a shell company, something Roger taught them how to do. They reckoned it was a useful place to stash dead people during an emergency. That's right, this wasn't the first time they'd hidden a stiff, let alone in this place. Even in the daytime, the place was amazingly quiet and secluded, considering it was only a few blocks away from the swankier parts of Notting Hill, where the media mafia and glitterati hang out. We parked the car and Clive unlocked the front door.

"There's something I should tell you first," he said.

"Look," I said. "We all know what we have to do, and we can pretty much kiss our chances of claiming that twenty million good-bye."

"Yeah," he said, subdued.

"Okay," I said. "First thing we should do is— Fuck me!"

"What's wrong?" Ken said.

"What's—? Where do I start?"

The far end of the lockup, where the metal worktable was, had been smeared with blood, like Jack the Ripper had taken up finger painting while on a cocaine jag. If I hadn't been shitting myself by then, I might have thought there was a kind of abstract expressionist beauty to the way the crimson was smeared and spattered all over the wall and the floor, and if we had decided to submit the tableau as an art installation, it would probably have qualified for a Turner Prize. But no, at that moment, all I could think about was how much deeper in the shit we were than I had originally thought.

"Ken? Clive?" I said very calmly. "What the fuck did you do?"

"Stay calm, mate," Ken said.

"What happened here?" I was still perfectly calm.

"Well, after you left, we were still awake from all the adrenaline, yeah? So we decided to, well, take the initiative a bit and . . . cut up the body with a chainsaw," Clive said.

"I see," I said, still very calm. "Were you bored already? After everything else we went through last night?"

"We just thought he'd be easier to transport, if he was, you know, in more conveniently transportable pieces . . ." Ken said.

"Listen, lads," I said, very calmly. "I'm up for a chainsaw massacre as much as the next bloke, but how do you suppose we're going to explain that?"

"Weren't we going to say he met with some trouble or had an accident or somethin'?"

"Oh," I said, calmly, "you mean like he went for a walk in the middle of the night and ran into a bunch of muggers who happened to be armed with chainsaws?"

"Stop yelling at us, Ben," Clive said.

"I'm not yellin'," I said, totally not yellin'.

"You really need to chill out there, mate," Ken said.

I stopped to take some deep breaths while Clive went over to open the freezer unit.

"We were very careful," he said. "Took off our suits and put on leather aprons and everythin'. So's not to get blood on the clothes, yeah?"

"I don't need to know the details, thank you. And I really don't need the *image of you two wearin' nothin' but aprons and swinging chainsaws in my head. I bet the after-dismemberment sex was fantastic, wasn't it?"*

My phone rang. It was Olivia calling to remind me about the fitting for our outfits for your wedding. Such a stickler for rules, that girl.

"Benjamin," she said. "Do not be late. I don't want any excuses. You are going to wear that tux I picked out for you if it kills you. It will be a rental. You don't need to pay for it. I've put it on my card already. All you have to do is put it on and keep your mouth shut during the wedding. Is that too much to ask of you?"

"No, it's fine," I said. "Did I say I wasn't going to wear it?"

"Only for the last two bloody weeks," she said.

"Come on, sweetie . . ."

"Don't you 'sweetie' me, you arsehole. After all that fuss you kicked off, now you're just going to roll over? Are you planning something, Benjamin? If you are, I swear I'm going to make your life hell."

"Nah, babes, it's just that I've come to see how much work you're puttin' into everythin', not to mention this is Ravi and Julia's wedding, I ain't gonna make it all about me, yeah?"

"What's with this sudden attack of maturity?" she said.

"Well, I can't be a dickhead all the time, can I? Like you said, it's exhaustin'."

"Too bloody right," she said.

"Love you, babes."

Click.

"Now you're actin' so suspiciously Olivia's bound to think you're up to somethin'," Ken said.

"Leave it out," I said.

We had to go through a change of plans now. We were going to have to ditch the body parts somewhere, preferably in the river to be recovered by the authorities later. We could report back to Roger and Cheryl that we'd heard al-Hassah was somehow intercepted by some extremists who were pissed off at him, who chopped him up to try to stop his proposed defection to the infidel West, and we would direct Marcie, who would then have to direct her CIA colleagues, to recover the parts. We would be then paid for *fulfilling our brief, even if we didn't find the fucker alive, which probably meant we wouldn't get the full twenty mil, and that would be the end of it. I would probably spend the rest of our days rubbing it in at Ken and Clive that if they hadn't snuffed al-Hassah, we still would've had a shot at the original reward for capturing him.*

I noticed that for the last few seconds, the two of them had gone silent, which was never a good sign.

"Um . . ." Clive said, standing over the freezer unit.

"Now what?"

"He's gone."

"What do you mean, he's bloody gone?"

"Just that. He's gone."

Ken went over to take a look.

"I need more. Do you mean some of the parts have been misplaced?"

"More like all of him."

"All of him?"

"He's gone! The fucking body's gone, man! All of 'im!"

"Okay, let's just think for a minute," I said, very calmly. Again. "Are you sure you didn't just put him someplace else and forgot where?"

"Fuck, yeah!" Clive said. "Ain't too many places to misplace a fucking body in here!"

"You weren't hopped up on uppers or caffeine and just mis-remembered where you stashed him?" Ken said. "We know what you're like when you imbibe your pills on the job . . ."

"No! I wasn't takin' any bloody pills!"

We looked all over the warehouse for any errant body parts, blood trails, anything that might have indicated where the pieces might have strayed to. Clive assured me that he'd put them all in black plastic bags and wrapped them up all nice and snug and put them away in a neat pile in the freezer unit, if that sort of thing could be considered reassuring. Could he have absentmindedly put them in the cupboard by mistake? Could he have put them in another container? The answer was a firm no to all the above.

"Well now," I said. "As far as savin' our arses go, things just got a lot

more complicated, didn't they? This is all my fault. I should have made it a point to tell you not to take the initiative and leave the planning and thinking for this mess to me."

"You're not exactly a brain trust on this kind of shit, mate," Ken said.

"You're good on the hardware, Ben," Ken said, "but a bit iffy on the big picture stuff."

"Well, I'm sorry it wasn't Mark or Ravi here with you instead of me," I said.

"Actually, Ravi would probably just say 'call the fucking police!' and be done with it," Clive said.

"You didn't tell anyone about last night or this place, right?" I asked.

"Course we didn't. We're professionals," Clive said.

"Could have fooled me," I said. "You're the ones who are supposed to be the experts at making sure bodies disappear forever, and here you are fucking this all up! Did the thought of twenty million dollars make your brains flop over and go stupid?"

"I admit we got a bit carried away," Ken said.

"All right," I said "We have to backtrack. This means someone must've followed us last night."

"Fuck! Who do ya reckon?" Ken said.

Ken and Clive had a funny look on their faces. They weren't looking at me, but over my shoulder. I turned to find four Asian guys running towards us with knives.

The next few minutes were a bit of a blur, to be honest with you.

ELEVEN

Benjamin continued:

When you have someone rushin' at you wavin' a knife, the thing to do is to rush right at them, not try to back away or run. This is because they fully expect you to try to get away from them. They would then adjust their forward momentum to come after you. To suddenly rush at them takes them by surprise, and if they weren't well trained, you have the edge. Their adrenaline rush will make them clumsy and imprecise, and they will miss you if they try to slash at you, as long as you stay calm, watch their hands, and dodge them.

This was just what Ken, Clive, and I did.

Ken and Clive, being big, went right for two of them, while I ran at the third fucker, who was, fortunately, sort of scrawny. There was panic in his eyes as he tried to slow down and slash at me to make me jump back. I let the blade wave past me before I trapped his arm under my armpit as I spun him around and used his own momentum to throw him to the ground. I stomped on his knife arm to make him let go of the weapon, then kicked it away from him. I noticed he was barely out of his teens as I kicked him in the face. That put him down for the time being, while I looked over to see how Ken and Clive were doing.

Ken and Clive were in their element and having fun. Way too much fun. It was too late for me to save one of the kids, but I was hoping to keep the third one breathing so we could interrogate at least two of them for corroboration. Ken had managed to turn the second one's knife back on him and stabbed him to death, and as he died, Clive grabbed him and used his body as a shield, swinging his knife arm against the other one, who was freaking out by then. I was coming up to the next one, hoping to grab him from behind and call a halt to the fight, but he saw me coming and panicked, brought his knife around to swing at me to drive me off, and that was when Clive threw the dead one at him like a spear.

It was one of those moments where what happened was so bonkers that time seemed to slow down so you could fully appreciate how fucking mad the situation was. I saw the dead one hit the kid like a cannonball. He fell forward as his friend slammed into him, pushing his own knife into his chest before the two of them fell in a heap on the ground.

Clive and I ran over to him and pulled the dead one off him. His knife was buried in his chest when we turned him over.

"All right," said Clive. "What's the game, eh?"

"Bastards . . ." he coughed, a spit of blood flecked on his lips. "We'll get you in the end . . . We are many . . ."

"Who's 'we'?" I said. "Do we know you? Have we met?"

"It's God's will that we kill you," he sputtered.

"Bollocks," said Ken.

"I know who they are," I said. "They're pissed-off idiots who got radicalized by reading jihadi sites on the Internet."

"Al-Hassah is a great man . . ." the kid choked out.

"Your great man is a frozen dinner, sunshine," said Clive. "Who sent you?"

"Al-Hassah himself."

"Bollocks!"

"He activated us last night. Sent us here to wait for the infidels who would harm him and kill them."

"He activated you?" I asked. "He talked to you himself?"

"His emissary," said the kid. "We heard the name of our leader. We were given the honor."

"Who's this 'emissary'?"

The kid started to twitch and he couldn't fill his lungs anymore. His eyes went wide as Clive started shaking him to get him focused again, but the fucker just went limp and expired on us.

"We better wake up the third one," I said. "At least he's still alive."

But the last bastard was gone. We saw him rev up a beat-up motorcycle right outside and stream off.

"Shit!" I said.

"Didn't you kick him in the head?" said Ken.

"You know I did."

"Well, you didn't kick 'im hard enough!"

"If I'd kicked him any harder, he wouldn't have gotten up ever again, let alone answered any questions!"

"Well, we better piss off out of here. This place is starting to get ugly with stiffs."

"You're right," Ken said. "It's compromised. We can't use it again."

"Right you are," said Clive, and his eyes lit up all of a sudden. "Better torch it, then."

"Won't your family or the owners object?"

"Naah. Everyone'll be happy to be shot of it. Too many ghosts. Besides," he grinned, "insurance policy's still in place. Be a nice little earner."

So Ken and Clive poured gasoline over the walls and the dead martyrs and lit a match. They set the place to make it look like a gangland revenge killing and torch job. This was obviously not the first time they'd done this sort of thing. I just sat in the work car and waited. That gave me a few moments to think. In less than twenty-four hours, we already had a body count. That was not good. This was a situation we created, and someone out there knew more than we did about what the fuck was going on. That was also not good. There was a body out there that we had to get back, that had been divided into several portable pieces and may have been distributed to more than one location. That was extremely not good. As I watched Ken and Clive cheerfully walk out of the burning garage, I started thinking this was perhaps getting a bit out of hand.

"I dunno about you," Ken said as he got in the car. "But I'm feelin' a bit peckish."

"Now?" I said.

"Must be the little workout we just had," Clive said. "I could murder a curry."

TWELVE

The more Benjamin told this story, the worst my expectations became:

So we retired to Ken and Clive's flat to regroup and so that they could order a Vindaloo from the local takeaway.

"'Ere," said Clive from his phone. "Whatcha fancy?"

"I'm not hungry," I said.

"Aw, go on! Get summink! Our treat!"

"Okay, okay, order me a couple of poppadoms."

Ken ordered a Beef Biryani for himself and a Chicken Vindaloo for Clive.

"Be round in about ten minutes," Ken said as he hung up.

I decided to do some real investigative work for a change by reading over the reports Marcie had given us that I had on my laptop.

"Marcie said they think al-Hassah brought a laptop computer with him, which promised all sorts of goodies like how the terrorist networks are set up and where the most prominent cells are."

"So we ought to find it, then," said Ken.

"Well, first we gotta figure out who's on to us," Clive said. "Let's hope it's not the CIA running a double or triple game. I wouldn't put it past them."

"I reckon they're just hedgin' their bets hirin' us and Interzone and whoever else is in town on their books," said Ken. "Throw as much shit at the wall as possible and see what sticks. Us racin' against those other pillocks to see who finds al-Hassah first puts us in the lead. We know more than the rest of 'em."

"Well, we better be first," I said. "Or we could end up as Her Majesty's

Guests at Belmarsh Prison for the rest of eternity, and Olivia will forget me and go marry some tech billionaire from Beijing or something."

"'Ere, wotcha reckon when that kid said al-Hassah ordered them to kill us?"

"I dunno," I said. "It could've meant anything. I can't believe they saw him face-to-face. They could've gotten a phone call that used the code words to convince them it was him."

"Still, that doesn't answer how they knew about us."

It was at that moment that the doorbell rang.

"Right," said Clive. "That'll be our food."

He got up to the door and opened it.

"Christ on a bike!" he cried. "Come 'ere!"

I leapt to my feet and ran to the door, not sure what I was going to do. I had a horrible notion that Hotspur had finally lost it and started attacking hapless delivery boys, and that I might have to do something drastic to stop him. This latter thought had never been far from my mind whenever we worked with Ken and Clive.

The delivery guy from the local takeaway turned out to be none other than the sole survivor from the band of baby martyrs who tried to kill us earlier. I wouldn't have wanted to be him at that point, to see Clive open the door, recognize him, and to see those massive hands lunge towards him like God's Hammers. I almost felt sorry for him, but then I almost felt sorry for anyone Ken and Clive got their hands on.

Clive bundled the kid into the flat and kicked the door shut. He had him so tight in his vise-like grip that the kid couldn't move, his face buried in Clive's chest so any cries he let out were muffled.

"Finally," Ken said. "We have somebody to interrogate!"

"Right, then," Clive said cheerfully. "I'll fill up the bath."

While Ken and Clive did disgusting things to the kid in the bathroom, I patiently sat in the living and munched on the poppadoms. I put Ken's Biryani in his microwave to keep it warm for him and tried to block out the splashing and muffled screams coming from the bathroom as I ran the night's events through my head again. Once the kid was sufficiently softened up, we started the interrogation.

We didn't need to put the fear of God into him, since as a fanatic, he had that already. No, what we had to instill in him was a fear of unbearably painful, gory, ugly death where bits go missing. Fortunately, Clive was a master at that. Given that he was in the bathtub, we told him that he would at least leave a very clean-looking corpse by the time we were through with him.

He was your average Asian teenager, really. Not necessarily the hippest around, probably as into sports as any, but definitely pissed off with the racism he'd encountered growing up, the feeling of Muslim persecution he thought had gone up after 9/11 and the War, and, with his raging hormones and search for absolute answers, probably easy enough to recruit from the local mosque and manipulate. But I could see that there was still a little spark of doubt in his eyes. This had probably been exacerbated by my kick to his head this morning, and now the waterboarding session Ken and Clive had just put him through.

It wasn't hard to get him to sing. He and his friends had been called early in the morning by their handler, who told them they had instructions from the honored and revered leader Hassan al-Hassah, who had come to town and run into a spot of bother. They were told to come to this garage and kill whoever showed up.

"Yeah, we tend to take it personally whenever people try to kill us," Ken said.

I pointed out to him that Clive was always eager to remove pieces off those people. The kid was babbling by now, and unlikely to be lying. We asked him if he was told where al-Hassah was staying. He mentioned Vanessa van Hooten's address in Earl's Court.

"He's restin' there, with his most trusted allies . . ."

I raced over to my computer and typed in the URL for the webpage we'd set up to view the footage from the webcams we'd installed in Vanessa van Hooten's flat. I clicked on the option to view the cams live.

"Aw, fuck me!" said Clive.

There he was: Hassan al-Hassah in his black suit and tie, kicking back on Vanessa's couch, sipping a glass of the booze he'd brought over the night before. For somebody who was supposed to be in pieces from a posthumous encounter with a chainsaw the night before, he looked remarkably intact and lively. The worst he could have been suffering from, based on his body language, was jet lag.

The three of us stared at the screen in disbelief for a whole minute. We managed to watch al-Hassah get up and pour himself another drink from the kitchen counter.

"You know what we're gonna have to do, don't ya?" said Hotspur.

"Damn straight."

"I dunno how the fucker did it, but we're not gonna be fucking fooled again!"

"Er, Clive . . ."

"This time, we do it fucking right!"

"Wait, chaps . . . let's get on the same page here . . . you're not suggesting . . ."

"We're gonna have to kill 'im again!"

THIRTEEN

"**Y**ou waterboarded a food delivery guy?!" I said.

"To be fair," Ken said, "we interrogated a homegrown wannabe terrorist."

"Who earlier tried to kill us," Clive added.

"Why do you need to tell me all this?" I said.

"Ravi, keep your voice down," Julia said.

"This is karma catching up with you," I said. "Live by secretly murdering people, die by being secretly murdered?"

"Steady on, son," Ken said. "That's a bit unkind."

"I've turned a blind eye to what you two get up to," I said. "But this goes beyond the fucking pale! First you accidentally murder the most wanted man in the world, then you chop up the body, then you try to hide the body, then you lose the body, and now you torture a wannabe jihadist! I told Roger we weren't qualified for this! Marcie and her bosses must be fucking desperate to be hiring the likes of us! We are out of our fucking depth here! I have enough to worry about already with my cases and my fucking wedding as it is and now you dump this on me!"

"I'm startin' to get some mixed signals here, mate," Clive said. "Are you losin' it here or are you really just stressin' out about your weddin'?"

"Ravi, mate," Benjamin said. "You don't know how bloody scary Marcie really is, yeah? She's all smiles on the outside, but you know she's a ball of razor and barbed wire underneath. I know, all right? Olivia has that exact same quality, only she doesn't hide it like Marcie does."

Ken was nodding furiously in agreement.

"We need your help on this one, son," Clive said.

"We're at the end of our rope here," Ken said. "We may not look it, but we got stress, too. We need your whatever, whether it's the gods whispering in your ear or that thing you got where you suddenly just suss everything out when no one else can."

"Have you looked more into Vanessa van Hooten?" I asked.

"You what?"

"The original job," I said. "Or have you forgotten already? That was how you came upon al-Hassah in the first place. You were bugging her flat. You have video feeds. This started with her. She's the one who followed you when you grabbed him, followed you to the forest where you killed him, and followed you to your garage when you stashed the body."

"Fuck me, of course!" Ken said.

"We should have guessed," Clive said.

"Yes, you bloody should have," I said. "It could only be her who took his body."

"That was fuckin' obvious," Benjamin said. "I suppose we were a bit too stressed out to suss it on our own."

"So where's the delivery guy now? The one you tortured," I asked.

"Tied up in the bathroom," Ken said.

"Alive?"

"We didn't kill him," Clive said, somewhat defensively.

"Good." I dialed Ariel's number.

"Hey, hon. Change your mind?"

"I have something for you," I said. "Ken and Clive blagged a homegrown wannabe terrorist who's part of a cell that answers to al-Hassah. You might want to come and take him off our hands."

"See, Jarrod? Told you Ravi would come up with something," Ariel said. "Sorry, hon, Jarrod was skeptical as ever. So you want us to come pick this little shit up?"

"Please."

Ken, Clive, and Benjamin weren't keen on my bringing Interzone in on this, but this was better than telling Marcie. I decided our best option was to cut in Ariel and Jarrod and let them do the heavy lifting. The delivery guy didn't know al-Hassah was dead and thought his order had come from the man himself, so Jarrod and his bastards could sit on him and interrogate him to their heart's content before handing him over to the CIA, who would either vanish him to a black site or hand him over the British authorities.

As liaison for our firm and Interzone, it was up to me to call their liaison, which was Ariel. She was always a bit too happy to hear from me.

"We'll be over in fifteen minutes," she said.

We opened the door to Ariel and Jarrod. I knew I'd run into Jarrod since he was the one who commanded Interzone's troops in the field. He was as proficient a soldier and killer as they came, and that was why I never wanted to be near him. The mood in the room immediately cooled since Ken and Clive regarded Jarrod with a combination of outright hostility and grudging respect. Ariel was her usual cheerful sociopathic self who didn't give a shit about any of that.

"Hello, cutie," she said to the wet, duct-taped delivery guy in the bathtub.

We handed him over to her and Jarrod.

"How did you find him?" Jarrod asked.

"Ken and Clive are ex-cops, so they used their informants to ask around and turned up this guy," I said. "Ken, Clive, and Benjamin grabbed him before he could alert his mates, interrogated him, and found out that al-Hassah has been hiding out with Vanessa van Hooten. Turns out they're lovers."

Jarrod's face dropped in surprise. He was clearly a regular viewer of her father's TV channel back in the States.

"How deep do you think the girl's in on this?" he asked. "She a believer?"

"She believes in his lovemakin' skills, that's for sure," Benjamin said with a nasty chuckle.

That didn't improve Jarrod's mood.

"By a complete coincidence," I said, "her father is a client of ours. And these guys were in charge of watching over her and reporting on anything she might do to embarrass him."

"And how grateful do you think her daddy would be if we save him from an incredibly embarrassing scandal where his darling daughter was found having an affair with the world's most wanted terrorist?" Julia said.

"Lots of birds with one stone here, guys," Ariel said. "It's like the stars aligned to bring all of us together on this."

"Funny how that happens, isn't it?" Lord Shiva said, briefly looking up from tweeting on his phone.

Kali hovered over Ariel. Bagalamukhi hummed in delight at all the deceit in the room and took a photo of us with her phone.

"There's still the reward as well," Ken said, hopefully.

"I'll leave that to our bosses to discuss," Jarrod said. "And I'm guessing you want us to take this guy off your hands."

"So what's the play?" Ariel said.

"Looks to me we could be playing Knights in Shining Armor," I said. "Get al-Hassah for our biggest client, and save Mr. van Hooten's reputation at the same time."

I didn't tell Ariel and Jarrod about the night before, or that Benjamin already had cameras all over Vanessa van Hooten's flat, or that we already had footage of al-Hassah in the flat with her, or the elephant in the room: that al-Hassah was dead, his body was missing, and there was a double of him hiding out in the flat. We were going to let Interzone think al-Hassah 2.0 was the real deal.

"This is going to be tricky," Jarrod said.

"That's why they pay us the big bucks. And bigger bucks if we pull this one off."

"We gotta get back into her flat," Clive said.

"Not before we check her out," I said.

"What for?" Jarrod asked.

"We need to find out what she's like," Julia said. "See how she'll react if the shit hits the fan. If she's a believer and member of the sleeper cell or if she's a hapless girl in love with a substitute bad father figure. Is she going to be a basket case or is she going to play ball? How high-maintenance is she going to get? Is Daddy going to have to pay for extra counseling? All that stuff."

"How you gonna do that?" Ken asked.

"She's American and upper class," Julia said. "An exchange student from an Ivy League school. They all hang out at the same bars and restaurants, snort cocaine and get stoned at the same parties in town. She's in the same student union I am. Our universities are affiliated."

"Julia, I don't want you to do that alone," I said.

"Then you can come with me," Julia said. "Pose as the teaching assistant in my class."

"It just so happens we have her schedule," Benjamin said. "And we already know the pub she goes to regularly with her classmates. It's near her school in Central London."

"So while Julia and I are meeting her," I said, "you lot can go into her flat in Earl's Court."

"Okay," Jarrod said, satisfied. "We have a plan. I got Mikkelford, Reyes, and DuBois here with us if we have to go in hard and fight a terror cell. You leave that part to us if it comes down to that."

"Didn't you say you didn't want to be involved in all this, Ravi?" Ariel said. "What changed your mind?"

"I was dropped into this," I said. "It wasn't my choice."

FOURTEEN

We returned to the office. Ken, Clive, and Benjamin got back slightly before Julia and I did so that it didn't look like we all ganged up to plot something and came back at the same time.

"Marcie, what can you tell me about Vanessa van Hooten?" I asked. She was the one who'd introduced Lucas van Hooten to Roger, after all. Small world. Small and insidious world.

"Where do I start?" Marcie said. "Total wild child heiress. Couldn't keep out of the gossip pages in New York for years when she was a teenager . . . you know, getting drunk with the A-list, cavorting in clubs and strip joints, all the good stuff. Back in New York, she made Paris Hilton look like Doris Day!"

"Did you know her when she came over for school?" I asked.

"Yeah, I'd meet her at all kinds of functions where American ex-pats in London gathered. She's always pumping me for contacts, and shopping tips, and the best deals, not to mention the best people to buy weed and blow from. And she gives nothing in return. Total user. I'm used to that. That was most of my clients back in PR."

"I heard a rumor that she got all radical and joined the Socialist Workers Party," I said.

"Not a rumor, dude," Marcie said. "It's all true."

"Seriously?"

"I notice the Company guys at the US Embassy put a flag on her just in case, but they think it's just a phase she's going through. And I bet it's over some guy she's balling. Gotta be. Probably some douchebag extreme leftist with a posh accent. American girls go for that. She doesn't have a political bone in her body. She never talked politics at any of the parties I saw her at. And thank God for that. She can be pretty unbearable already. Imagine her talking politics."

So Vanessa van Hooten was as adept at compartmentalizing as a man was. A girl who could separate her Marx from her Manolo Blahniks. Why not? This was the twenty-first century, after all.

"Chicks like her are into Power, and Dudes with Power. Total Alpha Male fixation," Marcie said.

"Well, look who her father is," I said.

"And who her boyfriend is," Kali said, chuckling.

"Do ya reckon Daddy would pay us extra if we uncover somethin' really scandalous and help keep it quiet?" Benjamin asked.

Ken and Clive glared at him, like they were ready to strangle him if he said any more.

"That's up to Roger to negotiate with Mr. van Hooten," Cheryl said from her desk.

Olivia didn't even look up from her computer. She showed no interest at all in any of this. She was busy looking over the bank accounts of an offshore company she had been hired to do a forensic analysis for.

From what I'd observed, Marcie might be adept at networking and knowing everyone worth knowing in London, justifying her past legend working in public relations, but as a private investigator, she was rather lazy. She tended to leave the heavy legwork to the rest of us after bringing cases to the firm. They were often lucrative cases involving high-profile clients with large wallets, but I suspected that she took her work as an intelligence officer much more seriously than her day-to-day cover as a private eye here at Golden Sentinels. In the case of finding al-Hassah, she was really here as Roger's handler and to monitor any progress we might make. Benjamin was bursting to blab what had happened in the last eighteen hours, but even he had enough self-preservation to keep his mouth shut. Marcie would be pissed off if she knew we were keeping something as big as al-Hassah from her, but we were definitely better off with her not knowing till we could tell her what we wanted her to know, which should be a version that didn't land us in the shit with her or her bosses.

Julia's smartphone rang.

"Mum?"

She rolled her eyes.

"Honestly, Mum, I'm not going to wear white. It's the twenty-first century. I told you. I've already picked out my gown. It's from Louise's closet. That's right, I kept her clothes. She had a lot of designer dresses and gowns. There's one I set my eye on. No, it's not garish. And why should Ravi wear a bloody tuxedo? It's so cliché. Listen to his mother. She has some good ideas. Because we could use some color rather than white and gray and black. Ravi's relatives are coming in from India and they'll be wearing their formal attire. Mum, if you want to argue, I'm going to call the wedding off. If you kick up a fuss, Ravi and I are just going to elope."

"Nice one, sis," Louise said from the office sofa, but only I saw and heard her.

"Sorted," Julia said when she hung up.

"Marcie," I said. "Benjamin just asked me to back him up on the van Hooten case."

"What's up?" she asked.

"I think Vanessa might have made Benjamin, Ken, and Clive when they were doing surveillance on her flat."

"Did she confront them?"

"No, but here's the thing," I said to Marcie. "Benjamin found out that Vanessa van Hooten's current boyfriend is a very dodgy geezer, the type her father would hate, and could bring down a huge scandal. I feel I should warn her."

"Why not tell Roger so he can tell her dad?" Marcie asked, raising an eyebrow. "He's the one who hired us to keep tabs on his little girl."

"I don't think this can wait," I asked. "The guy's crashing in her flat and scrounging off her. It might be one of those situations where we send Ken and Clive in to put the frighteners on him."

"Point taken," Marcie said. "I'd break it to her, but that might blow my cover. She doesn't know I'm the one her dad hired to watch over her."

"Guess it's down to me," I said.

"Good idea," Marcie said, and texted Vanessa van Hooten to arrange for us to meet her after class that evening.

Julia and I exchanged a look. That had been surprisingly easy.

FIFTEEN

The objective was to lure Vanessa van Hooten out of her flat so that Ken and Clive could sneak into it to look for the body parts. We hadn't told Interzone that al-Hassah was dead and in pieces. Ariel and Jarrod were sitting on the delivery guy and waiting for us to call and tell them when to make their move. We didn't want them bursting into Vanessa's flat to seize al-Hassah's double and finding the body parts, and if she was there, there would be a particularly huge mess. We couldn't let them interrogate Vanessa, because she would probably tell them that Ken and Clive had killed al-Hassah, which would piss Interzone off since it would mean that nobody was going to claim the twenty-million bounty.

I had to think about what I was going to do for the next few hours. What to say to Vanessa? How to warn her about her boyfriend?

"She's in class all day," Marcie said. "Here's what we'll do. I'll meet her at the tapas bar she likes going to and have a drink with her, do the usual social thing. Then you can come into the bar and I can spot you and wave you over to say hello. Then you can take it from there. How's that?"

"Sounds good," I said. "Then you can find an excuse to have to leave so she doesn't know you engineered the meeting, and if it goes south, it won't be your fault. I'll take responsibility."

"Is this why Benjamin, Ken, and Clive have been acting weird today?" Marcie said.

"I think they're embarrassed that they were sussed by the subject they were tailing," I said.

"I have to meet Mum this evening," Julia said. "She's driving me barmy with all this wedding stuff. I have to calm her down."

"No problem," I said. "I'll deal with this and see you at home."

Marcie and I headed for the tapas bar in Earl's Court ahead of Vanessa. Marcie went inside first to wait for her while I went into the off-license across the road to watch the bar.

And in she waltzed.

Vanessa van Hooten was what you'd expect her to be from her reputation: incredibly well turned out in all the right designer labels, with blond hair and an all-American arrogance that some people might find attractive, especially if it's in a woman with a nice rack.

"Hey, you," she said as she and Marcie air-kissed.

"Hey yourself," Marcie said.

I walked into the bar, and as if on cue, Marcie pretended to be surprised as she saw me and waved me over. Introductions were made and wine was ordered.

"So what brings you to London?" I asked.

"Studying abroad and getting out from living under my dad's shadow," Vanessa said. "He's so controlling, and acts like I'm still a little girl. You know how people say, 'born with a silver spoon in your mouth'? I was born with a silver antenna in my mouth."

"You mean your father is *the* van Hooten?" I asked, feigning surprise.

"Guilty as charged," she said. "Mom is really Daddy's third trophy wife, and he already had a son by his first wife. Howard was always being groomed to take over the family business."

"Vanessa is a wild child as only the offspring of the insanely rich can be," Marcie said.

"Oh, shut up," Vanessa laughed.

"Come on," Marcie said. "Caught skinny-dipping in Central Park at the age of sixteen, then ending up with a stint in rehab?"

"Yeah, yeah," Vanessa said. "Daddy had to donate a whole new sports stadium to my school to keep them from expelling me when they caught me snorting and selling cocaine to my classmates."

"You did pretty well as a model when you were eighteen," Marcie said.

"That was at Mom's behest."

"Vanessa managed to out-diva nearly all the other supermodels on the scene," Marcie said.

I remembered the magazine articles: copious plastic surgery (apparently, someone had started a website detailing which body part and when), shoplifting, trashing hotel rooms with rock star boyfriends, catfights at Bergdorf's, screaming matches with rivals at restaurants, and a contract she was rumored to have tried to take out on a fashion designer who failed to ask her to model his fall line (no charges were filed against her. All actual charges were settled out of court with financial payouts from Daddy and nondisclosure agreements). Vanessa certainly supplied Marcie with a steady stream of gossip.

"I'm turning over a new leaf here in London," Vanessa said. "Dad's lawyers kept a lot of unsubstantiated stories about me off of the front pages of the tabloids."

She still got up to her usual antics whenever she spent a weekend in New York, but overall, the city party scene became a little more sedate with her away in London. That she'd made it to grad school was a kind of testament to her academic abilities, but then nobody ever said she was stupid, just batshit-insane. Maybe it was a matter of her finding something to which she could apply herself.

"What can I say?" Vanessa said. "I'm used to people doing shit for me, answering my beck and call."

"It's not really her fault," Marcie said.

"As Philip Larkin wrote," I said, "your mum and dad, they fuck you up. They don't mean to but they do."

"That is soooo right!" Vanessa said.

Here she was, the boozy, druggy debutante abroad, motivated solely by hedonism. How much of this was an act? She was putting on a show for Marcie and me to cover up the fact that she had been fucking a wanted terrorist. Not even one mention of her joining the Socialist Workers Party or talk of politics at all this evening.

I talked a bit about my short-lived career in academia when I did religious studies, then my years teaching secondary school before I lost that job. She talked about liking London since people still took books and reading seriously here. She wanted to pitch to the editor of one of her father's more prestigious magazines to write some feature article on Americans in London and the shifting attitudes of the British towards them since World War II. Funny how everything was getting a little incestuous in the usual way.

"Yeah," she said and laughed. "Our worlds get awfully small, right? Funny how everybody knows everybody here."

"That's for sure."

We continued the small talk for a little while longer, with Marcie playing my wingman.

I asked her how her classes were. It felt like uni all over again, when you met someone new and the first thing you asked them was what they were majoring in. She talked about the year abroad program she was doing at the London School of Economics, hence her easy access to the bars of Soho after class. I did the usual "I did international relations, too" routine to establish commonality and rapport. Her eyes seemed to light up, and we chatted about the books we read and that the European newspapers had a more interesting perspective than even the *Washington Post* or the *New York Times*, and she had a bit of a moan about which of her professors were the most pompous, and how British academics could be even more snobby than American ones were.

Bagalamukhi sat with us and listened closely to my act of social engineering. She would just call it deception.

I was doing my best to keep her preoccupied and entertained while Ken and Clive were breaking into her apartment. It would not be a good idea for her to get back to find them rummaging through the place and probably grappling with al-Hassah 2.0. I really hoped they wouldn't end up killing this one. I prayed that they wouldn't be performing any more neck-snapping or whatever other method of human disposal for the foreseeable future, or at least the rest of this evening.

As the evening wore on, the mood between us started to wind down, but I kept up the conversation as long as I could.

"Gotta run," Marcie said. "Meeting in the morning."

She said a quick good-bye and left me alone with Vanessa.

"Wanna go back to my place for a drink?" she said, finally.

"I should be heading back as well," I said.

I hoped I'd given Ken and Clive enough time to get in and out of her flat by now.

"Whoa," Vanessa said. "I think I drank maybe a little too much. Do you mind sharing a cab with me to get home?"

SIXTEEN

We took a black cab back to Earl's Court.

"Your heart's beating real fast," she said as she leaned into me.

My brain was racing as I pondered my options. I hoped I wasn't going to have to sleep with her to maintain my cover. Sex was her way of appraising someone who didn't bore her. It was almost a formality, so she'd know something about you when you next met up. I was going to have to make up some excuse to get out of it and leave. I had a wedding coming up, to a woman I loved, and I really, really did not fancy having it off with someone who loved another man so much she was hiding his dismembered parts around her flat.

I looked around the street when we got out of the cab and waited for her to unlock the front door.

We walked up the stairs arm-in-arm like it was a first date. I prayed our people were out of her apartment by now. Then we noticed the door to her flat was ajar. She tensed up.

"Get behind me," I said as I slowly pushed the door open.

There were no sounds from the inside, so I hoped no one was there.

What we walked into was what you'd expect. It was the least I was expecting.

"Oh my Gaaaaahhhh!" she squealed. "Oh my God! Oh my God! Oh my God!"

Her apartment looked like a hurricane had hit it.

And I knew the name of that hurricane: Ken and Clive.

The furniture and papers had been tossed, breakable things like vases had been broken—everything you'd want in a break-in scenario. No one was in the flat.

"Eewww!" she said. "They even took a shit on the carpet!"

Knowing Ken and Clive, that was probably a dog turd they'd picked up rather than one that either of them produced. They'd faked countless burglaries before on various cases and knew that a forensics team could extract DNA for a positive ID from shit. Ken and Clive always said that leaving a turd made a burglary look more horribly authentic. They knew all kinds of ways to fake forensic evidence from their days as coppers.

"It's a control thing," I said. "It's their way of asserting dominance over the territory."

"That's so gross!" she said. "Ew! Ew! Ew!"

"I think the police will want you to leave things be, preserve the crime scene and all that."

"I'm not gonna sit around with a fresh dump in the middle of my living room."

"Can't say I blame you."

She started pacing around the flat, looking over the place—into and out of the kitchen, into and out of the bedroom. I realized that al-Hassah 2.0 wasn't in the apartment. That set off a whole avalanche of questions in my head over where he could have gone, whether Ken and Clive could had taken him, whether he was still breathing. I really hoped they didn't commit another murder.

"God damn it," Vanessa shouted as she stormed out of the bedroom. "It's gone!"

"What's gone?"

"Something personal! Motherfucker took it! The most personal thing in my whole fucking life!"

"We better call the police."

"Yeah, guess we should."

"Maybe you don't want to be here," I said. "We can go someplace and call from there."

"Fuck that. I'm staying right here."

"Okay."

She switched on her cellphone and walked into her bedroom to talk. When she came out, she was different. A kind of steely determination had come over her, rather than the kind of shock and anxiety you'd expect from somebody who'd just been broken into and felt violated.

"They'll be here in about fifteen minutes."

She planted herself down on the sofa and sat with her back rigid and straight. I sat down next to her and thought about putting an arm around her to comfort her, but I didn't get the feeling she wanted to be touched or comforted. I felt sorry for her, that she should be caught up in the middle of this.

"Do you have someplace else to stay?" I asked.

"I'll be okay."

"You might be in shock."

Her lips curled into a smile, like what I'd said was the most inane thing in the world. It probably was. She just sat there and contemplated the dog turd as if it were an art installation that had somehow popped up in the middle of her living room. We sat together in silence, staring at it, since there was nothing else to do at that time.

The buzzer went off.

"Finally," she said, and got up to let the cops in.

She stood by the door as we listened to the footsteps coming up the stairs.

"C'mon in, guys," she said.

Only it wasn't cops who came in, but three large and surly men in jeans and hoodies who looked like a rejected Asianbeat hip-hop group.

"That's him," she said, pointing at me.

I was too shocked to move, just sat there as my brain did backflips to revise all the questions in my head. She must have been on to me all along. Al-Hassah 2.0 either ran or Ken and Clive had taken him. Judging from the mess around the living room, there was some sort of struggle. What did she mean when she mentioned the "most personal thing in her life"? The body?

Ken and Clive had finally, well and truly, landed me in the shit. They had all the cards at this point: the al-Hassah Assembly Kit and al-Hassah 2.0. They could easily call up Marcie and throw themselves at her mercy, with these offerings to deal their way out of trouble. Unless they stuck to the plan.

"Who are you?" Vanessa said. "MI5? Or are you a CIA asset?"

"What are you talking about?"

"I made you the moment I laid eyes on you, motherfucker. You think I don't know the way you were subtly interrogating me? Marcie knows you, so you must be a spook like her. Now it's my turn."

I had to endure a short beating before a hood was put over my head.

SEVENTEEN

We British have a very apt euphemism for when things go horribly wrong: "gone pear-shaped."

It not only makes you think of the fruit in question, but also conjures an image of a situation succumbing to gravity in the worst way. Things going south. Shit going down.

I think "pear-shaped" was an apt description for the situation I was in at that moment. It should've been so simple: blah blah blah get bad guy, blah blah blah rescue girl, blah blah blah collect money, blah blah blah go home. Somehow, none of these goals had been met, and none were very likely to be realized at this point.

By the time I was bundled into a car, driven around for God knows how long, dragged out into a building, then tied to a chair and the hood removed from my head, I was in a badly heated space I thought was either a garage or a backroom someplace. There was no way of telling where I was, if I was even still in London. I could feel the bruises forming around my face and my jaw where they'd hit me. They'd taken my phone, but when they tried to unlock it, it bricked itself, one of the security measures Benjamin and Olivia had concocted to keep out anyone trying to get the information off our phones. That also meant I had no way to call for help.

This was the perfect time to start feeling sorry for myself, and naturally, I seized the moment. I wished I had another life, cooped up at home writing reviews of boring novels about middle-class English people and their midlife crises. I wished I'd never gotten into the private investigations business. I wished I'd never followed the course I'd chosen in my ridiculous life. I wished I didn't have the mental issues I had. I wished I was in a cushy, dull teaching job in academia, worrying about cutbacks and tenure while still working on my religious studies PhD thesis examining different faiths and mythologies. I wished I was in an amusing but trivial academic feud with a professor just because I had said something sarky about him in print, because that kind of war was fought with keyboards and long-winded arguments, maybe even on social media, and not with fists or blunt instruments.

I'd caught my abductors' names by then: Baz, Amir, and Zeb. Zeb was actually white, looked English. They were barely out of their teens, but that didn't make them any less dangerous. Great. I was a prisoner of the chav homegrown wannabes. Whichever group they were from, I was about to have a really crappy time.

Vanessa van Hooten came in and looked at me.

"Is he ready?" she asked.

They nodded as she shrugged off her winter coat.

"Oh, good God," I said. "Are you cosplaying Ilsa, She-Wolf of the SS?"

Vanessa van Hooten was dressed all in black leather. She was playing a role as much to put on a show for these lads as for me. She was using her sexuality to keep the lads hooked, but she herself was living out a kind of fantasy here. She was utterly mad. I had the feeling she had taken a leave of absence from reality. Or maybe she'd done so a long time ago.

"Is this something you're into? I'm really sort of vanilla in my tastes . . ."

"Shut up," she snarled.

"You know, there are men who would pay good money for this sort of treatment, but I'm not one of them."

"Well, you're getting it for free, and for real."

"Nothing's free, Vanessa."

"You're right. You're going to give it up for us in return."

"Give what up?"

She slapped me in the face.

The gods weren't here. That was odd. Or perhaps that was how it should be. They were just in my head all along, and now that reality had overtaken the most outrageous thoughts in my head, they had gone away. Which meant that I was doomed.

"You son of a bitch. You didn't think I might have stuck my head out the window and seen your buddies grab Hassan off the street last night? You didn't think I could've jumped in my car and followed you to where you took him?"

"Who's Hassan?"

Slap!

"Can you stop that? This is going to get old pretty fast."

Slap!

"Where are they?"

"Where are who?"

Slap!

"You know who!"

"Do me a favor!"

Slap!

"I know you're MI5!"

"You what, love?!"

This wasn't exactly Standard Operating Procedure in Basic Interrogation. There was no real attempt to manipulate me or soften me up with coercion, nor did any of these guys try playing Good Cop to Vanessa's Dominatrix Bad Cop. In fact, she should've been playing Good Cop, since she was clearly the leader, and had them play Bad Cop, as she was more likely to gain my trust than they were.

Which meant this lot was a bunch of amateurs.

Which meant I was in *really* deep shit.

Amateurs were not well trained. Amateurs were not good at gauging the tolerance levels of their subjects. Amateurs make mistakes, such as accidentally killing the target during interrogation.

"Who do you work for?" she asked.

"I'm a freelancer."

"Bullshit! Freelancers don't do high-profile extraction or wetwork!"

"What are you talking about!"

"Yeah, right!" she snorted. "It wasn't you who killed the only man I ever loved. It was your buddy, and you're all just following orders. It's nothing personal. Well, it's fucking personal to me!"

"Where did you find these guys anyway?" I said. "On the Internet? Did they get radicalized from all those websites?"

"They're local boys, hiding in plain sight. They were more than happy to join up after they learned all about the war on Islam and how the West is targeting them for extinction."

"Yeah, bruv!" Amir said. "Kill or be killed."

"I'm pretty sure that's not what the Koran teaches," I said.

"What do you know about the Koran?" Baz said. "You're an infidel."

"Have you actually read the Koran?" I said. "I have."

"You're wasting your breath," Vanessa said. "All they've seen are the torture photos from the black-site prisons that the CIA inflicted on their fellow Muslims, and they're totally up for a little payback."

"So, what, these local lads just answered a recruitment ad on the Dark Web?" I said.

My plan here was to keep them all talking, because then at least they'd be busy listening to me instead of torturing me.

"You're not in a position to ask questions here, motherfucker," she said. "And you haven't answered any of ours."

"Look, if you want to ask me about comparative religion, fire away. Otherwise, I don't know shit."

Slap!

"Listen, honey, these guys are pretty pissed off about you and your buddies messing my shit up, and they want him back, so you better cut the bullshit."

So they didn't know he was dead. She didn't tell them. She merely activated them and told them they were needed for a mission.

"Is this being videotaped for an Internet fetish porn site? 'Cause if it is, aren't you supposed to get me to sign a waiver? And give me a safe word? And pay me?"

Slap!

"You know and I know you're a fucking spook, so stop playing being an asshole and spill already!" she snarled.

"Spook?" I was still drawing it out.

"She means spy, bruv," Zeb said.

"He's just playing for time," Vanessa said, irritated that she had to spell out everything to them.

"How would you know that? Unless you're a spook yourself," I said.

"Cut the bullshit," she said.

"Really," I said. "Who are you really working for?"

"That'd be telling. Why don't you take a wild fucking guess?"

I took a wild fucking guess and arrived at only one place.

"Oh, Christ," I said. "But didn't you, like, join the Socialist Workers Party a couple of months ago and wear burkas in sympathy with Muslim women and all that stuff?"

"Totally. What better cover than joining the most incompetent, irrelevant, and worthless left-wing political party around? You'll be completely under everyone's radar."

"But you were recruited by the CIA, weren't you?" I said. "As an asset. Do these guys know they're really working for a CIA asset here?"

"Nah, bruv," Amir said. "This is the beauty part, yeah? She turn double-agent-like, yeah? She's workin' for the cause now. The leader vouched for her."

Ah. They must have met the double.

"I've proven myself to them," Vanessa said. "We're bonded."

"She proved herself and everything, yeah," Baz said.

Christ, his tone meant she'd had sex with them. That was how she'd gotten them doing her bidding. They were already pliable idiots, and sex made them even more stupid.

"I have one more question," I said.

"Shoot," she said.

"Isn't this a school night?"

"Yeah, I have class in the morning. In fact, I have to hand in a paper, but I already cribbed one off the Internet. Anyway, I need my beauty sleep, which is why I'm leaving you in the capable hands of Zeb, Amir, and Baz here."

She turned to leave.

"Hey!" I cried.

"What?"

"Come back here."

I indicated I wanted a private word. She ordered the men to stand in the corner and turn away from us, then tilted her ear to my mouth.

"Did you follow my mates to the garage?"

"Yeah."

"I knew it," I said. "Then you're the one who took the body after they left, aren't you?"

She didn't answer.

"These guys don't know the real al-Hassah's dead, do they?" I asked. "You went in and collected the body parts yourself before you called up the Junior Jihad Brigade and got the double to order them to ambush my colleagues in the lockup, didn't you?"

I could see her face go red.

"These guys think the double's the real one, but he's just going to be a figurehead, isn't he? You're juggling too many grenades here, Vanessa."

"I had practice. I used to be a model in New York and Paris. So where is he?"

"Which one?"

"Both. But the dead one. I want the head. Just the head."

I suddenly had a vision of Ken and Clive waltzing back to the office with al-Hassah's head in a shopping bag. Somehow, I did not find this the most comforting image in the world.

"What do you want it for?"

"I LOVE HIM, MOTHERFUCKER!" Her shriek made even the men jump. "AND NOW HE'S DEAD! I AM GOING TO FUCK YOUR FUCKING CITY UP FOR THAT!"

"Yeah!" the three stooges cried in unison.

"Wait, you're going to bomb London?" I said.

She didn't need to say yes. The look on her face was the answer.

"Al-Hassah didn't tell you to do this," I said. "This is your idea. And you convinced these geniuses to go along with you?"

"They're into it."

"Even though it has nothing to do with Jihad or martyrdom? This is just stupid," I said.

"They're not gonna listen no matter what you say. They just wanna torture you. Payback for Western foreign policy declaring war on Islam. This is what you British intelligence fucks have been up to. They know. I'm going to have fun watching you die, after I finish blowing up London."

"By the time you get back, I'll already be dead."

"I'll just watch the video. You can bet they'll circulate it on the Web."

As she put on her coat, a thought occurred to her that she just had to share with me.

"You know, they'll probably cut your head off. Muslims believe that your body has to be intact for you to enter Heaven. A beheading is considered the ultimate defilement, since it condemns you to Hell or Purgatory. Consider it karmic payback."

"I know far too much about karma."

"Well, I am going to be London's karma, and karma's a bitch," she said. "We're going to give them the payback they deserve."

She turned and walked out.

Now it was time for Amir, Baz, and Zeb to advance towards me.

"You know, all this isn't really necessary," I said. "I'll tell you what you need to know, which isn't much, actually."

They didn't look like they cared.

"Okay, okay, do you really want to perpetuate this cycle?" I said. "The thing is, the cycle is endless! That's why it's a *cycle*! It's going to keep going after we're gone, because the system of subterfuge and deception was designed to be self-sustaining and self-perpetuating! You kill us or we kill you, there's always going to be people who will carry on after us! There's always going to be someone to do the killing, someone to get killed, someone to do the covering up, and someone to lie to the general public to keep them scared and docile! We are not special! So fuck duty and patriotism and all that shit! The only thing I'm in for is staying alive! You can torture and kill me, and I won't be very happy about it, but you are just a bunch of sadistic dickheads getting off on violence!"

Where were the gods through all this? You'd think they'd want a ringside seat here.

The three idiots seemed to contemplate this for a few seconds as they continued to stare at me.

"You talk a lot of Western decadent rubbish, bruv," Amir said.

"We're not stupid," Zeb said. "It's about sending a message, yeah?"

"Okay, okay, maybe all of that was a bit too existential for you!" I said. "I get it! Relativism can be a dead end! That's why there's such a need to find some belief system to embrace! Oh! Oh! Hey! Electrodes! I hate electrodes! Who doesn't? Say, weren't you supposed to start with the small tortures before you move on to the big, flesh-ripping mutilation stuff? I'm just saying, that's all! You don't wanna peak too soon—!"

I spent the next eternity screaming.

EIGHTEEN

Being tortured is exhausting business. I really don't recommend it. At least I think I was still in London, or somewhere in England. I seriously doubted they could have spirited me off to downtown Baghdad or anything like that, thank God, but I still had images of Abu Ghraib–style torture pictures in my head, and I started to realize it didn't matter where I was while they were cutting and tweezing and electrocuting me. I could have been in South Kensington or Peckham or Bromley, but in the long run, I was going to be dead, so what did it matter at that point?

But then it's hard to feel better when you're in excruciating pain. My only alternative was the image of Ken and Clive waltzing into the US Embassy carrying al-Hassah's head in a bag and collecting the $20 million reward. Imagine how *that* one made me feel.

Everything was a blur. I didn't recall what I was shouting. My vision was all red with hellfire and demonic Rakshasas poking their spears at me. The gods were gone. I was in hell. I tried to shout at them in Hindi as their eyes blazed and tongues wagged and they punched and bit me with their razor-sharp teeth.

They weren't torturing me for information, but for some sort of ritual. I really hated it when that happened. And it really wasn't fair that I was a stand-in here for the sins the West committed on the rest of the world. I did try to empathize with my torturers' plight, being victims of imperialism, their sense of alienation and all that stuff, but they obviously didn't give a shit about any of that, and I couldn't say anything to them that would have any effect anyway.

All that stuff you hear about your life flashing before your eyes before you die is true, by the way. The problem was, I seemed to be caught in a loop, because I found myself watching the same parts of my life again three times, probably because, let's face it, I hadn't been on this Earth for *that* long. I desperately wished I would pass out or go into shock, so my brain would shut down. Well, perhaps I did a few times, but I kept waking up and getting tortured with spears and claws and teeth again, at which point the life-flashing-before-your-eyes part started all over again. Huge chunks of my life were really boring! I'd lost all sense of time, had no idea whether hours had passed or if it was just twenty minutes since Vanessa van Hooten walked out. My entire world was contracting into Pain and Bad Memory Reruns as the flames of hell raged around me. Rakshasas with their burning eyes rushing at me in a frenzy and tearing away at my flesh down to the bone, until there was nothing left, then I would awake to see it happen again in an endless loop. The smell of my flesh burning from the hellfire, or was it the electrodes? I watched them eat my heart again and again, my cries and protestations the same each time. And then everything went dark every time they swallowed the last bites of my heart.

When I opened my eyes, the three idiots were cowering in the corner of the room.

"Fucking hell!" Amir cried. "What the fuck was that?"

"That was fucked up, bruv!" Baz said. "We barely laid a finger on you!"

"Why are you so obsessed with nipples?" I cried.

"You what?" Zeb said.

"All that biting and clawing!" I said.

"What are you talking about, bruv? You just went into some kind of trance! And what was all that you was babblin'?"

"Like you was fucking possessed!" Zeb said.

I was confused.

Then I noticed I wasn't bleeding, and no real pain from my body, other than the dull aches I'd already had when they first brought me here. Did the gods do this? Did they send me into some kind of fugue state and have me babbling in tongues? Was this their way of protecting me? If it was, where were they? Wouldn't they be here with me now?

"I ain't touchin' him no more, nah," Baz said. "Fucker's fucking scary."

"What if he's contagious?" Amir said.

"What you saw," I said, "was the real ecstasy of martyrdom."

They looked at me in shock. Of course I was making this shit up as I went along, still dancing as fast as I could to stay alive.

"This is what you have to look forward to if you truly believe," I said. "This is that transcendent state you get to achieve if you really, truly believe."

They looked at each other in confusion.

"Nah, you're just fucking mad, bruv," Zeb said, unsure.

"Or you could just walk away," I said. "It's not too late. Just don't do what it is she wants you to do. Go home. Go back to your lives. You have that choice. Go on."

I was using my old Teacher's Voice, the one I used to admonish students when I caught them during break planning something naughty. If I could keep it up and draw them in, I had a chance.

They conferred in the corner in whispers again, then seemed to reach a decision.

"She said we should kill him," Zeb said.

"Oh, come on!" I said.

"Shut up, you! Don't question us! We got our priorities!"

This was bad. I was in an already ridiculous situation that was about to get truly dire. The gods were still nowhere to be found. Radio silence when their presence might have reassured me.

"Yeah," Baz said. "We kill him. You know, cut his head off. Film it and all."

So that was it. I was about to die. I was about to be murdered by a bunch of idiots for no good reason.

"Hang on," I said. "Aren't you forgetting something?"

"Do what, bruv?" Zeb asked.

"Look at my skin!" I said. "I'm dark-skinned. If you kill me, no one will give a shit!"

"What are you on about?" Baz said.

"If you kill me on video," I said. "Yeah, sure, it'll be horrible, because you're cutting my head off, but I'm not a white guy! They won't care! They think dark-skinned people kill each other all the time! They don't even care if I'm not Muslim just because of my skin color! You'll have wasted your time!"

"Yeah, that's a good point, bruv," Baz said. "I mean, we're not prejudiced, yeah? We'll kill anyone."

"I know," I said. "But it's all about the optics, isn't it? It's all image and branding!"

"But she wants us to kill him," Zeb said.

"If we just kill him without any publicity, it's just a waste, innit?" Baz said.

"My point exactly!" I said.

"Vanessa still wants 'im dead, though," Amir said.

"How? We stab him? I don't want to hear him screaming again, bruv," Zeb said.

"I don't ever want to hear all that weird shit he was shoutin' again," Baz said.

"Yeah, and we don't want to make a mess," Zeb said.

"I know, let's just stick 'im in the oil drum. He'll run out of air. That should take care of it," Amir said.

"Good idea. No muss, no fuss," Baz said.

"Are you fucking kidding me?!" I cried.

I shouted and protested, kicked and struggled as they stuck me in the drum and shut the lid. It got stuffy immediately, then I was rocked and spun as they shifted me to wherever it was they stored the drums.

NINETEEN

This was it. I was going to die. On the eve of my wedding, alone, in the dark, in silence and hidden away. No gods, no voices. Just my head as I ran out of air.

How long had I been stuck in here dying? It felt like an eternity. I didn't remember how long it took to suffocate to death in an airtight drum. It wasn't something I'd ever thought to look up.

I had nothing to do but think about how this was where my life had led. Maybe this was comeuppance for my hubris, my moral compromises, my complicity in all the nasty shit we got up to at Golden Sentinels. I was at last paying for the lives I'd blown up, the people whose deaths I'd been party to, the chaos I'd caused and unleashed into the world. This was the price for my hypocrisy. I had no one to blame but myself. I had made the decisions. No one forced me. I chose to work at Golden Sentinels and not quit as soon the first morally fucked up decision had to be made. I had known and done too much to be able to consider myself a good person by now. I felt guilty about the grief Julia and my family were going to be put through once they found out what had happened to me.

Breathing was getting difficult. It probably wouldn't be long now. It was just going to be darkness and nothingness. No gods, no heaven or hell, just a total loss of Self. As an atheist, I didn't believe in any afterlife. No comfort for me. No reincarnation, no respite. No reward or punishment. This end was the punishment.

I was so preoccupied with losing consciousness that I barely noticed the shouting and banging outside the confines of the drum. I assumed it was auditory hallucinations as my brain fired off its last desperate synapses before shutting down from oxygen depravation, until the scraping of metal screeched over my head and the lid of the oil drum was forcibly removed.

"There you are," Ariel said, as she and Jarrod pulled me out.

And now the gods were here, gathered together and taking photos with their smartphones.

"Hurrah!" Shiva said.

Great.

I coughed and took breaths.

"Easy, brother," Jarrod said.

"How long was I in there?" I asked. "Felt like hours."

"About ten minutes before we came in," Jarrod said.

"Christ, felt like a lot longer than that," I said.

"Time flies when you think you're dying," Jarrod said matter-of-factly. "Your adrenaline's just firing like crazy. Its normal."

I looked around at the hideout. A pair of Rakshasas—no, it was Mikkelford and Diaz, the Interzone mercs I'd met before, a year ago in Los Angeles. They were busy putting zip-ties around the wrists and ankles of Amir, Baz, and Zeb. Interzone had breached the door and shot them all with nonlethal beanbag rounds. They knew not to kill anyone on British soil, as it would have raised too many questions.

My legs were a bit wobbly, and Jarrod and Ariel had to hold me up.

"Seriously, Ravi?" Ariel said. "You thought you could use your good looks to lure Vanessa van Hooten into a trap? You have majorly overestimated your Chick Magnet Rating."

"I wasn't trying to seduce her! I was just trying to distract her long enough for Ken and Clive to get out of her flat!"

"You say she was the one who seduced you? Honey, aren't Julia and I enough for you?" Ariel said, smiling in mock jealousy.

"I was trying to do my fucking job! Seduction was not on my mind!"

"Sure, brother." Jarrod chuckled.

Even Mikkelford and Diaz were grinning.

Julia was waiting in the van when Ariel and Jarrod brought me out. She put her arms around me and kissed me, then draped a blanket around my shoulders.

"I don't need this," I said.

"You're in shock," she said.

"I'm not in shock," I protested.

"Babe, you're in shock," Ariel said. "You were nearly murdered. Your adrenaline's spiking. You'd have to be a psychopath with a low heart rate to not be in shock. You're gonna crash in a moment."

"That was more than the Banality of Evil back there," I said. "That was sheer bloody Stupidity of Evil! A combination of mental instability and idiot malice! Never thought I'd ever see it up close and personal!"

"Calm down, brother," Jarrod said as he started the engine. "You're in shock."

"I'm in shock," I said, deflating, feeling the crash at last. "Wait, how did you find me anyway?"

"Kali told me," Ariel said, grinning.

"Bullshit," I said.

"That's what I said," Jarrod said. "But however way she did it, we found you. She even knew which drum you were in."

"You must have had a drone or some kind of GPS or you tapped their phone or something," I said.

"Nope," Ariel said. "Kali whispered in my ear. Told me who had you, where, and how many of 'em there were. How do you think we knew where to hit in the room so we'd avoid you?"

"You're just fucking with me now," I said.

Ariel laughed.

"Ravi honey, I loooove fucking with you, but I don't need to lie to fuck with you. I just have to tell you the truth and it'll fuck with you."

"Very true!" Kali chuckled, suddenly beside me, in my ear. "My poor darling boy, I wasn't going to lose you so carelessly."

Julia gave me a phone and a Bluetooth earpiece that I put in immediately.

"To be fair," Benjamin said on the Bluetooth. "You did have a tracker in your belt buckle. I helped them track you via GPS."

We were speeding towards Central London.

"Where the hell are we going now?" I asked.

"Where do you think?" Jarrod said. "Get you secured, get back on the hunt."

"And where do you think you're going to look?" I said.

"We got a couple of leads," Jarrod said.

"Rubbish," I said. "You don't have shit. You have no idea where to look next, do you? Or did Kali tell you?"

Jarrod and Ariel stayed silent. Kali must have only told them where to find me. If I wasn't in the picture, Kali didn't bother.

"Benjamin," I said. "Did Ken and Clive find what they were looking for in the flat?"

"They found the double," he said. "And all the parts. Had to pack them back into black bin liners so they wouldn't leak and stink up the place."

"We need to find Vanessa van Hooten," I said. "She's going to launch a terror attack on London."

I didn't tell them al-Hassah was dead since I wasn't sure if they already knew. We were in enough trouble as it was. What I was sure of was that Vanessa had to be keeping al-Hassah's corpse at home where she could be with him. I didn't need the gods to tell me that.

"How do you know that, brother?" Jarrod asked.

"She's completely off her rocker and he's the love of her life. If he hasn't shown up at the meeting with the CIA, then perhaps she stopped him from going to keep him from getting taken away from her."

"You mean she *Single White Female*'d him?" Ariel asked. "That's so fucked up it's kind of hilarious."

"It's the only logical answer," I said. "And the only proper lead. Somebody pass me a laptop."

I logged into the server where Benjamin stored the footage from the cameras he had hidden in Vanessa's flat.

"Damn," Jarrod said.

"He's not lookin' too lively there," Ariel said.

There she was unwrapping the black bin liners and taking out the pieces of al-Hassah, including the head, which she cradled to her chest and started primal screaming over.

"Somehow, this still doesn't make the list of Top Ten Most Fucked Up Things we've ever seen," Mikkelford said.

Interzone, being efficient as ever, came in two SUV vans. Mikkelford and Reyes packed Baz, Amir, and Zeb into one while the rest of us got into the other. As we drove out, I noticed that we were in a garage in Hammersmith. I knew we'd never left London.

TWENTY

I was now doing something I'd vowed I would never do again: ride in a van with Jarrod and his murderous cohorts from Interzone. I also had to be grudgingly grateful to him and Ariel for saving my life. For the first time in my life, I had nearly been deliberately murdered. It was not a pleasant feeling. I wondered if I would get PTSD.

"You thought Vanessa might have been a damsel who needed rescuing, didn't you?" Julia said.

She didn't need to hear an answer from me.

"We always told you your White Knight Complex would get you in trouble," she said.

"First rule," Ariel said. "You don't try to rescue a bunny-boiler."

"That's a man for you, sister," Diaz said.

"Damn right!" Dubois said, chuckling.

Lord Vishnu and Rudra were there in full SWAT body armor, cosplaying as special ops guys just for a laugh. They were gleefully fist-bumping each other, quoting bad Hollywood action movie dialogue, and laughing their heads off.

Seriously?

At that moment, I hated everyone.

I looked out the window and saw it was morning. Julia looked at me and didn't say a word. She wanted to hold me and make it better but knew I was in too shitty a mood for that.

"Were you holding out on us?" Jarrod said. "How did you get cameras in that girl's apartment?"

Before I could say anything, Julia stepped in.

"The cameras were already there," she said. "Vanessa's father had them installed without her knowledge. Benjamin managed to find the feed. Ken and Clive went in there last night and found al-Hassah's double tied to the bed and covered in air freshener cakes bought from the local chemist's to cover up the smell of the body parts she had there."

Julia was always good at improvising and selling a story, much more than I was. This got Ken and Clive off the hook for how al-Hassah had ended up dead.

"They didn't want you breaking into the flat since they felt it was their tip. Ken and Clive are territorial like that. Besides, they never liked you after you ambushed them when you first met."

Jarrod grunted.

"Do they have the body parts and the double secured someplace?" he asked.

"I'm sure they do," I said.

"So now we have this chick running loose in London all set to pull off an act of terror," Ariel said. "Fun fun fun."

"They don't have access to guns," Jarrod said. "They're probably going to use a car and just drive it into a crowd somewhere in Central London, maybe go on a stabbing spree. That's even if they don't have a bunch of explosives."

"Benjamin, do you have a ping on Vanessa's phone?" I asked.

"Yeah, I've been trackin' her since this morning. She's been on campus all day. Looks like she's keepin' up appearances by going to class."

"What about her car?" I asked. "Do you have it on GPS?"

"Hang on," he said. "Yeah. Looks like she drove it to school this morning. It's in the college car park. Must've been the one she used to follow us the other night."

"Okay," I said and addressed everyone in the van. "I believe Vanessa van Hooten is planning to use her car to pull off an attack on London later today."

"How do you know that, brother?" Jarrod asked.

"I saw it in her eyes last night when she was slapping me about," I said. "The man she loves is dead, so she wants to take it out on the world. It's revenge."

"What makes you think she's going to do something today?" Mikkelford asked. "An attack usually takes months for a cell to plan. Lot of recon, mapping."

"Because she's impatient," I said. "She's not operating on a rational level here. It's an off-the-cuff act of nihilism."

"She could have explosives in that car that she's planning to detonate," Mikkelford said. "Maybe drive it into a crowd of people somewhere, run as many over as she can, then blow herself up and take out a whole city block."

"Okay," Jarrod said. "We need to get to that car and check it out, defuse any explosives if it has any."

"Or," I said, "we could phone the police and report the car and let them send in the actual bomb squad to deal with it."

They all looked at me for a second, then laughed. Even Benjamin was laughing, a bit too loudly, on the Bluetooth.

"Good one, brother," Jarrod said.

Even Julia looked at me rather piteously. The gods laughed longer than everyone else. Louise shook her head.

"I had to put that option out there," I said, and off their blank stares: "Really? You're going for it? You're not getting paid for this. We tell Marcie, she tells her station chief, he calls the local authorities—"

"Who will fuck this up," Ariel said. "Your cops are good at acting after something happens. We've never been too impressed with their response when shit is actually happening."

"She's right about that one, mate," Benjamin said.

"We're actually doing this?" I said. "We're going after a bunch of terrorists?"

"What if Marcie's station chief decides not to call the Brits for whatever reason?" Ariel said. "Like they don't want to tell the Brits how they got the information or why it was happening? They might just let it happen and see where the pieces land."

"And why do you care?" I asked.

"A messed-up London is bad for us," Ariel said. "It's one of Colonel Collins's favorite cities. He'd hate to see this place plunged into chaos. It'd make his coming over for high tea really suck. And we have major clients here."

"And you can defuse a bomb?" I said.

"Not our first rodeo," Dubois said. "I'll handle any explosives if we find them."

"Dubois," Jarrod spoke on his Bluetooth. "Would you kindly ask the three gentlemen if they were all the members of their sleeper cell so we don't have any unexpected company when we do this?"

"Way ahead of you, Sarge," Reyes said. "Answer's negative. They think our guys killed about three of 'em yesterday and they were the other half apart from Ms. van Hooten."

Jarrod looked at me and raised an eyebrow.

"We didn't kill anyone yesterday," he said. "Would that be your two alpha gorillas' handiwork?"

"That was how they ended up with the one you picked up in their flat," I said.

"For civilians, you folks have been awfully busy since this job started," Jarrod said, a mix of mild irritation and respect in his tone.

TWENTY-ONE

Jarrod drove the van to the campus and dropped off Ariel and Mikkelford. Mikkelford, with his ginger beard, jeans, and backpack, and Ariel, with her tattoos and jeans, easily passed for grad students milling around the entrance of the school building, chatting and checking their phones.

We then dropped Dubois off in the car park. Benjamin fed him the license number and color of Vanessa's Golf GTI, which was a surprisingly modest car given she could have bought a Mercedes or a BMW. Everyone communicated via Bluetooth headset. The gods didn't need Bluetooth. They could hear us all just fine.

Dubois found the car and pretended to get down to tie his shoelaces so he could inspect the undercarriage.

"Not seeing any wires or explosives on the underside," he reported. "I'm guessing it's inside the car. She might be driving this thing into town, like over to the Embankment, plenty of targets nearby. She could go to the West End, Picadilly, Westminster, and blow herself up where it'll make the biggest statement."

"Class should be over in about fifteen minutes," Benjamin said.

"Sarge, I could open the trunk or the driver's seat," Dubois said. "Don't know if she might have booby-trapped the door. What's your call?"

We were a few hundred feet away from the car, but if it went off, we'd still be caught in the explosion if the GTI was packed with Semtex in the boot.

"When Vanessa comes out," I said, "we have to distract her in case she tries to remotely detonate the car."

"Stand by," Jarrod said.

"Copy that."

"You can't let Vanessa see you," Julia said to me. "She thinks you're still in that garage or dead."

"I could snipe her from the roof across the street when she comes out," Ariel said. "Got a clear view of the front entrance. Put a bullet through her brainstem before she can reach a detonator. Mikkelford could be my spotter."

"Too many witnesses and bystanders," Jarrod said. "Too many variables for what kind of chaos that could unleash."

"Guess we have to do up close and personal, then," Ariel said. "My favorite."

"Can somebody give me a phone?" I said.

"What are you going to do?" Julia asked.

"I'm going to be the distraction," I said. "Benjamin, give me her number."

When the students came out of the building, it took four minutes before Vanessa van Hooten walked out.

"Let her walk past you," Jarrod told Ariel and Mikkelford.

I dialed.

"Vanessa, we didn't finish talking when you left the garage last night."

"What the fuck?" she answered.

"We have the head. That's what you want, isn't it? Let's make a deal."

"The only deal you're getting is death, fucker," Vanessa said.

"Okay, then we'll just toss it in the Thames, shall we?"

"NO!"

"All right, here's my offer. Let's meet in Trafalgar Square, by the fountain, and I'll bring the head in a bag."

"Fuck you. You don't even know the kind of hell I'm about to send you to."

"Let her walk clear of the building and the bystanders," Jarrod said to Ariel and Mikkelford, who were now following Vanessa.

"If you want the head, you don't want to set anything off. I'm offering you a chance to walk away."

"It's too late for that. All my life I've seen what bullshit everything is. My father and his TV news and papers, the whole fame thing. Nothing meant anything till I met Hassan, and you took him from me."

Vanessa could have ransomed me for the body parts the night before, but she thought I was MI5 and wanted to kill me for revenge and to send a message. It didn't seem to have occurred to her to make that play.

"So, what, you're just going to throw an epic tantrum?" I said. "Grow the hell up."

"Listen, motherfucker, I'm sick and tired of assholes like you always trying to make a move on me thinking you can glom off my name or my money—"

Ariel quietly walked up behind Vanessa and stuck her with a stun gun. It happened so quickly that the passersby missed it. Anyone looking over would have seen Ariel and Mikkelford supporting Vanessa as she went slack, then grabbing her under the arms and walking her into the van. They put her in the back, shut the door, and bound her wrists and ankles with zip-ties as Jarrod drove into the car park, towards Dubois.

This was the second time in as many months I'd witnessed Ariel sneaking up on someone. That seemed to be her specialty, that and her skills with a sniper rifle, which I hoped never to witness.

Ariel took Vanessa's purse and searched it.

"Found a detonator," she said.

She passed the car keys to Dubois. He smashed the window on the driver's side and checked inside to make sure there were no wires before he opened the door and popped the boot.

"Looks like C-4," he said. "Wired to a detonator, but no timer. Basic job, totally analogue. Give me two minutes."

"Take your time," Jarrod said.

Dubois cut the wires connecting the C-4 and removed the detonator rods. Then he got in the car and we drove off to Interzone's safe house, where he secured the explosives.

TWENTY-TWO

We returned to Golden Sentinels and told Roger, Cheryl, and Marcie what had happened, leaving out the part about Ken and Clive grabbing and killing al-Hassah two nights before.

"I always had faith in my boys and girls," Roger said, beaming.

"And you managed to grab one of the doubles as well?" Marcie said.

"We recorded him on video and everything," Ken said proudly.

He opened his phone and played it.

On the screen, al-Hassah 2.0 sat on a chair facing the camera.

"My name is Mohammed al-Hassah. It is true, I am the sixth cousin of Hassan al-Hassah. Our fathers were brothers. I was given plastic surgery so that I would look more like him, in order that I can serve as a double for him. I do not know how many doubles he kept. I may have followed him for years, but I never had the heart for the acts of violence and bloodshed he advocated. I had made contact with the Americans a year ago and told them I wanted to defect, in return for all the knowledge I could give them on the network my cousin had established. They were not very interested in what I could tell them. I was eventually contacted by Vanessa, who told me that they needed me to continue to live as a sleeper in Paris until they needed me. She said when the time came, my being a double to Hassan could be very important. I just did not want to get killed. I thought they might order me to act as a double agent, to deliver false information or inform them of any imminent danger, but they never did. I was left alone for more than a year. They told me to 'sit tight.' It was very difficult for me, as I looked just like Hassan after the plastic surgery. Occasionally, I would be required to stand in for him in a videotape, reading out a statement pledging to continue our struggle against the 'infidels' of the decadent West. For the rest of the time, I would remain in hiding in the mosques and safe houses around the city, barely seeing any sunlight at all.

"I had been in hiding with another sleeper cell in Paris when Vanessa van Hooten phoned me a few days ago, and told me to come to London immediately, that she needed me to pose as my cousin in London. She told me that this was part of a grand plan the Central Intelligence Agency wanted to play on the British MI5. My blood became like ice, because I could tell she was mad. I believed if I went along with her plans, I would likely end up dead. I finally made contact with the French Secret Service and offered to defect to them. Unlike the Americans, they were overjoyed at my offer, since I knew almost everything Hassan knew, including his training at the hands of the Americans, and the French very much wanted all the inside information on the CIA. However, before I could arrange to give myself to them, Vanessa had some men take me to a private airfield and fly to England. I was taken straight to Vanessa's flat and told to wait there, until your friend broke down the door and took me out of that place. I will be forever grateful to you for that."

"See? Aren't you glad you didn't kill him?" I said to Ken and Clive.

"We're a pair of fuckin' heroes," Clive said. "Still bothers me, him lookin' like that piece of shit, though."

"I told you they'd pull it off," Roger said to Marcie. "Even Ravi."

I realized that Interzone had not killed a single person here, while Ken and Clive had racked up quite the body count in just two days. Cheryl had told me previously that Ken and Clive did not usually kill people on a case, that was more their outside hobby, so this kind of thing was an exception rather than the rule for them. It would have to be someone truly irredeemable to drive Ken and Clive to want to snuff them. This had never reassured me before, and it certainly didn't now.

"Huh," Marcie said. "I thought it was going to come to nothing. Trail was stone-cold."

"Now, if you'll excuse us, we have some calls to make," Roger said and went into his office. Cheryl shut the door so we wouldn't hear through the soundproof glass.

I had a thought and walked over to Marcie.

"The real al-Hassah has been dead for ages, hasn't he?"

"I can neither confirm nor deny,' Marcie said, smiling.

"That report in the German newspapers six months ago that he died in that bombing in Basra," I said. "That was one of the last sightings anyone had of him before we got the case four days ago that he'd snuck into the UK to turn himself in to you lot."

"Or someone who claimed to be him," Marcie said.

"Your people wouldn't say it was him unless there was evidence or he'd sent some kind of proof it was him," I said. "Or it was one of his doubles, who was one of his relatives anyway. You decided it was no longer necessary to have the narrative that al-Hassah was out there terrorizing the world when there are so many other bastards out there."

"Again, I can neither confirm nor deny," Marcie said.

"I get it," I said. "Al-Hassah has become such a bogeyman for the West, a symbol for people to invest all their fears and paranoias in, that it doesn't matter if nobody has seen him for over a year. In fact, it's *better*. He gets to be the symbol of Ultimate Evil for the politicos to wave around every time they want more funding for the War on Terror or to pass through some insane legislation. Meanwhile, nobody really knows where the real guy is, if he's dead or alive, and you end up with the myth. And even if it gets out, it doesn't matter, because there's so much bullshit surrounding the myth that the truth is buried."

"Welcome to my world," Marcie said.

"Christ," I said. "That makes everything relative. And once again we're the only ones who know what really happened."

"Well," Marcie said. "It's our job to make sure the public doesn't."

"And you must have known Vanessa was having an affair with al-Hassah," I said. "She was a CIA asset, must have been recruited when she entered college."

"She hadn't even finished her training," Marcie said. "Don't look at me. I didn't recruit her. I would have recommended we didn't."

"Did you even know she was carrying on with al-Hassah?" I asked.

"Actually, she hid the affair from us," Marcie said. "You saw how good she was at compartmentalizing."

"You lot missed that when it was right under your noses."

"Yeah, yeah, rub it in," Marcie said with a slight hint of exasperation.

"That means we just helped the Company hide away one of its own embarrassing failures as well, didn't we?" I said.

"Some days I think I trained you too well." Marcie said.

You have no idea, I thought.

TWENTY-THREE

"**Y**ou're just going to let her go?" I said, barely stifling my outrage.

"I had a long talk with Mr. van Hooten," Roger said. "He's still our client, and all this started because he hired us and we stumbled upon what his little girl was up to. In four hours, dear old dad is flying her out on his private jet and taking her back to New York, and no one's going to be the wiser."

"It would have been really embarrassing for the public to find out she was having an affair with one of the biggest terrorists in the world," Marcie said. "Roger told Mr. van Hooten that you guys discovered the insane shit Vanessa was up to and that you stopped her from doing something even more embarrassing—"

"She tried to blow up Central London," I said. "Understatement of the century."

"And I'm going to get her out of the country and back to New York before the shit hits the fan and the news finds out," Roger said. "That way, van Hooten gets to dodge a major scandal about his daughter and the al-Hassah mess. The CIA won't ever admit she was one of theirs, and she'll be out of their clutches once she's back in Daddy's."

"She doesn't even get held accountable for nearly killing dozens of people."

"I wouldn't say that," Marcie said. "We all know Vanessa's elevator doesn't reach the top floor. There's going to be a team of doctors and psychiatrists waiting for her when she touches down. Chances are, she's gonna be spending the rest of her life in a big, bouncy room, pumped so full of drugs she'll practically be a vegetable. She'll be so brain-fried she'll probably have to wear a diaper. She's just going to be the madwoman in the attic that no one talks about. A dirty little secret we're all glad was swept under the carpet."

In the end, our story held up: Roger, Marcie, the CIA, and Interzone would continue to think Vanessa killed al-Hassah and kept his body around because, well, she was completely fucking mad. Bunny-boilingly mad. Daddy van Hooten suddenly had a scandal on his hands, what with his daughter bonking the world's most wanted terrorist, commanding a small cell of homegrown would-be terrorists, and keeping her lover's corpse in her flat that Daddy was paying for, and probably having sex with it before trying to turn it into a bomb to blow up Big Ben. Golden Sentinels had the video of al-Hassah visiting and the two of them bonking like bunnies. Benjamin even had the footage of her destroying al-Hassah's laptop, so kiss whatever intel he was bringing over good-bye. You would think there would be some bonus in the four homegrown wannabe insurgents that Interzone and Ken and Clive captured, but they didn't know anything, and Marcie's bosses were going to have to negotiate with the British authorities to take them off the Americans' hands, since these idiots were UK citizens and what they knew was not worth holding on to them in a black site somewhere. A suitable cover story was going to be needed to explain how they were caught, where the Americans were left out of it and the British police could take credit for it. Marcie found doing that rather tedious, since it didn't involve any A-list stars, but she did it anyway because it was her job.

Roger had van Hooten by the short and curlies. There would be another negotiation: What did Roger want for the video and audio to prevent any of this from ending up in the news, published by van Hooten's rival news outlets? Roger could use his pull—in truth, Marcie Holder's PR skills and CIA contacts—to keep all this secret, and to hold off anyone who might try to sniff it out. Van Hooten's papers could report that poor Vanessa had had her heart broken in London and suffered a nervous breakdown, so she had to go back to the States to enter a mental institution for treatment. Marcie's bosses at the CIA would cover up the fact that there was nearly a major terror attack on London right under the British authorities' noses, and no one would be any wiser. It wouldn't even occur to the Metropolitan Police to hold a press conference to announce that an attack in London had been prevented. All's well that ended well.

Except for the matter of the $20 million reward for the capture of al-Hassah.

"Sorry, guys," Marcie said. "The stipulation was for his capture *alive*."

Ken and Clive sulked, but Marcie didn't know why. The rest of us did.

"We wanted to debrief him and get all that intel. With him dead, and with Vanessa cuckoo-for-cocoa-puffs, we got zip other than what we already get from on-the-ground recon. Golden Sentinels gets paid the usual fee for this."

That meant no bonus for us, just the same amount Roger usually got for jobs Marcie brought to the firm. Roger still got some benefits, though. He had gained a new influential friend out of this job, a media tycoon with deep pockets who would call on him more than ever. I nearly got murdered, my head cut off by some idiots, but I didn't and it wasn't. The gods were not going to let that happen. This was only the start of what was to come, and I had some part to play in it, whatever it was. We would all find out in the months ahead.

"Ravi, me old china," Mark said. "Did it occur to you that your near-death experience in the oil drum could have been your final rite of passage in your journey to become a shaman?"

"What are you on about?"

"In many cultures, shamans usually had to undergo a ritual of symbolic death to strip away their former lives before they could take on their new role."

"I can't say I felt any different, other than being seriously fucked off about the whole ordeal," I said. "I certainly didn't feel like I gained any new insight or superpowers. My ego wasn't stripped away, my personality didn't go through any transformation. I'm still stuck being me. The gods are still here hanging about watching me like I'm their favorite reality show."

"But you didn't enter some kind of altered state?" Mark asked.

"Well, I did hallucinate a bit when I thought I was being tortured. Don't know what that was all about. What?"

Mark had that look on his face.

"How do you know that wasn't an intervention?" he said, a bit smug.

"Perhaps now you'll listen to us more often," Shiva said.

No chance.

Roger didn't seem to bat an eyelash at the news that we weren't getting the twenty million, but then Interzone wasn't either, so that was a win as far as he was concerned.

"Job well done, children," he said. "Onwards and upwards."

He went back into his office and got on the phone to his new business partners. He'd shut the door, so we couldn't hear what he was laughing it up about.

The gods leaned back on the sofa, contentedly exhausted from this whole drama.

"Wow, that was intense," Louise said. "I feel like I should light up a cigarette."

"A marvelous display of deception and duplicity," Bagalamukhi said. "Best case ever."

TWENTY-FOUR

And so, to our wedding.

It was as if the last case was but a distant dream. My bruises had almost completely healed. Now I was in a new dream, a much more pleasant one where I wasn't threatened with murder. David and the lads gave me a stag night, of course. We weren't the idiots we were in our twenties anymore, so there was no flying off to Ibiza for a drugs-and-booze-filled night of debauchery where someone ended up getting killed. I'd already nearly gotten killed on this last case and had no desire to repeat that experience. And none of us was interested in becoming another statistic in the crisis of fatalities on stag nights. This was a uniquely British phenomenon. As Marcie would say, only us Brits would overdo the booze and turn what should be a joyous rite of passage into a horrible tragedy. My stag night was a surprisingly sedate affair at a club David booked in Soho. We'd had enough excitement on this past case, and my friends from university, including David, were all past the need to drink ourselves stupid. Most of them had kids to go home to. Instead, Ken and Clive served as chaperones and bought us whiskey. Instead of a stripper, Mark booked a burlesque dancer who depicted a sexy fairy godmother who danced on strands of aerial silk as she removed her layers of clothing in an elegantly choreographed display of Olympic-level gymnastic skills. Ken and Clive were in charge of making sure everyone present got home in one piece, and in one or two cases, they picked up one of my friends like a football and installed him into a taxi. No one was driving.

For her hen night, Julia was taken to a bar in Hoxton with a muscular male stripper doing an Ali Baba routine. Or was he a genie? I forget. Julia was a bit vague about the details. Much wine was drunk, then champagne as Julia was presented with a tiara and a sash. From what little she told me, it was much, much raunchier than my stag do. Marcie and Olivia, who were there, wouldn't tell me anything at all. Julia's friend Angie from college copped off with the stripper at the end of the party. At the end of the evening, Julia went to her parents' house so that we could observe the tradition that the groom didn't see the bride the night before the wedding.

By the time my parents came to pick me up in the hired car in the morning, I was already dressed and only mildly hungover. Dad had actually persuaded Mum to let Brenda get on with the fashion choices. Our relatives who had come in from India all wore formal attire, and that was going to lend the proceedings a nice splash of color. They were also quite keen to experience an English wedding.

David had the rings ready and we got to the chapel. The guests were all in their pews, my relatives on one side, Julia's on the other. Anji and Vivek held their kids. Mum wept. So did Brenda. Dad had a look of relief on his face that I had managed not to end up in a mental institution and was getting married. Julia's father smiled and looked stoical. The gods were there, all in formal attire. Louise sat with them, her dress and hat far more glamorous than anyone else's, of course, as she beamed at her little sister.

It was an Anglican wedding, but to please Julia, her parents agreed to a multicultural look. Mum had sat with Brenda as she worked with the vicar at the parish to plan out the service. It didn't matter that the groom and more than half the attendees were Hindu.

"That's the beauty of the Church of England," Mark said. "Faith is optional."

Yes, Ariel showed up, dressed extravagantly and in a large hat as expected of women attending British weddings. Considering she saved my life, it would have been churlish of us not to invite her. She had been unsubtly angling for an invitation all that time. She seemed to enjoy the whole experience since she found it all delightfully alien. Then again, I had the feeling she found most normal human social gatherings alien.

"But I think in her own way," Julia said, "she loves you."

I honestly didn't know how to process that. I still don't.

The organist played to signal the arrival of the bride, and when I turned to greet Julia, I was gobsmacked. Julia was dressed in a stunning golden Zac Posen dress, her face behind a gold veil. The dress had belonged to Louise, from her days as a supermodel. I was reminded here that with her looks and body, Julia could have pursued a modeling career herself but had chosen not to. The décolletage plunged deep to reveal her cleavage and back; the gold patterns of the dress were tiny seashells. She looked like a princess that had risen from the seas as she walked towards me. She looked almost naked, the dress an illusion. I felt the temperature in the whole church go up. When she turned it on, Julia could reduce men to gibbering wrecks. Louise had made a career out of doing that herself. Perhaps it was a good thing Julia had chosen not to do that. The world might not have been able to withstand two Fowler sisters at once.

"Fuck me," Benjamin muttered, and Olivia smacked him on the arm.

Julia winked at me from behind her veil. I was in a sherwani, a traditional Hindu groom's outfit. It was also gold, and complemented Julia's dress. There was no gray or white at this wedding. It was gold and bright colors, the way the gods liked it.

At the back of the church, Louise sat with the gods and beamed with pride at her sister. She even dabbed her eyes with a handkerchief while Lord Shiva gave her shoulder a squeeze. They were sitting behind our people from Golden Sentinels. Strange to think we were tied to them now, to the point where some of them had nearly gotten me killed. And Ariel.

The organist played an intro to signal the start of the ceremony. The vicar welcomed the guests and began the ceremony with a prayer. This was the first time my relatives had experienced a full Anglican wedding and prayer service. They found it all fascinating.

A hymn was sung. The vicar offered another prayer, then the preface:

"In the presence of God, Father, Son, and Holy Spirit, we have come together to witness the marriage of Ravi Chandra Singh and Julia Annabel Fowler, to pray for God's blessing on them, to share their joy, and to celebrate their love . . ."

My relatives were experiencing firsthand how long prayers and sermons at an Anglican wedding could actually be. My cousins' kids got bored and fell asleep. For our part, Julia and I were not unaware of the paradox that we were both atheists getting married in this ceremony because her parents always wanted one for her. She was baptized when she was a baby, and they had begun putting aside money for a wedding that long ago.

"First, I am required to ask anyone present who knows a reason why these persons may not lawfully marry to declare it now."

Julia's racist grand-uncle who had dementia didn't say anything or start a scene. I was more worried about Ariel pulling out a gun and shooting up the church and everyone here, but that was just one of my flights of fancy from stress.

"Will you, Ravi Chandra Singh, take this woman to be your wife? Will you love her, comfort her, honor and protect her, and, forsaking all others, be faithful to her as long as you both shall live?"

"I will."

"Julia Annabel Fowler, will you take Ravi Chandra Singh to be your husband? Will you love him, comfort him, honor and protect him, and, forsaking all others, be faithful to him as long as you both shall live?"

"I will."

"Will you, the friends and family of Ravi Chandra Singh and Julia Annabel Fowler, support and uphold them in their marriage now and in the years to come?"

"We will."

Then the vicar led the prayer and read a passage from the Bible before Julia and I spoke our vows. Then the exchange of rings, and Julia and I held hands while the proclamation was said.

"In the presence of God, and therefore this congregation, Ravi Chandra Singh and Julia Annabel Fowler have given their consent and made their marriage vows to each other. They have declared their marriage by the joining of hands and by the giving and receiving of rings. I therefore proclaim that they are husband and wife. Those whom God has joined together let no one put asunder."

Then the blessing of the marriage, and final prayer, then the dismissal.

This was a full-on Church of England wedding, since Julia's parents took this awfully seriously. We even kneeled for the proclamation and everything. It took a lot longer than you might expect. Or it felt longer because everyone was standing or sitting in the same place through the whole ceremony. It was actually a relief that Julia and I didn't have to write our own vows. We were too knackered and stressed out anyway. I'd recently nearly been murdered and Julia helped save me, so we were not worried about our devotion to each other.

Julia's friends and family were all weepy and happy. My relatives were enjoying the ritual of it all.

Reception dinner in the hotel ballroom.

As best man, David got to make the speech totally taking the piss out of me.

"Back when we were friends at university, Ravi was always the mad one. We had some wild times didn't we, mate? Ravi's had his ups and downs, he's been around the block a few times, but if I ever get into deep trouble, he's the one I'm going to call, if only because he's going to make things even worse by doing the right thing. Because he can't help himself. He's what our boss Roger would call a mensch. He's the most ridiculously straight-up bloke I've ever met, and I'm a lawyer, all right? I meet all kinds of people who are morally less than pure. Not Ravi. He has his code and he sticks to it. Therefore, it's a bit of a mystery how Ravi could have landed someone as fabulous as Julia. It's as if she's tamed the wild lion that's our Mr. Singh here. Seriously though, the two of you make a great team. It's like you complete him in a way I never thought would happen. Here's to you both."

He raised his glass in a toast. All in all, it was very politic, more gentle than I'd expected or deserved, no talk of my seeing gods or possible insanity. No way was David going to even hint at the types of things Julia and I got up to at Golden Sentinels.

"A speech written by a lawyer," I said. "That's going to serve you really well when you run for office."

"Piss off," David laughed.

We cut the cake. Of course there was a large cake. They saved us the top tier for the christening of our future firstborn. We tried not to wince. Catering for the reception was esoteric, to say the least, a surreal combination of English roasts, hors d'oeuvres and Indian dishes. Our mothers had made sure both families were catered to. My mother told me that Mrs. Dhewan had gotten them a discount on the food.

The night ended with dancing. Ken and Clive smoked at their table and traded stories about serving in the military with Julia's uncle. Mark rolled a spliff. Marcie mingled with our parents, which made me wary, but what could I do? Julia held me close as we slow-danced together.

As we held each other, we observed our friends and families intermingling. Ken and Clive were too old-school to dance with each other, but danced with nearly all our aunts through the evening. Olivia had to teach an extremely uncoordinated Benjamin. Marcie went from table to table socializing and trading gossip, or rather gathering intel, as she always did. Roger didn't show up though he sent a gift. I hadn't expected him to show up, somehow. Cheryl, however, did. She wore a yellow floral dress and hat, and smiled and projected a warmth we rarely saw in the office as she spoke to our parents and congratulated them. Julia's mother and mine were new best friends. Somehow, the arguments about the wedding plans had brought them closer. Mrs. Dhewan gossiped and played grande dame with my relatives, catching up on news from India. Mark was a hit with my female cousins. Ariel was being hit on by nearly all the single men, especially amongst Julia's guests, which I'd sort of expected. It was her playing with all the kids that I found disturbing. Perhaps that was her way of passing for human?

"Look at that," I said. "I never would have expected our work and home lives would cross over like this."

"Let's just be happy tonight, Ravi," Julia said. "Accept everyone's kindness while we can. We can go back to dealing with the chaotic evils of the world later."

Who was I to disagree?

Finally, the end. The departure. Barrage of confetti. David and the guys had tied cans and old sneakers to the back of the BMW Julia and I usually drove to cases.

Before we left, Julia turned around and tossed the bouquet at the outstretched arms of the bridesmaids and guests, and who should happen to catch it?

Ariel. Of course it was Ariel.

She held up the bouquet like a trophy and winked at us.

As we drove away, Julia and I both breathed a sigh of relief.

"Glad that's over with," she said.

"I'm so glad Laird Collins didn't show up like he did at my sister's wedding," I said.

"You know, I think Ariel might be more turned on by us being married than us not being married."

"Oh God. We're never going to be rid of her, are we?" I said. "It's like Kali sent her to mess with our lives."

"Or keep you on your toes," Kali said from the backseat, sipping champagne with Louise. When the other gods went off, Kali and Louise always stuck with us, probably because they were our patron gods.

"Now it's official. We're stuck with each other," Julia said.

"Until death do us part," I said. "Are you okay with that?"

"Ravi," Julia put her hand over mine on the steering wheel, "after everything we've been through and everything we know, who can replace either of us if the other goes first? You and I know each other better than anyone else on earth. I don't want anyone else. If and when death comes, we're not parting. We're going together."

"Agreed," I said, and squeezed her hand.

That night, we made our own heaven. And we didn't need the gods to do that.

THE DEIFICATION OF
KAREENA MAHFOUZ

ONE

When the world you know falls apart, it can happen very quickly, suddenly, when you're least expecting it. You might have seen the signs and portents, but you didn't know what they meant.

"Things fall apart, the center cannot hold," Julia liked to quote. "And mere anarchy is loosed upon the world."

"Yeats," I said. I used to teach that poem. "Curse your talent for choosing the most appropriate literary quote when the shit hits the fan."

"Stress relief," Julia said.

It was a damn sight better than jumping on the first bloke she laid eyes on and bonking him senseless, which she told me she used to do. That would have been a serious relapse in her sex addiction. And stress was certainly what we were experiencing that morning.

Anyway, life proceeded normally enough. We were at my parents' for Sunday dinner as usual.

"So where are you going for your honeymoon?" Vivek asked.

"More to the point, *when* are you going on your honeymoon?" Anjita asked.

"We haven't quite decided yet," I said. "We haven't even had a chance to unwrap all the gifts yet."

"Or decide which ones to return," Julia said.

"Come on, Ravi," Anji said. "It's up to the groom to pick the honeymoon. It's been a week since the wedding and you're still here."

"Well," I said. "We still have some work to finish off at the firm."

"We're probably going to go to a beach resort somewhere," Julia said.

"Didn't we say that was a bit of a cliché?" I said.

"Sun, sea, and sex," Vivek said. "Don't knock it, mate."

"You're always working," Mum said. "You're such a workaholic. You haven't taken a holiday for ages. You owe it to your wife to take one with her."

"I know, I know. We'll pick a place and go off and do nothing."

Why were the gods so interested in what my answer would be? They stood by the dinner table listening very intently. Did they know something I didn't? Even Louise looked impatient and a bit annoyed.

"Do your duty as a newlywed," she said. "Take my sister someplace fun and bonk her brains out."

My wife's late sister became a goddess so she could come back and nag me. In truth, Julia and I really couldn't decide where to go. Her fugitive heart was too restless to just chill out on a beach somewhere. I was afraid we might wind up in the type of place where we got into some insane situation. I'd already been nearly murdered by would-be terrorists just a few weeks ago, and I wasn't in a hurry to rush into another insane scenario. Julia was being very patient with me.

"Do you remember the old house our family owned in Mumbai?" Dad asked.

"You told us about it," I said. "Anjita and I have never seen it."

"I thought Granddad lost it gambling or something," Anji said.

"Well, it was left with your great-aunt after we left for London, and she just passed away," Dad said. "She left it to us in her will."

"That's great!" Vivek said.

"With the money we saved from not having to pay for Ravi and Julia's wedding," Mum said, "we thought we'd fly over there to look at the place."

"It's been a long time since your mother and I have been back in India," Dad said.

"It's changed a lot," Vivek said.

Vivek and Anji's baby cooed. Louise was fussing over her as she sat in her baby chair. I could swear my niece could see her and was reacting to her smile and funny faces. The gods were milling around us, as usual.

"Great-aunt Aparna's husband wasn't the most responsible man in the world," Dad said. "And the lawyer warned us the house was in disrepair for years."

"Sounds like a fixer-upper," Vivek said.

"What do you reckon?" Anjita said. "Thinking about making it a second home? Maybe retire there when you get sick of London?"

"The thought did occur to us," Dad said.

"So we'll be off this week," Mum said.

"That's quick," I said. "Where are you staying?"

"At my brother's," Dad said. "Since everyone already saw us when they came for your wedding, we don't need to do a big song and dance about visiting. It should be nice and leisurely."

"And Mrs. Dhewan asked me to deliver some gifts to her sister," Mum said.

Dad and I both stiffened.

"Mum, no!"

"Why are you looking at me like that?" Mum said. "It's just some presents from Fortnum & Mason's and Selfridges. It's not drugs or contraband. It's jam, biscuits, scarves. I went shopping with her to pick them. I helped wrap them. I'm not smuggling drugs, for heaven's sake."

"I just don't want you getting involved in any schemes that woman is cooking up," Dad grumbled.

"She's not cooking up anything," Mum said. "It's all completely innocent."

"Nothing is ever completely innocent with that gangster," Dad said.

"Don't be so melodramatic," Mum said.

The rest of the dinner was the usual bickering.

"I'm calling our office in Mumbai," I said as Julia and I drove back from my parents' house. "Have them keep an eye on Mum and Dad."

"Good idea!" Lord Shiva said from the backseat.

My phone rang. I put it on the hands-free.

"Grab your passports," Marcie said.

"What's going on?" I asked.

"Get your asses to Heathrow. Cheryl's booked tickets for you two on the next flight to JFK tonight."

"New York? Why?"

"Golden Sentinels in New York knows you," Marcie said. "They'll put you guys in a safe house in Manhattan. Once you get there, we can figure stuff out. Dump your phones. You can get fresh phones and laptops when you get there."

"Wait, what's going on?" I asked.

"I got word that Roger's getting busted first thing in the morning."

"For what?" Julia asked.

"It's going to be all over the news, but I might as well tell you now. Two days ago, a plane full of mercenaries, trained by Interzone, got intercepted by government troops leaving Nigeria. The mercs were on their way to Niger, one of the smaller resource-rich African countries, to overthrow the government and install a new puppet regime in the pocket of one Roger Golden."

"What the fuck?!"

"It was like if the Keystone Kops were mercenaries, from what I heard," Marcie said. "They had problems with the plane they chartered to fly them out. It wouldn't take off the runway. And a bunch of white guys with guns on a plane whose engine nearly fell off was kind of conspicuous. You can't blame the local cops and military for surrounding it with their guns drawn."

Kali and Shiva whooped and clapped from the backseat.

"Roger tried to finance a coup to take over a third world country," Marcie said. "That was what that weekend party at Alfie Beam's mansion was about all along. Roger didn't tell us about his 'business plan' so we'd have deniability. He probably wanted to make sure none of us would rat him out."

"Well, someone's grassed on him anyway," Julia said.

"He had us collect dirt on his partners for leverage," I said. "That makes us complicit, even if we didn't know what was going on."

"I'll tell you something else," Marcie said. "Two weeks ago, Roger had David draw up some papers to sign ownership and control of Golden Sentinels over to Cheryl."

"For what?" I asked.

"To separate the firm from whatever company he formed to front the coup," Julia said. "That way Golden Sentinels wouldn't be caught in the net if the coup went pear-shaped."

"What about the others?" I asked. "Mark, Olivia, Benjamin, Ken, Clive, David? Cheryl?"

"Everybody's fine," Marcie said. "They're in the wind like you."

"What about the office?"

"Cheryl is holding down the fort, but she's kind of expecting Special Branch to show up and take away the computers and files. Benjamin already triggered the kill switch on the computers. All the hard drives are toast. They're not going to get shit."

A wave of déjà vu washed over me—I suddenly remembered a dream I'd had a year ago where we blew up all the computers after Roger was taken and the world was ending. Was that a prophetic dream the gods sent me? Suddenly it all seemed to fit.

"Marcie, are the police or Special Branch coming for us?" I asked.

"Not yet. Right now, they're looking at Roger's shell company. They might decide to look into his other companies, like Golden Sentinels. And you don't want to be around when they decide to."

"We're going on the run? Honestly?" Julia asked.

"You know what would have been worse?" Marcie said. "If those mercs made it into Niger and launched their attack thinking they had a chance when the locals were waiting for them. It would have been a massacre. The failed coup would have been a lot messier, and Roger would probably be in even deeper shit."

"Marcie, where are you now?" I asked.

"At the US Embassy. We're having an emergency meeting about this whole mess."

"Are you in trouble, considering Roger's your asset?"

"Don't worry about me." Marcie said. "I got your back. Now get your asses on that plane."

TWO

Julia and I got home, grabbed our passports, and each packed a small bag with basics, mainly clothes. Best to travel clean.

"Do you see anyone watching the flat?" I asked.

"Not a soul outside," Julia said, peering out the window.

We took a taxi to Heathrow so the company car couldn't be traced. Our tickets were waiting for us at the British Airways desk.

It was the middle of the night and we had two hours before we boarded our flight. We watched the news on the screens in the empty departure lounge. Roger and the failed coup were the big topic. "LONDON BUSINESSMAN ARRESTED FOR PLOTTING COUP IN AFRICA" ran the chyron. Roger had been arrested as the mastermind behind the attempted coup in Niger. The British authorities were cooperating with the government in Niger to determine how deep the plot was to overthrow them. Arrests had already been made there, and investigations into the shell company that financed the failed coup had been traced to London businessman and former private investigator Roger Golden. Authorities were investigating who his partners and co-conspirators were.

When our plane took off, we could finally relax.

It wasn't a full flight, so there was plenty of room for the gods to kick back in first class. Louise was right at home with them, looking every bit the glamorous world traveler.

I managed to fall asleep, but it wasn't peaceful.

"Wake up, mate," Mark said. "You'll want to see this."

I opened my eyes. Mark was shaking me.

"Mark? What are you doing here?"

"I've always been here, Rav," he said. "David's going mental. Everything's gone pear-shaped."

I sat up on the office sofa.

"What's happened?" I asked.

"We happened. Chickens come home to roost."

"Finally pissed off the wrong people," David said, walking in and gathering up another batch of files. "I knew this would happen one day. Bloody Roger."

"Roger said this day would come," Julia said.

The office was a mess. Cheryl was busy pushing papers and files into a shredder, as fast as Ken and Clive could pass them to her. David added his to the pile. Benjamin was whacking away at the computers with a fire axe, a manic grin on his face.

"Wa-hey!" he said. "Nice of you to join us, Ravi!"

"Honestly, Benjamin," Olivia said, irritated. "I told you, the best way to get rid of evidence on a computer was thermite or C-4."

With that, she pushed the button on a detonator and all the computers in the office exploded in puffs of smoke.

"Let's see them try to recover the data," Olivia said, satisfied.

"What the hell did we do?" I asked.

Mark chuckled.

"More like what *didn't* we do," he said.

"Where's Roger?"

"Gone," Cheryl said. "They've taken him."

"Who's taken him?"

"Who do you think?" Ken said with a sneer.

"All his fancy friends in high places," Clive said. "They fucking sold him out, didn't they?"

I looked around.

"Where's Marcie?"

"Her masters called her home," Cheryl said. "In disgrace. Nothing left for her here. Probably her fault."

"Bloody typical," Olivia said. "She comes here, makes a bloody great mess of things, then buggers off to do the same thing somewhere else."

"So what's going on here?" I asked.

"What does it bloody look like?" Ken said. "It's the end, innit?"

"Gotta cover our arses," Clive said.

"Golden Sentinels is toast," David said. "And we have to get out of here before they show up."

"Bloody right," Ken said. "We don't want to be here when Special Branch shows up."

Benjamin helped Ken and Clive pour gasoline over the whole office. Once finished, they tossed the cans aside and joined us at the exit.

"Cheryl," Olivia said. "Will you do the honors?"

Cheryl lit a match and tossed it into the office. We didn't stay to watch as everything went up in flames.

"No forensics for them to recover," Benjamin said.

"Parting is such sweet sorrow," Mark said as he blew a kiss at the burning office.

Mark and David led us through the door out into the street.

Farringdon was in pandemonium. Black smoke was everywhere, billowing into the sky. Sirens in the air. Burning cars. Riot police chasing protesters with placards that read "NO MORE LIES!" I heard helicopters overhead.

"Yes," Mark said. "It's gone a bit J. G. Ballard, hasn't it?"

Somewhere in the distance, clear as a bell, a boy was singing "Jerusalem."

"And did those feet in ancient time,
Walk upon England's mountains green:
And was the holy Lamb of God,
On England's pleasant pastures seen! . . ."

As I looked around for where the singer was, Julia pulled at my arm.

"Ravi, look."

"Roger?" I said. "What are you doing here?"

In the middle of the street was a metal table at the top of a twenty-foot wicker man, and there sat Roger, handcuffed to it. Gone was his expensive Savile Row suit and tie. In its place were the orange overalls you found in American prisons. Roger was unshaven, his eyes red from lack of sleep and from weeping.

"Ahh, Ravi old son, the bastards finally got me."

"I warned you everything would come a-cropper one day," Cheryl said, her rage barely contained. "You just had to chance everything."

"What's the point in saying sorry, eh?" Roger said.

We all stood in front of the table like a tribunal, judging him. He looked like an exhibit, a cautionary tale in the middle the street, an art installation by some Goldsmiths College graduate who used found objects to capture the times.

"All your wheeling and dealing," Cheryl said. "All your favors, all the dirty laundry you had us hide and clean, and this still happens."

"Yes, yes," Roger said, all fight gone from his body. He looked shockingly frail, broken.

"You're not takin' us down with you," Ken said. "I'll tell you that."

"I'm not taking you down," Roger said. "It's all me. Just me."

"Too right," Clive said, and began to pour gasoline over the wicker man, Roger, and the table.

"Listen," Roger said, spluttering. "I can still get out on top. It all depends on you, Ravi."

"Me? What the hell can I do?"

"You know what the big picture is. You know where the bodies are buried now. I want you to use it. You'll know what to do with it all. We can still come out a win. Work with Olivia."

"Sorry, Roger," Olivia said. "I'm off to run a bank in Shanghai. This is all my past now."

"And I look forward to being your kept man, babes," Benjamin said.

"We'll see how long that lasts," Olivia said with a sniff.

"Come on," Roger said. "Just one last hurrah, eh? What have you got to lose?"

"Enough!" Cheryl said. "We've lost everything thanks to you! I followed you for over twenty years, you bastard! I loved you! You were always a disappointment! I waited for you to become the better version of you! But no, you liked the gutter too much because scraping for leftover power was all you ever went after! Once a chancer always a chancer! Now everything we built has gone up in flames! Only one last thing left to burn!"

Ken passed Cheryl a box of matches.

"Is this absolutely necessary?" I asked.

"We have to get rid of all evidence that comes back to us," Cheryl said. "It's every man for himself after this."

Roger just nodded sadly.

We watched the wicker man burn in this final ritual. Roger disappeared in the smoke and the flames. I bet he'd never thought he would end up a sacrifice to the forgotten pagan gods of the British Isles. We all turned away.

"And did the Countenance Divine,
Shine forth upon our clouded hills?
And was Jerusalem builded here,
Among these dark Satanic Mills? . . ."

Where was the singing coming from?

It felt like this would be the last I would see everyone. I thought of Ken and Clive. What would become of them now, unleashed from the restraints of Golden Sentinels, where they were barely restrained to start with? They were going to sink back into the fabric of the land, become murderous urban legends, hunting the truly wicked. Why was I so certain of that now?

I had to call my parents. I desperately wanted to hear their voices.

"Ravi?" my dad said on the other end of the line. "Is that you? How is London?"

"Falling apart. You and Mum picked the right time to move to Mumbai."

"We saw the writing on the wall," Mum said. "Are you and Julia all right?"

"We'll be fine, Mum."

"Good. We're off to see your grandparents for dinner."

"Um, didn't Dadaji and Dadiji pass away ten years ago?"

"Good memory, Ravi. They're cooking tonight. It's going to be a nice dinner. We'll send them your love."

"Thanks, Mum."

"And Ravi," Dad came on, "keep listening to the gods. You can't go wrong."

"I will, Dad."

And with that, they were gone.

And still the singing in the air.

"Bring me my Bow of burning gold;

Bring me my Arrows of desire:

Bring me my Spear: O clouds unfold!

Bring me my Chariot of fire! . . ."

"Good morning, ladies and gentlemen, this is your captain speaking. We are making our final approach to John F. Kennedy Airport. The time is now 7:40 a.m. Temperature is a mild sixty-five degrees Fahrenheit. If you'll put your seats back upright and store your tray tables, the flight attendants will be along to collect your headphones shortly. I'd like to thank you for flying with us and hope to see you again soon. Flight attendants, prepare for landing."

We got through passport control and customs without a hitch. Of course, they eyed me a bit suspiciously because of my skin color, but they must have consulted whatever list Marcie had put me on, and they waved me through, their demeanor changed after they looked me up. I had half expected to be snatched at the airport, and the fact that we weren't meant nobody was coming after Golden Sentinels just yet.

THREE

Julia and I took a cab to Golden Sentinels' New York City office. It was Downtown, near One World Trade Center, and had a similar design to the offices in London and Los Angeles, open plan, brightly lit, and ultramodern, with the best feng shui, though the investigators were dressed slightly more formally than we were at the London office, suits and ties for the men and pantsuits for the women, to convey the maximum air of professionalism. We said hello to everyone there. Hector Camacho and Dave Kosinski, their version of Ken and Clive, also ex-cops, only much less homicidal, greeted me with bad British accents as they always did. Julia introduced herself to the gang, since this was her first visit to the New York branch.

"Omigod, you're the hot English Rose Roger talks about in his newsletters," they said. Julia was immediately the object of male lust around the New York office and an object of jealousy amongst the women.

Their tech guy issued us with fresh smartphones and laptops, complete with Olivia's security programs installed to keep the connections secure when we had to communicate.

Before we even settled in, Ed Serrano, the boss, told us we had a job.

"The client specifically asked for you when he heard you were in the country," he said.

"How did he know?" I asked. "We didn't even know we were coming till last night."

"Guess he's just really well informed," Ed said. "They sent a car to pick you up."

"Who's the client anyway?" Julia asked.

"You're about to find out," Ed said. "Car should be here any minute."

When we went downstairs, we found a stretch limousine waiting for us, and standing next to us was Ariel Morgenstern.

"Oh Christ," I muttered.

"Isn't this great?" she said. "We never get to see each other this much in a year."

She kissed both Julia and me and ushered us into the back of the limousine.

"Look at us, traveling all fancy," she said, gleeful like a teenager out on the town, and called to the chauffeur, "Steve, let's jam."

"Where are we going?" Julia asked.

"Midtown to pick up the client," Ariel said. "He's in town to attend upfronts for the new TV season. All the buyers and advertisers are here."

"Were you the one who told the client we were in town?" I asked.

"I mentioned you when we were assigned as his bodyguards," Ariel said.

"Marcie must have told her what happened in London," Julia said.

The gods sat with us in the limousine. It was big enough to fit everyone.

"Now you know what your boss was up to for the last few years, right?" Ariel asked. "He was drumming up partners, finance, sponsorship for his coup."

"And that's why he didn't want us to know," I said. "That bloody madman. He actually wanted to own a whole country?"

"The business plan Roger kept hinting at to us was to take over an African country that produces twenty thousand barrels of oil a day and is also rich in uranium," Julia said. "That's Bond villain levels of madness."

"That's megalomaniacs for you," Ariel said. "To run a whole country via a puppet government you put in play, own an entire economy and its natural resources? To be a player at the global table?"

"Right," I said. "Roger couldn't resist dreaming big. He must have spent years putting the pieces in place for that. That must have been what the investors were for."

"And what was your boss doing there?" Julia asked.

"Roger needed soldiers," Ariel said. "So he asked Interzone to provide training to some cheap-ass army he'd hired."

"Roger must have negotiated the use of some 'advisors' from Interzone for the coup," I said. "In exchange for a cut of the profits and a slice of the country?"

"Money speaks louder than hate," Ariel said. "Roger offered Interzone a piece of the country. Collins is a lot more power-hungry than Roger. For a PMC to co-own a country with oil and uranium, that would be a good place to store a lot of weapons outside the eyes of the US. And I bet Roger was looking for a way to fuck us over later, after he got everything he wanted."

"So how did it fail?" I asked. "Roger wouldn't be so careless as to get caught just like that."

"Somebody must have blown the whistle on him," Ariel said.

"Who?" Julia asked. "One of the partners? Could Collins have done it just to fuck Roger over?"

"Not my boss," Ariel said. "He stood to lose from this deal falling apart. And Mr. Collins ain't in much condition to pull any double-dealing shit right now."

"Oh? What's wrong with him?" I asked.

"Let's just say he hasn't been the same since that weekend in the country," Ariel said.

"How's that?"

"Turns out the boss doesn't take naturally to mind-altering magic mushrooms."

"Did he have a nervous breakdown? Some kind of trauma?" I asked.

"I really shouldn't say," Ariel said. "Let's just say he's going to need to take medical leave to get his shit together."

"Then who's running Interzone right now?" I asked.

"We do have a board of directors." Ariel said.

"The board doesn't run the company," I said. "Who's in charge of the operations?"

"Right now, it's mostly Jarrod and me," Ariel said. "Jarrod hates the contract and admin stuff, so it's been mostly up to me. I've been picking our contracts for the last month."

I suddenly felt nauseous.

"You okay, Ravi?" Ariel smiled, reading my mind.

"This means that both Golden Sentinels and Interzone are in free fall right now," I said. "Two of the most dangerous private organizations around and both without proper leadership."

"Hey," Ariel said, mock offended. "What am I, chopped liver? Jarrod and I are holding up the fort."

"We're on the run and scattered to the wind to avoid the British authorities, and you're . . . Just what the hell are you doing?"

"We still have contracts," Ariel said. "Jobs with various governments. Busy as ever. We just don't have Collins around to make speeches about the Second Coming and the Rapture, which is kind of a relief, I can tell ya."

Behind Ariel, Kali snickered. That made me wince.

"Don't look so lost," Ariel said. "You're living the dream, babe. You don't have Roger giving you assignments you're afraid are going to get you in trouble. You're Arjuna cut loose and free after he kills his guru."

"What, that bit in the Bhagavad Gita where he kills Dronacharya, who taught him the bow and arrow? Great."

"To win the battle at Mahabharata," Ariel said. "Arjuna kills his teacher. The pupil becomes the master at last."

"What are you talking about?" I said. "You mean Roger? He's not my bloody guru. He's my boss."

"Not for much longer," Julia said.

"And you gotta admit you learned a lot from him," Ariel said. "He kind of molded your worldview in the last three years. With Dronacharya gone, Arjuna has to come of age and make his own moral decisions."

"Look, I'm not going to kill Roger, figuratively or literally," I said. "And anyway, he's fucked himself. He doesn't need me to end him."

"That's just the beginning," Ariel said. "The point is, once he's out of the picture, you're free to make your own decisions about what to do with your life. Golden Sentinels is done."

"You're forgetting that I might still end up in jail with Roger if everything keeps going horribly wrong."

"That's if you go back to the UK," Ariel said.

"I have no intention of becoming an international fugitive."

"Don't knock it till you try it, babe," Ariel said.

"How did the authorities know Roger was behind the coup?" I asked. "The mercenaries they arrested at the airport in Lagos wouldn't know he was the boss of the coup. He must have set up shell companies to write the checks, hire people. Who would have had the know-how to suss out it was Roger?"

We all had the same thought.

"The Americans," Julia said.

"More specifically, the CIA," I said.

"Did Marcie know?" Julia asked.

"She didn't," I said. "You saw her. She was as much in the dark as we were. That must have pissed her off. Then she must have found out. There are a number of ways she could have done it, like simply interrogate David. He would have folded immediately and told her everything since he was terrified of the whole deal."

"Think about it," Ariel said. "You piss off Marcie Holder, you piss off the CIA. They're the biggest clients of both our companies."

"Does that mean we have the CIA pissed off with us now?" I said. "Just how fucked are we?"

"La la la la la!" Kali sang as she twirled around.

"I think you're good," Ariel said. "Marcie's the one who warned you and put you on the plane out of there, right? Means she's keeping the rest of you guys separate from this meltdown. She's a goddamned undeclared intelligence officer in London. She needs her assets to back up any play she might make."

"But why would the CIA grass Roger up?" I asked, my head spinning.

"The US has bases in Niger," Ariel said.

"Is Niger a US ally?" Julia asked.

"Well, they've been kind of having talks," Ariel said.

Lagos. Nigeria. That was where David's family came from. Now it all began to fit: Roger was using David's family's connections for an in over there, so he could use Nigeria as the staging ground for his coup. No wonder David was getting more and more nervous in the last few months. He had to help Roger put together the deals to make this happen. David was in deep shit. More than the rest of us at Golden Sentinels, because he actually *knew* what was going on.

Or could he have been the one who grassed Roger up?

And to Marcie, perhaps? It would fit.

The coup had fallen apart so quickly and unexpectedly this morning that someone must have talked to the CIA at least days if not weeks in advance. The CIA must have gotten in touch with the governments in Niger, then in Nigeria. The Nigerian president would have mobilized the army to grab the mercenaries boarding the commercial flight to Niger, and the whole scheme would have gone to hell from there. The CIA then made a call to the British government, who then got the authorities to issue an arrest warrant for Roger. This meant MI5 might be involved as well. Police, Special Branch, scrutiny would be on all of Roger's businesses, including Golden Sentinels. We were all in the shit.

"You've just sussed it out, haven't you?" Julia said.

"He's totally worked it out," Ariel said. "He's got that look on his face."

"I wish I didn't," I said. "Because it might mean we're in deeper trouble than we imagined."

"How deep?" Ariel asked, that amused, knowing look on her face, like she was the American Punk Rock embodiment of Kali.

"So who's the client you're taking us to anyway?" I asked.

"Oh, you've met him," Ariel said. "You could say you bonded last year when he nearly got us all killed."

FOUR

"**R**avi, Julia, it is so very good to see you again."

Hamid Mahfouz looked relaxed and totally in his element when he got into the limo. He had the look of a man relieved to no longer have to worry about people trying to kill him. That was how we'd first met him last year. We inadvertently became his babysitters as we ran around Los Angeles dodging assassins while the city was surrounded by brushfires in the hills.

Interzone had had the contract for protecting him ever since.

"The minute he heard you were available," Ariel said, "he asked for the two of you."

"Mr. Mahfouz—"

"Please, call me Hamid. We're all friends here, after what you did to save my life in Los Angeles."

"I thought you might have ended up back in your country being forced to take over as the dictator," I said.

"That ship has gloriously sailed," he said. "As I predicted, the factional infighting over there became so out of control it was obvious that nobody from my father's family would be suitable to rule the place. The rebels that overthrew him have split into several factions and are at war with the other groups the CIA are backing. My presence there would not serve any purpose."

"So all you had to do was wait it out until they couldn't use you anymore," I said.

"Good things come to those who wait," Julia said.

"They saw the light," Hamid said. "So they're not insisting I try to even form a government-in-exile. Whatever regime change they want to prop up, they have to do it without me. I'm free to continue my life as a decadent playboy layabout here."

"Congratulations," Julia said.

"Thank you, my dear. This leads me to why I've asked for your services."

"What do you need us for this time?" I asked.

"It's my sister Kareena."

"The one who led the rebels to overthrow your father?" Julia asked.

"I only have one sister."

"Wasn't she the one who sent those killers after you that chased us all over Los Angeles when it was on fire?" I asked.

"The same. Well, her standing amongst the Maoist rebels has also taken a tumble, and they tried to have her killed as well."

"Talk about karma," Ariel said, amused as ever. "Plan a revolution, overthrow the government, execute your dad, execute your nasty older brothers, try to have your last remaining brother killed, try to be the power behind your boyfriend in his bid to take over the government, and it all comes crashing down around your ears."

"Indeed," Hamid said. "The CIA had a hand in her boyfriend getting killed. He was leading the rebels, though he was useless without Kareena calling the shots behind him. She tried to take over, but the rebels were too sexist to accept her as their true leader and tried to kill her in turn. They accused her of being a CIA asset as well, which prompted the need for her to leave the country."

"So where is she now?" Julia asked.

"Here in America," Hamid said. "I used my last favor with the CIA to have her flown over her and placed under my protection."

"But she tried to kill you last year," I said. "Why would you take care of her now?"

"She's still my sister." Hamid said. "We've always been close. I'm not going to abandon her now, especially if there are people who might want to kill her. Our mother has no interest, since she was never much of a mother to start with. She's perfectly happy playing Jackie O with her new billionaire boyfriend, gallivanting around the South of France."

"What do you need us for?" Julia asked.

"Kareena is at a very delicate stage in her life. She's lost everything. I have to help her sort out what's next. I need you to babysit her in the meantime."

"Um," I said.

"I may be a lazy playboy," he said, "but I still have work to do. I've just finished talking to advertisers and sales representatives who want to buy the next season of *Ultimate Times*, my kids' variety show. It's the biggest kids' variety show, that's sold to over one hundred and twenty markets around the world and earns my production company and the KidTime network tens of millions of dollars in revenue. I have my hands full trying to find a new star to host the show since we lost the last two. The head of network is playing hardball with me about the next season of my show because we don't have a new star. So I can't look after my sister full-time while I deal with my day job."

"But why us?" I asked. "You have Interzone on retainer to be your bodyguards. You could just get them to babysit her."

"She hates private military contractors," Hamid said. "And you have an ability to gain people's trust, as if you were blessed by the gods. I'm hoping you might have the same calming effect on my sister."

"How do you know your sister won't try to kill us all?" I asked. "She orchestrated those hit squads we had to run from last year. Now we're going to be in the same room with her?"

"She's, well, not like you expect," Hamid said. "She won't kill us because we're her benefactors now. It would just be rude. And my sister was raised to show good manners, just like me."

"If you say so," Julia said, still a bit skeptical.

Hamid seemed to enjoy the observable fact that Julia tolerated him rather than liked him.

"When you meet her, you'll understand."

"Where are we going?" Julia asked.

"Why, to meet my sister for lunch, of course."

Out of the corner of my eye, I saw Louise wink. Kali and Shiva laughed their arses off. Bagalamukhi raised her glass in a toast. Ganesha took a picture of me with his phone to catch the look on my face.

FIVE

Hamid brought us to a five-star restaurant on Fifth Avenue where he had made reservations. Ariel accompanied us, her eyes alert as we walked past the diners to scan for threats. We were brought into a private dining room at the back where we could talk privately. Two Interzone men in suits sat with Hamid's sister as she waited for us to arrive.

"All done pressing the flesh of the bigwigs who run the TV industry, then?" she said, her accent revealing the British private schools she was sent to when she was younger.

Kareena Mahfouz was not what I was expecting at all.

To hear Hamid talk about her, and see the results of her actions, including the trouble she sent our way last year when we had to outrun scores of killers across Los Angeles, I was expecting a fiery, rage-filled militant. Instead, Julia and I were presented with a slim, athletic woman in her twenties, dressed in jeans and a blouse that made her look like a PhD student. The only thing that suggested otherwise was the intensity of her eyes, how they seemed to burn into you with their unwavering, unblinking gaze.

She shook Julia's and my hands with a firm but gentle grip.

"Please accept my apology for nearly having you killed," she said. "That was a different time. I was on a war footing."

"That's one way of putting it," I said.

"You were on the opposing side, and I was intent on eliminating it."

"The 'opposing side' was your brother, and you sent killers after him," I said.

"Well, now I'm on the same side as him, and I have no army. That war is over for me," she said.

I never thought I would ever meet someone like Kareena Mahfouz. Hamid had told us she studied political theory and philosophy in college. She was particularly taken with the Suffragettes and Rosa Luxemburg, and wrote a paper on the Russian Revolution, the Chinese Revolution, and the Red Brigade of the 1970s and the Baader-Meinhof Gang. No one thought she was preparing herself for leading a revolt against her own father back home. She was a genuine revolutionary, driven by ideology and moral certainty, cool and ruthless in her moral calculations when it came to casualties and deaths. This made her uncompromising and dangerous. She was the most dangerous type of killer, one that commanded armies and sent people to their deaths without hesitation.

"I've been reading up on my brother's world," Kareena said. "Hollywood is rather like Babylon, isn't it? All that money and glamour and everyone fighting to get their share of it. And the abuse of power is astonishing. I've been following social media feeds, and it seems the film and television industry is full of sexual predators."

"Surely no different from any other industry," Hamid said.

"Show business more than most," Kareena said. "All those men in positions of power preying on women who just want to have careers. This epidemic of sexual assault just won't do."

"Baby sister," Hamid said, "I can assure you I never harassed or assaulted any of the women I slept with. It was all consensual. And I compensated them well for the service."

"I know," Kareena said. "It was never in your nature. It was in our older brothers' nature, and I made sure they paid for that. If you were like them, I would have had you killed long ago."

The older brothers, Kabil and Mirza, had both been publicly and messily killed by the braying mobs when their father was overthrown. Hamid was actually relieved when his psychopathic brothers were dead. He mentioned that Kareena was more than relieved. She was downright delighted that she had engineered their deaths.

"They were torturers and rapists and our father enabled them,"

Kareena said. "You can't have change in a society without justice being seen to be done. And a civil society needs to be founded on social justice."

"Yes, yes," Hamid said. "We've had that discussion God knows how many times."

"If I was religious," Kareena said, "I would like to think there was a special corner of hell reserved for rapists and abusers. But I'm an atheist, so I'll settle for the glee of being the one who arranged for their horrible deaths."

"My little sister," Hamid said with a combination of pride and horrified awe.

"I was just reading about the head of the network that produces your little show," Kareena said. "He's been accused of abusing several of the actresses who were in their shows. And they were underage. They were practically children at the time. Monstrous."

"Yes," Hamid sighed, "Herb always had a reputation for being a bit of a creeper for young girls. It's only just coming out that he was much worse than the rumors suggested."

"Is he going to be arrested?" Kareena asked.

"The police are investigating," Hamid said. "But this is going to take time. And he's hired an expensive lawyer to act as a firewall. Right now, he's more preoccupied with keeping his job than fighting any criminal charges. Those haven't been brought yet."

"I would hate to think he's going to get away with it," Kareena said. "Is there anyone in charge at your children's TV studio who's not a pedophile?"

"Now, Kareena," Hamid said. "You promised you wouldn't get up to any mischief while you're here. That's the deal I struck with the CIA, remember? You're going to keep a low profile and not do any of the things you got up to back home."

"Don't worry, brother," Kareena said. "I'll watch my Ps and Qs. I won't do anything to cause you any trouble."

Kareena possessed a kind of clinical calm as she talked about this. She had been dispassionately analyzing and absorbing information to acclimatize herself to the new world she had entered.

Hamid turned to Julia and me.

"Now, do you see why I need you to babysit her?" he asked. "I can't keep her prisoner, but she needs a minder to get through the next few weeks."

Lunch was expensive steaks and roast lamb, salads and buttered vegetables. Ariel and her men ate beefsteak tartar, but they never let down their guard, always keeping an eye on the door and ready to draw their guns at the hint of any trouble. Julia and I had the salmon. Kareena had a chicken salad, the cheapest item on the menu. It wasn't the calmest lunch I ever had.

When Kareena got up to go to the loo, Ariel went with her.

"What do you make of her?" Julia asked.

"She's rather mad," I said. "But this might be what it felt like to meet Che Guevara."

"I like her," Kali said.

Of course, she would.

"I see righteous wrath and vengeance in her," Rudra said. "She is one of mine!"

And he laughed a hearty bellow that only I could hear.

"In case you were wondering," Hamid said, "she didn't become that way. She was always like that. Somehow, ever since childhood, she honed her anger at our dad and the world at large into a kind of focused, rational calm because she was always planning to bring it all crashing down."

"The problem with that is the world is likely to crash down on her as well," I said.

"It has," Hamid said. "She's actually rather subdued now that she's lost everything. She's at a loose end and doesn't know what to do with herself. What she needs now is a second chapter."

"I think what she's looking for is a purpose," Julia said. "A mission in life."

"Another war to fight," Julia said.

"How long is this job supposed to be?" I asked Hamid.

"Only until she gets a new face and a new identity," Hamid said. "I know it's a big job, but you're in need of one, given your boss's current problems in London, no?"

SIX

Hamid's private jet headed for South Korea. Everything from here on in was clandestine. No one would think to follow Kareena to Seoul, and no one would be nosy enough to expect her to get her new face there. Ariel accompanied us; her seniority in Interzone meant she could pick and choose which jobs to look in on and whom to accompany.

Kareena took advantage of the in-flight WiFi and quietly read websites on her laptop during the flight. Hamid was flying separately back to Los Angeles to get on with casting a new leading lady for his show. Julia and I were still in the dark about what was happening to everyone at Golden Sentinels in London.

I had to check on my parents. It was morning in India. I put in a video call to Golden Sentinels' Mumbai branch and talked to Sanjiv Mishra, one of the investigators there. Sanjiv was a bit of a Jack the Lad about Mumbai and always eager to try out new things as an investigator. He also liked to switch between English and Hindi when he spoke to me, always throwing in Mumbai slang in between as if he felt it was his job to keep me up to date on the patois over there.

"Ravi! To what do I owe the pleasure of hearing from Golden Sentinels' holy man!"

Oh God. Roger must have mentioned me seeing the gods in the intercompany newsletter that Cheryl sent to all the Golden Sentinels branches across the world.

"So you want us to follow your folks as they go around town, *beedu*?" he asked.

That was like the equivalent of "dude" in English.

"That and check up on the Dhewans they're supposed to give gifts from Fortnum & Mason's to," I said.

"Ah, the Dhewans. Big family."

"The way you say it, should I be concerned?" I asked. "Please tell me they're not a major crime family."

"Well . . . let me ask around," he said. "If it sets your mind at ease, shall we just say they're a perfectly 'respectable' family here in Mumbai?"

"I'm not sure, mate," I said. "But you'd be doing me a big favor here."

"Least I can do for a colleague," Sanjiv said. "I could be serving the gods here, maybe get a blessing from Lord Shiva."

"Yeah, why not?" Shiva said, beside me all along. He gave me the thumbs-up.

"The gods will be pleased," I said, wincing.

"First class!" Sanjiv said and rang off.

Kareena was reading up on more reports naming executives, casting directors, studio bosses in Hollywood being accused of sexual harassment and assault. She seemed to be absorbing it all. Kali and Rudra were reading over her shoulder. The stewardess served her tea. She didn't drink alcohol.

"It's not just actresses," Kareena said. "It's actors and young boys who are vulnerable as well. It's remarkable that this went on for decades, but the victims are finally coming out in force to name their tormenters. This is an example of collective action, a popular uprising. It has the public's support. Who's going to speak against the victims of sexual assault? The ones who do just reveal their own callousness and monstrousness."

I found her dispassionate tone a bit chilling.

"I'm amazed you can be so calm as you read all this," I said.

"I am calm because I'm absolutely furious," Kareena said. "Inside, I'm screaming for blood. But all my life, whenever I get angry, I become very calm. The angrier I am, the calmer I become."

Her tone of voice was so cool it could freeze lava. I had no doubt in my mind she was capable of murdering hundreds of people if she believed it needed to be done for the greater good. And make no mistake, it would still be murder, no matter how justified she believed it to be. And the worst part was that she would feel perfectly justified when she got around to doing it.

Julia and Ariel took her in their stride. They were both capable of a similar ruthlessness, so it wasn't new or shocking to them. And here I was, witness to it all.

New York to South Korea was a thirteen-hour flight. Kareena passed the time on a video call with Dr. Kim at his clinic. They were already prepping for her surgery. Hamid had picked one of the best cosmetic surgeons in Seoul because no one would think to hunt his sister to a clinic in South Korea. They expected her to be in Europe or the States. Kareena spent an hour on the video call reviewing her medical file with Dr. Kim to make sure she didn't have any allergies to medications or preexisting conditions that might be a hindrance to her surgery. He sent her a link to his interactive computer program where she could pick the mold and shape the 3D model of the face to show what changes she wanted in her surgery. They went over the procedures to resculpting her face—her cheekbones, her nose, her eyes, her mouth. He went over the process of bleaching her skin to lighten it and the type of maintenance it would require.

"I just want to become a different woman," she said. "It's been a burden being me for so long."

Nobody wanted to be a dictator's daughter, witness to her father's crimes and atrocities but pretending to be blind, living in complicity and denial until it was no longer possible. What was in Kareena's wiring that had made her different from her mother and her brothers, that had driven her to decide this wouldn't do and to take the responsibility of assuming her family's karma and righting that wrong, by leading a revolt that overthrew the government, then overseeing the execution of her father and brothers for their crimes? Was this what she was put on Earth to do? Was this what she was always going to be? And if so, what next? Or was she to immolate herself, and reenter the cycle or reincarnation to start anew? No, here she was deciding to put herself in the hands of her surviving brother, to make herself into something else and leave that life behind. But that wasn't going to change what she was. She was always going to be a revolutionary. She had a vision of the world she wanted to create, and she still burned to lead a revolution. I saw it in her and so did the gods. They were rooting for her, egging her on. She was going to be a good show.

SEVEN

A car was waiting for us at Incheon International Airport and drove us right into the heart of Seoul. We checked into a hotel in Gangnam-gu. Hamid had arranged the reservation and paid extra to keep our real names hidden. Ariel took the room with Kareena, since she was the one who would pull a gun to protect her if anyone came after her. Julia and I took the adjoining room.

It was night when we settled in. While everyone else rested, I set to work. The excellent Internet services in Seoul enabled me to set up my new laptop and establish a portal for getting in touch with Golden Sentinels in London. Olivia had established a protocol for creating a secure video conferencing hub if we ever had to go underground and still needed to get in touch. I hid the computer's ISP behind a VPN as I sent out messages to everyone via an encrypted email server using their backup email addresses. Then it was just a matter of waiting to see who responded.

In less than an hour, my smartphone rang. Unknown number.

"Ravi old son, the bastards finally got me."

"Roger? They let you go? Where are you?"

"I'm out on bail. They've placed me under house arrest. I'm under curfew and can't be out in the evenings. Took my passport because they think I'm a flight risk. Can you believe the bloody cheek of it?"

"How did you get this number?"

"I have my ways. You should know that by now."

"Why are you calling, Roger?"

"You're the only one I can trust, my son. I think Cheryl and the others are all narked off at me."

"Good-bye, Roger."

"Ravi, wait! Hear me out!"

"What? You tried to take over a country in a coup! What the fuck were you thinking?"

"I've been hearing about how weak their government was for ages. Seemed ripe for the pickings."

"That's it? That's all you have to say? You're unbelievable. This is colonialism. How can you, a white guy in the twenty-first century, ever presume to think you can take over a country in Africa to exploit its resources?"

"Come on, I was backin' a decent lot to take over the place."

"And give you dibs on resources. Is your moral compass so broken that you don't see any problem with being an imperialist?"

"You sound like my rabbi."

"Did you even think about how that makes you look?"

"If I'd won, nobody would have known it was me. I would have offered a good deal to the Americans so their troops wouldn't need to fight. The new government would have declared themselves a US and Western ally, open to trade. It would have been a win for everyone."

"And you collect the profits. You're arguing in favor of imperialism with me?! Me of all people? Seriously? Have you forgotten who I am? Where my family came from? England exploited and fucked with India for centuries! And you had David, whose family is from Nigeria, draw up contracts to legally raise money for your Great Game? You've got some bloody cheek, Roger! And you talk about this like you failed to order a pizza? You like to talk to me about righteousness and doing the right thing! There is nothing righteous about trying to overthrow someone else's government! Go talk to your rabbi. Leave me out of this!"

"He's bloody sick and tired of me by now. No one else will talk about this to me. My wife won't talk to me. Come on, Ravi. This is important."

"This is the fucking limit, Roger! You said we didn't always do stuff we were proud of, but we were never going to go after innocent people! All your talk about using the Dark Arts for good where we can is just a pile of bollocks! You almost had me convinced! And now you land us, the entire firm, in this shit?"

"I kept your names out of this fiasco so they don't know about you lot, all right? You genuinely didn't know about the business plan—"

"The coup! *Your* coup! Stop beating around the bush! They're going to look into all your businesses now, including Golden Sentinels! We're all implicated!"

"Now, hold on. I look after my people, Ravi. And I make sure everyone is always properly compensated."

"Until you land us in shit we can't crawl out of! It's one thing if we make the mistake! That's our call! This is something you put us in without a say!"

"Listen, I signed over ownership and control of Golden Sentinels to Cheryl a month ago in case things went pear-shaped."

"So you did think you might fail!"

"Always be prepared. That's the first rule, remember? I also signed all my assets over to my wife and family members so they wouldn't get seized, just in case. And don't you think Cheryl deserves the firm? It's her baby, after all. She poured her whole life into Golden Sentinels. See, I think of my people. I know my people."

"Sounds like you have it all under control. What do you need me for?"

"There's something I need you to do, Ravi. It's going to put things right, I swear on my mother's grave. I can't be seen to be doing it. It can't come from me. They don't even know about the phone I'm usin' to talk to you."

"Why do you think I'll help you?"

"Come on, Ravi. You're my boy, aren't you? My protégé. I took you under my wing when you started. I always saw greatness in you. You see gods and that's a rare quality. Speaks of your character. You're a *mensch*. You always do the right thing. That's your nature. I can't do fuck-all right now, so it's got to be down to you. I don't know how Cheryl or the others will react because they're all taking it a bit personally."

"I'll ask you again. How do you know I'll agree to whatever this is?"

"Because you don't have an agenda, son."

"Yes, I do. I want to not go to prison."

"That's not an agenda, that's a goal. It's a good goal. Everyone should have that goal. You don't have years of emotional investment in the firm so you're not as pissed off as they are. I know that about you, old son. I'm just askin' you to help me put everything right and get everything back to the way it was. That's what everyone wants, innit?"

"You're assuming a lot."

"Now, I have friends in high places, very high places, as in 'senior in the government,' who owe me favors," Roger said. "They could make all this go away with a few phone calls. Except they refuse to take my calls. I told you they were never going to let me into their club, I'll never be one of them."

"Don't give me any more of your class divide talk, Roger. I've had enough of that."

He wasn't even listening to me at that point. He just had to monologue.

"Ungrateful bastards. This is my Plan B. You see, I've kept files on 'em all. Just in case they forget they owe me. These files will remind them."

"So where are those files? I'm out of the country," I said.

"That's the beauty part, my son. They're in the cloud. I got Olivia to create a cache on a server based in Finland. I need you to download those files for me. These aren't just any files, old son, these are the mother lode that will get me out of jail and make the bastards leave you lot alone."

"Why can't you do it yourself?" I asked.

"Because my Internet activity is bein' closely monitored. Also, it needs a password that I don't have."

"How can you not have a password to your own doomsday emergency files?"

"Olivia set up the server for me when she started working at the firm, and she said the files were too tempting for me not to touch, so she and I did a deal: when the shit hit the fan, she would download the files for me and I would use 'em as leverage to get us out of the fire."

"So why not talk to Olivia?"

"She won't take my calls. None of the others will except for Cheryl, and she doesn't know the password. Olivia ain't going to give her the password."

"So it's down to me because I'm the mug who takes your calls."

"You know how to get in touch with 'em. You know the protocols for gettin' in touch with everyone. We taught 'em to you when you just joined."

"You're ducking and diving, fucking and skiving, dancing as fast as you can, hoping that things will work out by the time the music stops."

"Story of my life, old son. That's the way the game's always been. The whole point is to live to dance another day. Don't let anyone tell you different."

"Not everybody wants to dance with you, Roger."

"Come on, Ravi. I'm beggin' you here. I'm a man of pride, but I'm at the end of my rope. If you could see me, you'd see I'm on my knees right now."

I sighed.

When I hung up, Julia was watching me. So were Ariel and Kareena.

"Jet lag," Ariel said. "Couldn't sleep."

"Did you hear all that?" I asked.

"So this is what you're like when you're really angry," Ariel said, smiling, and turned to Kareena. "See? I told you he was bags and bags of fun."

"All right," Kareena said. "I like him."

"It's a good thing the walls here are thick," Julia said. "You could have shouted the whole house down."

"I apologize," I said. "That was unprofessional of me."

"Don't worry about it, babe," Ariel said.

Kareena was looking at me with that unnervingly even gaze of hers.

"Imperialism," Kareena said. "We're all of us by-products of its legacy, really. My father was a product of imperialism and served its agents thinking he could carve out his own kingdom after growing up watching the country under British rule, then after I overthrew him, the Americans tried to make my brother their puppet to take over the country. I suppose you think I'm foolish to fight imperialism. And now I'm back at square one, all on my own."

"It's a little big, hon," Ariel said.

"Here we are," Kareena said, "in a country that was also a victim of Japanese imperialism. It's inescapable."

"What you really ought to do," Ariel said, "is pick the small fights, get through 'em one by one, do it stealthy so nobody knows you're there. And if you're still alive after each fight, do it again. And again. And again. Slowly work your way up."

Kareena glanced at Ariel.

"And here I am being protected by an agent of imperialism. Ironies never cease."

EIGHT

In the morning, we took Kareena to Dr. Kim's clinic near Gangnam Station, the heart of the Beauty Belt, the cosmetic surgery capital of South Korea. Kareena met Dr. Kim in person and he went over the last details of her procedure. She finalized the face she wanted on his interactive 3D system. She had followed his instructions to fast the night before. He talked her through the risks—of infection, of complications, or allergic reactions to the anesthetic—it would have been a horrible cosmic joke to have her survive assassination attempts and fleeing her home country just to drop dead on the operating table in South Korea. Kareena nodded with all the certainty of one who was just going to move forward, come what may. The gods stood behind her and listened to Dr. Kim's talk. They were very interested in Kareena for some reason.

The doctor's assistants wheeled her in for surgery. Since we looked a bit conspicuous, being an Indian bloke and two white women in Seoul, Julia, Ariel, and I decided to wait for her in the lavish reception area of the clinic.

Since I had nothing better to do, I phoned my father to check up on him and Mum.

"Ravi, my God, Mumbai is so hot," Dad said. "Living in England for so many decades means that your mother and I have become horribly used to cold weather. We have been sweating since we arrived. This is sad. We have become Englanders."

"How's everything else, Dad?"

"Here's another thing. The city is complete chaos compared to London. Traffic is unbelievable. It's like a denser, faster, madder, even more corrupt version of London. England has a pretense of order and rules. Mumbai doesn't. The UK may be a horrible mess, but the sheer madness here makes England look like a tea party. I can't keep up with the pace here anymore."

"What about the family house?"

"It's a tip. Practically a wreck. No one could possibly live in it now."

"Oh."

"The place is completely run down. I can't believe your uncles and aunts and I were born in this mess."

"Are you still thinking about fixing it up as a retirement home?"

"Better to just knock it down and get it over with," Dad said.

"Are you sure? That seems a shame."

"Actually, I went to the land registry office to look up the property. The land it's on is in fact worth a fortune. The lawyer is drawing up the papers to put it up for sale now."

"Weren't you thinking about retiring to India with Mum?"

"After what we experienced the last few days, we're better off staying in England."

"So I suppose you'll be going back to London soon, then?"

"As soon as I can pry your mother away from going shopping with Mrs. Dhewan's twin sister."

"Did they bond?"

"They're new best friends, Ravi. She's like Mrs. Dhewan in so many ways, except she claims she's not really a gangster. Those two gossip so much my ears are going to fall off."

"Not really a gangster. Huh. Does this mean when you dropped off the gifts from Mrs. Dhewan, everything went without a hitch?"

"They're a family of Anglophiles, Ravi. Totally mad for anything British. The moment your mother gave them that package, she became their new BFF. That's even how she's saying it. 'BFF.' I could swear they had people following us wherever we went. I think they were bodyguards keeping their distance."

"How did you know that?"

"You're not the only one with a sixth sense, boy. I could feel it."

"Oh dear."

"Nothing came of it. No harm done," Dad said.

"Did Mum just join a crime family?" I asked.

"You tell me, boy."

I didn't tell Dad that Sanjiv or his guys would have followed Mum to make sure she was fine.

"What about you, Ravi? When are you and Julia flying back?"

"Might not be for a few more weeks, Dad. We're escorting a client halfway around the world."

"What's that sound in the background? That doesn't sound like America."

"We're in Korea, Dad. Seoul. Client's here for plastic surgery."

"You mean you're in the Beauty Belt?"

"How did you know that?"

"Your mother and sister are addicted to those Korean soap operas," Dad said. "I can't help overhearing all the gossip those women talk about."

"Bet it'll be a relief to be back in London."

"You really can't go home again, but this is no longer my home. England is my home now."

"That's awfully melancholy, Dad."

"Wait till you grow old, son. Melancholy has its own comforts."

NINE

As we waited for Kareena's operation to finish, Ariel seemed unusually rapt with whatever was on her smartphone.

"Hey guys, you might want to look at his," she said.

She held up her phone. The screen featured a newspaper report of a producer found hanging in his penthouse in New York, a man who had been accused of assaulting multiple actresses. A suicide note confessing to it all was found next to his body.

"Good riddance," I said.

"There's more," Ariel said.

She scrolled to another news report of a manager accused of molesting young male actors for decades, found with a plastic bag over his face in either a suicide or a case of autoerotic asphyxiation gone wrong. The Los Angeles district attorney was still reviewing reports against him to decide whether to prosecute.

"All these incidents happened last night," Ariel said. "Within hours of each other."

Another report featured an agent at a major talent agency, whose rumored reputation for sexual harassment was considered an open secret around town, getting shot in what looked like a failed carjacking. He was in critical condition but expected to survive. He was unable to provide the LAPD with a description of his assailant.

"Why are you showing us this?" I asked.

"I'm bored," Ariel said. "Just wanted to see how you'd react."

"All this happening during the same time period is probably not a coincidence," Julia said.

"Guess who was reading up on all these guys for the last few weeks, since she arrived in the States?" Ariel said.

"So what?" I said. "Kareena and every woman in LA must have been reading up on all these bastards and keeping track on who was being named or about to be named."

"Homegirl is the only one who set up a forum on the Dark Web where she was putting out calls to people who thought the cops were taking too long to do anything, if they bothered to at all," Ariel said.

I felt the bottom drop out of my stomach.

"How do you know this?" I asked.

"'Cause I'm the one who set up secure access to the Dark Web for her when I was babysitting her," Ariel said. "And she's been dipping into a bunch of hidden bank accounts she had access to. Not enough to fund a revolutionary army, but more than enough for beer and pizza and the occasional hit job."

"Resources and motivation," Julia said.

"Homegirl's taking my advice about starting small and stealthy, after all," Ariel said.

"Oh shit," I said. "She's crowdsourcing hit squads."

"Every girl needs a hobby." Ariel shrugged. "Gotta hand it to her. She knows how to get shit done."

"Are we sure it's her?" Julia asked.

"Who else would have the strategic mind to do this?" Ariel said. "This is an op, through and through."

"Shouldn't we stop her?" I asked.

"We're not the cops," Ariel said. "And it's not the job. Our job is to babysit her and keep her out of trouble. So far she's not in trouble. Those guys are."

"And us reporting her to the authorities exposes us," Julia said. "Too many questions we can't answer."

"And there's no hard evidence to tie her to the deaths," Ariel said.

"Her messages to the hit men are all in code. None of them say outright, 'Hey, this studio exec is a rapist asshole. Go kill him and make it look like an accident.' Both she and the people she's been messaging on her Dark Web account don't use their real names. Her ISP is masked. She hasn't directly met any of these people, and you can't prove the ones behind the usernames she's replying to went out and whacked those guys."

"Not to mention she's not even in the country right now," Julia said. "She was on the plane when those bastards got hit, and now she's unconscious getting surgery. She never left our sight all that time. We are her rock-solid alibi."

"I knew there was going to be a shoe dropping with this job," I said. "We can't just get a simple babysitting gig, can we?"

Ariel's phone pinged.

"Oh hey," she said. "That TV director, the one who's been accused of sexual assault? They found him drowned near Santa Monica. Boating accident, they said."

"You set up an alert for stories like this?" I said.

"A girl's gotta keep up with current events," Ariel said, grinning.

Kali threw back her head and laughed.

TEN

As soon as Dr. Kim declared Kareena was fit to travel, we were off. The bandages hadn't even come off yet. We were never going to stay in Seoul long, it was always going to be in and out. We took Kareena in the Mercedes to the airport, where Hamid's private jet was waiting and flew us back to Los Angeles. Kareena spent the flight sedated and sleeping, which spared us another long debate about revolution and politics.

Hamid had arranged for us to stay in a house in a gated community in the Pacific Palisades, overlooking the sea. The community consisted of two movie stars, at least one tech tycoon, and three multimillionaires. The neighbors left each other alone, so we could spend our days there without anyone disturbing us, and they were used to armed guards patrolling the houses. The neighbors would just assume that Kareena was one of Hamid's mistresses and not ask any questions.

Hamid stopped by, partly to maintain that cover, and also to look in on Kareena.

"She's still asleep from the sedatives and painkillers," Julia said.

"Oh good," he said. "We don't have to listen to her speeches."

"That's what we said on the flight back," Ariel said.

"I have people drawing up a set of new papers for her," Hamid said. "New name, new life, new biography. She won't even be Middle Eastern anymore."

"She's going to be an American," Julia said.

"Her new name is Karen Radley," Hamid said. "Born in Irvine,

California. Parents deceased. There will be a birth certificate, social security number. Adopted. Grew up in boarding schools in Europe. Degree in journalism. She's going to have a quiet life, a quiet job, a house someplace where she can disappear. She can meet some boring middle-class chap, get married, and have children if she wants."

"I don't think she's suited for that kind of life." Julia said. "You know how she is, committed to revolution and social change."

Hamid sighed and buried his face in his hands.

"What, then? I take it she already hasn't been quiet all this time."

"She started a new campaign even before we left for Seoul," I said.

"Oh God, who did she send after me this time?" Hamid said.

"She's not trying to kill you anymore," I said.

"That's a relief," he said.

"She's been collecting all the reports about sexual predators and sexual harassment in the media industry," Julia said.

"Oh?" Hamid said, a curious look on his face.

"And she's been sending hit squads after predators," I said. "All under cover of anonymity."

"Is she paying them?" Hamid asked.

"Many of them are actually volunteering," Julia said.

"Though she's reimbursing them for their expenses and tools," I said.

"She does it all through the Dark Web," Julia said.

"What is all this?" Hamid asked.

"While you were in Seoul, Herb Shelberger, the head of the KidTime network, was found dead by apparent suicide. He'd been rumored to be a pedophile and sexual predator for years. His alleged former victims were speaking out."

"Kareena would have seen their posts on social media," Julia said. "Then read up on him."

"And arranged to have him taken care of," Ariel said.

"Huh," Hamid said. "She's actually done me a favor. Judy Yosemite is taking over as head of the network, and she's a friend of mine. She's going to give me a better deal when they renew my variety show, even before we cast the new star."

"Silver lining in every whack," Ariel said.

Hamid groaned.

"We have to find something for her to do," he said. "I'm off. Keep me posted."

He went back to his suite at the Four Seasons in Beverly Hills. He preferred to live in the hotel and only come back to this house when he had to, especially now that he'd temporarily installed his sister there.

ELEVEN

Kareena was using her intelligence contacts, or rather she was probably blackmailing them, to gather additional information on sexual predators in the industry, and then targeting them for retribution. She obeyed Ariel's orders to stay in the house. Two armed Interzone men were posted outside at all times. With her face wrapped in bandages Kareena haunted the house like a wraith.

Julia said she was the eyes without a face.

Kareena spent much of the day on her laptop corresponding with people on her Dark Web forum, exchanging information about sexual assaulters.

"There should be a sliding scale of punishments," Kareena explained to Ariel and Julia. "Sexual harassers get beaten up. Rapists get crippled or killed. Depending on their profiles, it can be made to look like accident, random crime, or suicide. The worst, most undignified deaths should be reserved for pedophiles, since they're abusing children."

"Don't tell me you're posting those as guidelines on your site," I said.

"It's best if the squads know the rules," she said. "We're not an indiscriminate mob. I prefer to have professionals who know how to make it look like an accident or a robbery, or a random act of violence. That can remain a mystery, a burst of chaos in a violent and unpredictable universe. However, I think the victims of these men will know, deep down. You can't achieve any change in society without justice being seen to be carried out. That's the only way to move forward."

"She isn't going to stop," Julia said.

"Well, considering a year ago she was ordering a hit on her brother," I said, "this is a marked improvement."

"Looks like we're going to be helping her do this by not giving her up to the law," Julia said. "Are you going to start feeling guilty about being complicit in whatever she brings down?"

"I assume that's a rhetorical question," I said.

My phone rang. There was a code on the Caller ID to indicate who it was.

"Olivia. Thanks for calling back," I said.

Julia joined me in our bedroom. I told Olivia about my conversation with Roger.

"You really are a soft touch aren't you, Ravi?" She sighed.

"I'm just the messenger here," I said.

"All right, I suppose my poor old godfather has been punished enough."

"So you'll do it?"

"We can't not do it. We don't want to be on the run and looking over our shoulders forever," Olivia said.

"Where are you now?" I asked.

"Tokyo," Olivia said. "I'm helping out my dad with sussing out this bank here in Japan. I'm looking into them before my dad does any deal with them."

"So you'll be hacking into their servers, I take it?" I said.

"What I do best, darling," Olivia said. "And I've got Benjamin with me. We really needed to get his arse out of London. He's not well pleased about being a person of interest."

"Do you know where everyone else is?" I asked.

"Mark's gone into hiding with his anarchist squatter friends, moving from one place to another. I think he's rather enjoying that, actually. Did you know his mates are squatting in a really posh building in Grosvenor Square? Used to be an embassy. Imagine that! Right in the heart of London! Probably only a matter of time before they get thrown out, but Mark's been larging it up in there. They've been throwing rave parties. And nobody but us knows that Mark is hiding amongst them."

"I actually had a dream about that," I said.

"Did you? Interesting. Anyway, Marcie's cover is intact. When she was questioned by the coppers, she played the chirpy American PR girl act and they bought it. Cheryl put up a good front of cooperating with the authorities and pleading ignorance about Roger's coup scheme. Since there was no evidence of it in whatever files we didn't nuke at Golden Sentinels, they had nothing on her."

"What about David? He drew up the contracts and was at the meetings. They must want to talk to him."

"David got himself a solicitor. The lawyer got himself a lawyer. Extra firewall. He's answered their questions through his lawyer and is holding them off."

"Do the authorities know about Roger's investors, the ones at the party at the mansion?" Julia asked.

"They all lawyered up to the hilt, and the ones who could get out of the country have done so, just holing up in their tax shelter houses in places like the Caymans. I think they'll keep their mouths shut because of what Roger has on them from the video recordings he had Benjamin make of them at Alfie Beam's manor."

"Fuckin' Roger and his fuckin' blackmail," Benjamin muttered in the background.

"Benjamin," Olivia said. "You better not throw another tantrum. If you behave, I'll let you go buy some hentai anime at Akihabara with my credit card."

"Oh God," I said.

"Too right," Olivia said. "So leave the server and the password to me. I built the whole protocol, after all. You don't need to go through the hassle of sifting through it. There's actually more than one, so it's all rather complicated. Keep in touch, yeah, darling? We're all in this together."

"Either we all get out of this or we all end up in jail," I said.

I suddenly saw an image of Kwan Yin, the Chinese goddess of mercy, sitting behind Olivia in Tokyo. She looked serene and utterly confident. Olivia was the other person in Golden Sentinels who had a patron god. Unlike me, she was a believer. Taoism was her thing, and she prayed to the moon goddess for luck and guidance whenever she got the chance.

"Oh ye of little faith," Olivia said, and rang off.

TWELVE

If you've ever had to spend time with people who have had plastic surgery, you will have discovered that it takes time for them to recover before going out in public. For a full facial makeover like Kareena's, where she had a rhinoplasty to reshape her nose, some cheek implants, and work on her eyes to change their shape, she was going to need a few weeks. When the bandages first came off, there was still a lot of swollen tissue all over her face.

But when she looked in the mirror, she was utterly delighted.

"I look like an orc who's been in a bar fight!" She laughed. "Or an ogre! Or a bridge troll!"

"Or a mutant baby!" Ariel said, and the two of them laughed like a pair of mad banshees.

"What is this mutant baby going to grow up into?" I muttered.

Julia shushed me.

Kareena reveled in looking this grotesque, temporarily freed from the shackles of beauty.

"I wish I could look like this forever!" she said. "Let me be the Monstrous Feminine! Freed from the burdens of beauty! An avenging demon conjured up by all those abused women demanding retribution!"

"Perhaps it's the drugs talking," Julia said. "She's completely off her head on the painkillers."

"Great," I said. "We're getting a tour of her id."

The gods loved it. They applauded and made gifs of her with their phone cameras.

She didn't slow down her pace with the website she was running on the Dark Web. After all, it wasn't as if she had anything else to do other than recover from the surgery. She continued to expose sexual predators and organize hit squads for them after studying surveillance reports of their movements so she would know when and where to send the squads, and they always made the deaths look like accidents, road rage, or random robberies.

Then there was the night a scream woke us all up.

Julia and I leapt out of bed and ran for Kareena's room, where the scream came from. Ariel was ahead of us with her gun drawn.

When we got inside, we saw the two Interzone men wrestling a terrified man in denim to the ground just outside the window. He was screaming as his gaze was directed into the room, at Kareena. She was standing at the window looking out, her long black hair streaming down her back like a veil.

The Interzone men restrained the man and tied his wrists with zipties. Kareena just stood in her room, completely calm, watching. Later, when the police arrived to take the man away, we got his story: he was a meth addict who had been breaking into expensive houses up and down the Palisades for weeks. He'd managed to climb over the locked gates of the neighborhood and snuck past the Interzone men after noticing their patrol patterns. He was all set to break into this place via Kareena's bedroom when she was awakened by his attempts to open the window and got out of bed to see what was going on. When he saw her in her white sleeping gown and grotesquely swollen face and eyelids, the poor bastard must have thought he'd wandered into an Asian horror movie and screamed bloody murder. Nerves already frayed from drugs and adrenaline, he was seized with a primal, uncontrollable, pants-wetting terror.

He was still screaming that he had seen a demon out to take him to Hell when the police packed him in the back of their car and drove away. Of course, we kept Kareena from being seen by the coppers or any of the neighbors who came out to see what was going on. After they left, Kareena and Ariel laughed their arses off.

"I wish I could be like this forever and haunt the streets as a demon, become an urban legend," Kareena said.

That was the last bit of excitement we had. The days passed with a certain routine. When she wasn't directing her army of anonymous avengers, Kareena would make a video call to Hamid just to watch him squirm at her swollen, discolored face.

"Look at me, brother! Don't I look absolutely monstrous?" she would declare with glee. "I can be a monster of our times!"

"Oh my God, stop pushing your monster face at me!" Hamid would moan and quickly hang up.

Later, he would call me and plead, "Ravi, can you please stop her from calling me on video until she recovers?"

Louise leaned in and looked closely at Kareena's swollen face.

"I think she can make it work," Louise said. "She doesn't have to, though. She's going to look very nice when she recovers."

I wondered if Louise had been this unflappable when she was alive. According to Julia, she was. Nothing would ever faze a trans goddess of glamour.

"Hamid," Ariel asked. "I gotta ask, why are you protecting her anyway? She killed your dad and brothers and tried to kill you. You don't owe her anything."

"She's the only family I have left," Hamid said. "She and I were the only refuge from the rest of my horrible, murderous family. Our mother was no help. She checked out mentally long ago. I don't take her trying to kill me personally. It was an abstract thing for her. Once I was no longer going to take over the government over there, she didn't need to kill me anymore and she said she was glad about that. At the end of the day, she's all I have and I'm all she has."

To Ariel, that was just sentimentality. But he was the client, so she didn't argue.

I got a call from my father rather than the other way round.

"Dad? Is everything all right? What's that noise?"

"Hello, Ravi! Say hello to your mother!"

"Helloooo, Ravi!"

"Mum? Are you drunk?"

"We are having the most marvelous time! Your father and I are burning down the old house!"

"What? Why?"

"To make a clean break," Dad said. "This may be the old family house, but it has seen so much drama and tragedy, it's no wonder none of the rest of the family wants to live in it. Since we're selling the land, we don't need the house anymore."

"But to burn it down, isn't it arson?"

"On a plot of land no one comes to. Whoever buys it is going to build an office or luxury condominiums," Dad said. "I decided to make this a cleansing ritual. To burn away all the bad karma of the family. All the dramas, all the fights, all the tears, just be done with it."

"And he's invited the whole family!" Mum said. "It's a party! Say hello, everybody!"

A cacophony of cheers rang down the phone. It really was the rest of the family. I'd only seen them weeks ago at my wedding.

"Aren't the police going to be pissed off?" I asked.

"I still have some friends; they're old like me and retired, but I called in some favors so we won't have any trouble."

"I haven't had so much fun since your father beat up those gang members with a cricket bat!"

"Back to the party!" Dad said. "I just didn't want you to worry, and don't believe anything if you read it in the papers!"

"Papers? Dad, what—?"

He hung up.

"Everything all right?" Julia asked.

"I just found out my family is big on grand, mythical gestures," I said.

"Now we know where you got it from," Julia said.

THIRTEEN

As the days passed, the swelling on Kareena's face subsided and the scars faded, and she looked more and more human. Dr. Kim's work made her look like a new person, totally unlike Kareena Mahfouz. She didn't look at all like the other women in Los Angeles with the obviously fixed pencil-thin noses, implanted cheekbones, or pumped-up lips. The point of Dr. Kim's method was to make her look like an individual beauty rather than a generic one, and not like she'd had work done. The only trace of her old appearance was that intense gaze in her eyes. That was never going to disappear, and it was that gaze that lent her charisma.

Hamid hired a beautician who dyed her hair from dark to a lighter color. Her skin was already fair, so her ethnicity now had an indeterminate, if slightly exotic, quality. With her new lighter skin, she could pass for a slightly tanned Caucasian, a Latina, or someone of mixed race.

When she saw her new face in the mirror, Kareena became pensive.

"So that's Karen Radley, then?" she said. "Is it really the face of an American? Hm."

She spent her days watching television to absorb what she called "the grotesquerie of American Culture." She changed her accent to knock out the Britishness and began to sound more and more American.

Julia and I were witnessing her becoming a different person. Karen Radley was a new persona gradually being layered over Kareena Mahfouz.

There was still something incomplete about her transformation, though, and Julia and I had an idea.

Meanwhile, a casting director who had been accused by multiple women of sexual assault had had his car run off the road in the middle of the night in a secluded part of Glendale. There were no witnesses and he was not expected to wake up from his coma.

Eventually, Hamid called Julia and me in for a meeting at his office.

"She's not going to stop with her campaign, is she?" Hamid asked.

"She has a mission," I said. "And she has a whole network of contacts and the money to pursue it. It's the same type of revolutionary campaign she carried out when she overthrew your father. She's out to get justice for victims of sexual assault by enabling secret acts of vigilantism. She's still a revolutionary. That's her calling."

"What am I going to do with her?" Hamid buried his face in his hands.

"We have a suggestion," Julia said.

"You know your sister," I said. "She's a force of nature. She won't ever be quiet. Sooner or later, she's going to do or say something that puts her in the public eye in a big way, and it could be a world of trouble for the both of you. Those assassins you're so worried about would know where to look for her."

"What do you suggest?" Hamid asked.

"Cast Karen Radley as the new star of *Ultimate Times*," I said.

Hamid's eyes went wide. He looked at me like I'd gone mad.

"Think about it," I said. "It's better than casting drug addicts and toxic narcissists."

"Hazards of show business," Hamid said. "They're the ones who possess that mad charisma about them that the public loves. I don't set out to cast addicts. The most compelling actors keep turning out to be mentally unstable, outright insane, or addicts."

"But for a children's variety TV show?" Julia said.

"Kids love them," Hamid said. "By the time we find out they have problems, it's too late, until their problems make them unable to do the show anymore."

"Karen has the wholesome good looks that the networks like," I said.

"You already know she's mad as a hatter and charismatic as hell. You also know she's disciplined enough to sustain the type of work ethic needed to star in a show. After all, she managed to spend the years needed to whip a whole revolutionary army into a state where they were capable of overthrowing your father's dictatorship. She wants to influence hearts and minds. She'll be more than willing to support causes that lift up children, girls, and women. She'll use her celebrity as a platform for her revolutionary impulses. She's a fanatical believer in social justice. She has the presence of mind not to film a sex tape. She knows how to use the Internet and social media to organize people for her causes. She knows how to fight trolls and harassers and she's not afraid of anyone. She'll be the perfect star."

"And it lets you keep her close by so you can continue to watch over her," Julia said. "She'll effectively be your employee."

Hamid's face stayed frozen while we spoke.

Then he let it sink in.

"This is so crazy it can only work." Then he started laughing. "Mine eyes have seen the light!"

FOURTEEN

It took a bit of wrangling, what with some of us stuck in different time zones, but I finally managed to get a video conference call with the rest of the firm. Olivia and Benjamin were calling in from Japan. Cheryl and Marcie from London. Mark from an anarchist squat in Cornwall.

"It's nice to see you all again," Cheryl said. "I've had everyone doing their bit investigating Roger and his shenanigans."

"We sent Ken and Clive following a paper trail we found in Roger's safe," Marcie said.

"Benjamin and I have been downloading the files Roger had me upload to the cloud years ago," Olivia said. "They date all the way back to the nineties."

"A lot of the recordings are from usin' the bugs I made for the firm," Benjamin said.

"And Roger'd been supplying drugs to his clients from my stash for years," Mark said. "He bought them off my friends and paid them not to tell me. I never sell drugs, and he turned me into a drug dealer."

Benjamin and Mark were particularly pissed off.

"You know what Ken and I found?" Clive said. "A bloody private military contractor company registered in Reno, Nevada, under Roger's name. It's the same ex-Interzone blokes wot got nicked on that plane in Nigeria!"

"I see Roger's game now," Mark said. "Fuck up Laird Collins's head at the party in Sussex, then start quietly poaching mercenaries from

Interzone when they start doubting Collins because he's gone off his rocker. Roger didn't just want revenge on Collins. He wanted his own Interzone. He wanted it all."

"I knew it," Cheryl said. "No wonder he was so cagey. He knew I would never let him do that, so he kept the pieces from me so I couldn't put it together till it was too late. He'd been plotting this for more than twenty years."

"We got Roger's files off that cloud server," Olivia said. "Nearly every government scandal you can think of that's been covered up in the last fifteen years is here, and a few nobody ever even thought of. It's Roger's nuclear option. We can use them to leverage his release. The question is which files to release and how much."

"All of them," I said.

Everyone went quiet.

"Seriously?" Marcie said, almost laughing.

Benjamin burst out laughing.

The gods burst out laughing.

"Why not?" I said. "If we want a change, this is our chance."

"Bloody hell, Ravi," Mark said. "That's the nuclear option."

"There ain't no takin' that back, son," Clive said.

"I know," I said.

The ensuing silence was broken by Cheryl.

"I'm tired of Roger's playbook," Cheryl said. "We can do that and go back to the old status quo, continuing Roger's game, and he compiles even more files like this like he's been doing for twenty years."

"But he's not the head of Golden Sentinels now," I said. "You are."

"I've put up with this rubbish long enough," Cheryl said.

"Too bloody right," Ken said.

"Are we all in agreement?" I asked.

Everyone grunted, not a hint of reluctance among them.

"Are we really doing this?" Olivia asked.

"You know what?" I said. "I'm sick of this. Just release the files. All of them."

And with the push of a button, Olivia did what she'd done when she was a teenage hacker. She created an anonymous email account and used it to dump the files at every major newspaper and online outlet that had a trusted correspondent. It took two days before the papers raced each other to release their files.

For the next few weeks, we watched the world go mad on the news. Roger's files were like a nail bomb that exploded on the political carpet, sending shrapnel into both the British and American governments. Politicians were scrambling. In London, questions were being asked in parliament. The papers were running new revelations every three hours on their websites in the twenty-four-hour news cycle. Lawsuits and writs were threatened to no avail. The prime minister was completely gobsmacked by all the dirt about the party that Roger's files had exposed. Half the cabinet were former clients of Roger's, and he'd collected secrets of theirs they hadn't expected him to find. There was dirt that went back ten, fifteen, twenty years. Adultery. Underage kids. Embezzlement. Suspicious deaths. Bribes from foreign companies. Sex trafficking rings. The City was in turmoil from all the dirty deals that Roger's files detailed. He'd gathered them using Olivia's hacking skills for years, based on gossip his clients told him, long before I arrived at Golden Sentinels. Roger's instincts as an investigator told him there were trails to follow, and he used people like Mark and Olivia to sniff out the dirty little secrets that he then banked for a rainy day like this one. In America, politicians were fighting over the most expensive lawyers to prepare for questioning about their donors, the lobbyists whose pockets they were occupying, the business deals that earned them money they shouldn't have been making.

I wondered if Roger had predicted that I would go nuclear and release all the files. If this was the end of my career as an investigator, I might as well just vomit it all out to the ether. The investigations and inquiries looking into Roger's coup would quietly stall and go away. News coverage would fizzle to the point where everyone conveniently forgot about it. Roger would be off the hook in a few weeks, and eventually we would receive a call from Marcie.

"Cheryl says the heat's off Golden Sentinels," she said. "Come home when you're ready, kids."

FIFTEEN

I put in a call with Sanjiv at Golden Sentinels Mumbai to see how things were.

"All's well, *beedu*," Sanjiv said. "Hey, you never told me your father was hardcore, yaar?"

"Well, I didn't know about that either."

"Burning the house to the ground for the whole city to see, that sends a message that he and your mother are nobody to be messed with."

"I suppose it does," I said.

"Hey, just for the hell of it, yaar? I looked up your father's history? Before he emigrated to the UK, he was a seriously badass man, you know that?"

"What are you talking about? I thought he was a professor at the university."

"He was—what? Did he never tell you? He was what they call a firebrand. He had his own crew, he led protests against the police, against the authorities, when he was younger, he was in so many street scraps. I think he left for England because there was nothing for him here anymore, yaar?"

"I didn't know about that at all," I said.

"You come from a family of interesting people, *beedu*! You should ask your parents about that more."

"But things are sorted with them, right? They've left?"

"You have nothing to worry about. Your parents are on their way back to London now. They have a reputable agent handling the sale of their property. Everything is sorted out A-OK."

"So what did you find out?" I asked.

"The Dhewans are one of the bigger families in Mumbai who somehow manage not to be considered a major crime family, if you can believe that. They deal with trading goods, luxury items, food stuffs, entertainment products, 'off the back of a lorry' types of things."

"Do you mean smugglers? Black marketeers?"

"Sort of," Sanjiv said. "At least the Dhewan family is benign."

"What makes you say that?" I asked.

"They don't kill people."

"Fair enough."

"They don't deal drugs, which would bring them the attention of the law, and so their people don't get arrested often. They don't engage in violent gang wars like you see here in Mumbai, so they don't get beaten to death in custody. As far as the law is concerned, they're pussycats who pay a bit of bribe money to the police to turn the other way, and they sell goods at a discount to people who aren't rich. They're a vital part of the city's economy if you can believe that."

"So my 'auntie' back in London is just carrying on a branch of the family business, then?"

"Just doing what they do best, yaar? Another thing: while we were watching after your parents, our boss here made contact with the head of the Dhewan family in Mumbai."

"Oh, no."

"It's good news, *beedu*. It looks like the Dhewans are now Golden Sentinels Mumbai's newest clients. They've hired us to do checks on their business partners, due process to check they're not getting cheated, make sure the goods they receive aren't fake. It's all *jhakaas*."

I shouldn't have been surprised that the bosses at every Golden Sentinels branch would be cut from the same cloth as Roger, always with an eye for deal-making. I just hoped not all of them became megalomaniacs who tried to take over a country in a coup.

"Sanjiv, mate, I owe you one for helping out my parents with the contract stuff on the house."

"What are friends for, eh, *beedu*? We're all Golden Sentinels. We do our bit."

Julia and I continued to work with Hamid to prepare Karen for her entrance into the world. Hamid hired coaches to teach her to sing and dance, and media consultants to teach her how to hold herself and speak during interviews. Given that Kareena had attended the best private schools in Europe, half the work was already done. The rest was how to conduct herself on camera. Again, she had learned that already, when she was a revolutionary who appeared on video as she overthrew her father. She already had good posture, and she knew how to sit and stand in the most poised manner that would draw people's eyes to her. Her father had expected her to be married to a rich and powerful man and made sure she learned how to act like that girl.

And Karen Radley agreed to all this without any resistance after we explained to her that this was how she could be a revolutionary in plain sight. It didn't occur to her to become a TV star, but once she got the idea, it made perfect sense to her. That was why she agreed to learn to speak in an American accent, to hide her past self under this new persona.

Karen spoke to us in Kareena's voice, the one with the British accent from the years at school, perhaps for the last time.

"This is what I am now, but the real me will always be lurking at her core. I will continue to hide and plot, and this is how I will fight each battle in the shadows. Karen will be the creature the world sees, and she can do her part to make the world better while I do mine."

The gods gathered to observe her final transformation with great interest, as if they were watching a highly rated talent reality show. There was something in it for all of them. Shiva and Kali noted the death and rebirth of her life. Bagalamukhi admired the layers of deception in the creation of Karen Radley. Louise Fowler oversaw her learning to become glamorous, her charisma growing. Lakshmi saw the abundance of wealth around her. Rudra was there for her righteous vengefulness, a girl after his own heart. Ganesha was impressed by the way she swept aside obstacles.

Hamid was well versed in the art of cultivating the image of a new star. By the time he brought Karen to the network as the new lead of his show, she had the executives eating out of her hand. She was sexy, yet wholesome enough to appeal to kids. She had a little bit of an edge in her strength of personality, so we had to coach her to downplay how strong and aggressive she could get. She knew how to get her way with a smile. We watched as they filmed her first shows, held press junkets where she was interviewed by the celebrity press. She was the new face of Hamid's show and, in a few months, the face of the network. In six months, she would be on the cover of every magazine on the stands. Product endorsement deals flooded in. She supported causes like children's education, women's health, and of course the exposure of sexual predators and help for their victims. She would cause as many headaches for the network for her outspokenness as she would earn them tens of millions of dollars, so they put up with her. Her entire being was a massive feat of social engineering.

She was on her way, and our work was done. Julia and I packed our bags and said our good-byes. Karen thanked us for our help without a hint of sentimentality. Hamid paid us handsomely for coming up with the solution to save his sister.

"I knew you had the right touch," he said. "It takes a certain kind of madness to come up with your solutions. Truly top service there."

We drove away leaving Interzone in charge of Karen's protection.

"Do you think we'll meet her again?" Julia asked.

"I hope not," I said. "And anyway, she's got Interzone as her bodyguards. All we did was witness all that weirdness. She doesn't need us anymore."

"You sound like you're trying to convince yourself about that," she said.

"Well done, my son," Shiva said. "You have created a god."

"We always knew you had it in you," Kali said, beaming with maternal pride.

"Your own transformation is now complete," Ganesha said. "There's no going back now."

"Best shaman we ever had," Bagalamukhi said.

"You're really good at this stuff," Louise said. "Stop denying it."

"Ravi?" Julia said. "Is something wrong? You look like the world just exploded underneath your feet."

SIXTEEN

Once upon a time, there lived a princess in a faraway kingdom. Her father the king was an evil tyrant who ruled with an iron fist of terror. Her two older brothers, the princes, were even worse than their father. They tormented and terrorized the people for pleasure. The princess and her third brother were not like that at all, and took the opportunity to spend as much time away from the kingdom as possible, going to the best schools and learning the ways of the world.

The princess burned with a righteous anger at the evil her father and brothers caused, and she refused the custom of being married off as chattel to cement relationships with neighboring princes.

So she ran away.

She knew there were people who opposed her father's rule and were secretly planning to overthrow him, so she found them and taught them all the innermost secrets of the castle her father thought himself safe in as he plundered the kingdom and reveled in his subjects' suffering. In time, the princess became one of the leaders of the rebellion and led the uprising that deposed her father, and captured her two brothers. She did not hesitate to oversee the execution of her father and brothers to ensure they would never rise to take control again.

Unfortunately, with her father gone, the kingdom did not settle down into peace. The deep divisions amongst rival factions that had been present for hundreds of years erupted, and chaos ensued as they all fought over ultimate control. Her surviving brother, a gentle soul with no desire for power, had fled abroad years before. When she heard that plotters were trying to make him the new king so they could continue the kingdom's old status, she sent assassins and tried to have him killed. He escaped these attempts on his life, and announced he would not try to take power. The princess soon found herself in danger from assassins herself. Even though she had no great desire to take the throne, the warring factions in the kingdom believed she posed a threat to their bids for power. Her brother, who still loved his sister, arranged for her to escape to the country where he was living freely.

When she arrived in this new land, her brother told her she was still in danger from assassins and she would need to change. He kept her hidden in a castle and arranged to give her a new name so she could start a new life. He introduced her to a wizard who weaved a spell to prepare her. The wizard altered her face so no one from her old life would recognize her.

But the princess wanted more than just to live a normal life. She wanted revolution. She wanted to fight in opposition to the war that was being waged against all women and girls, and she could still command armies in secret, the way she had when she led the revolution that overthrew her father. She still wanted to change the world.

The wizard listened to her wishes and weaved a spell that turned her into a goddess. She would be celebrated and worshipped as a goddess of light, bringing joy and hope to children, but she was also a goddess of justice. She would still send out armies in the night, this time to destroy the men who would hurt women. Thus reborn, she had found a new purpose, and henceforth, she would fulfill her new role.

His work done, the wizard bid her farewell, for he, too, had battles to fight and a war to win. His war was deep in the underworld, and whether he survived victorious or not, the goddess would never know.

"Is this how you're writing it up?" I said as I read Julia's notebook.

"Just a bit of fun," Julia said.

"One day you're going to have to write a proper book," I said.

"Of course I will," Julia said. "I'm not your manic pixie dream girl."

"I never said you were."

"Come off it, Ravi, I know the way you've always looked at me. You keep calling me an English Rose as if that was my defining characteristic."

"Sorry," I said.

"I know that's all people think I am, the better to trap them. That's why Roger hired me, after all. I'm not going to be an investigator forever."

"When you took the job, I was worried you did it to get involved in risky situations as a substitute for your addiction," I said.

She rolled her eyes.

"It's a job with flexible hours, Ravi. I still have my degree to finish. And it gives me time to think. And bear witness."

"What for?"

"What for? Everything. Ever since I got in recovery, I've been wondering what to do with my life. When Louise died, I didn't know how I was going to carry on without her. She was my rock, and now she was gone. I don't want you to be my rock, Ravi. You're my husband now. I want you to be my partner."

"Well, I'm here for that," I said, trying not to sound defensive.

"I watch you go about worrying that you're losing your mind. I watch everyone at the firm secretly chasing their own agendas, and I think about my own agenda all the time. I collect everyone's stories, including yours, and I keep them to myself. I keep to the background so I can watch everything. When Ariel and Interzone come into our lives, I wonder if they'll be the death of us this time. Then I'm not an observer, I'm waiting. I'm waiting to see if I might have to kill her to save both of us. And no matter how frightened I might be, I never show it because I learned to detach long ago. When you're in trouble, I'll back you up and do what's needed to save you. If you ever betray me, I'll never forgive you."

"What's brought this on?" I asked. "Are you thinking about getting out? Of investigating? Or this crazy life? If you are, I'll support you."

"You're still not hearing me, Ravi. I'm telling you that I'm here and I'm not going away. I have my story and you're part of it. But one day I might decide not to play anymore. And when that day comes, you may not be as big a part of it. It'll be mine and mine alone, and perhaps I'll tell it. That's when I'll write a 'proper book,' as you call it."

I looked at Julia and couldn't read her face. I was at a loss. She could see that.

"I've been having the time of my life," she said. "I wouldn't trade what we've been through for anything in the world. All I'm asking, Ravi, is that you not take me for granted."

"Never," I said, and hoped I wasn't lying.

We were on a flight back to London. Cheryl had given us the all clear. Golden Sentinels was no longer under scrutiny. The government was in so much chaos that they'd quietly dropped the case against Roger and he was going to be released from house arrest.

Julia and I had witnessed how a person could become a god. This wasn't a light show with magic and special effects like a fantasy novel or TV series, this was the real thing. Kareena Mafouz had given up her old life, her name, her face, to become someone new and mythical. She became a celebrity, and her fame made her a myth. Fame was the religion in Hollywood, after all. The public would never know who she really was, only the pretty, cheery children's TV star. They would never know she used her resources and connections to outsource hit squads against the sexual predators of the world. And the gods would claim her as a living embodiment of one of their own—Lakshmi for her wealth, Rudra for her unending wrath and vengeance, Shiva for her ruling her world, Bagalamukhi for her turning her entire life into an origami of deception, and Kali for her orchestrating a whole cycle of chaos and destruction, with her own life a rebirth from the old one. Even Louise was impressed with her effortless masquerade and role-play as a harmless and friendly children's TV star.

"When you think about it," I said, "Kareena, in becoming Karen Radley, has become every bit a god as any we might create for our myths. That she did it all for the sake of survival just adds to her mystique. It isn't money or resources that make her a god. Anyone could get a new face or identity if they set their mind to it. It's intent and will. Kareena, now Karen, has a mission that she's intent on fulfilling, to influence hearts and minds, and to exact justice on the patriarchy. Magic is the focus of intent and will, and that is what defines a god."

Forgive me if I keep repeating all this. I'd had a few glasses of wine down me during the flight and couldn't help rambling.

"You've done a shaman's work, my son," Kali said proudly. Of course she presided over this case. She was the goddess of death and rebirth, after all.

After helping Kareena's rebirth to this new life and identity, Julia and I were gratefully dismissed to go back to our lives. The pay we got was a clean parting of the ways. We had no more obligation to Karen Radley, newly minted goddess. This was probably the most metaphysical case I ever had as an investigator.

"She might just change the world," Julia said.

"If she does, it'll be our fault."

"She's every bit as mad as Vanessa van Hooten, and just as dangerous."

"Vanessa was obsessed with her lover, and everything she did was to serve him," I said. "That's how she came a cropper. Kareena served a cause she believed was greater than her and devoted her life to it. She had the will, the intent, and the drive, and you could say that was what enabled her to transform into a god. As an atheist, I don't believe in an afterlife. I believe we create heaven and hell here on Earth, and we pretty much create gods from living people. They become ideas that transcend their lives."

"Whereas Laird Collins wants to destroy the world to create paradise in its wake," Julia said.

"I think that is where Collins fails," I said. "For all his striving for power in his twisted notion of serving divinity, he fell well short. He lacked the vision or imagination to become truly mythical. Instead, he chose to pursue a perverse dogma in the most literal way. And he didn't see God in his nightmarish trip that weekend in Alfie Beam's mansion because deep down, he really didn't believe in the God he so fervently insisted he was doing everything for."

"I'm glad he didn't see himself as a god," Julia said.

"He wouldn't even admit he had a God Complex," I said. "That night in the mansion where he nearly shot me exposed his failing. His bad trip held up a mirror to his emptiness. Being forced to face that might be what broke him. His hubris had come to naught, just as Roger's hubris brought him down. Collins's and Roger's fates ran in ironic parallel paths."

"You know you've unleashed Kareena—sorry, Karen—on the world, right?" Julia said.

"More chaos on the world." I sighed. "Perhaps I should feel guilty, but I don't really feel bad about being complicit in ridding the world of some rapists and sexual predators."

Did the gods know all along that I was the one who would provide the last detail to complete Kareena's transformation into this new entity? Was this what they were waiting for? I didn't want to think about it.

I asked the flight attendant for a top-up on my wine.

SEVENTEEN

Sunday dinner with my parents.

It was as if Julia and I hadn't spent a month on the run abroad and the world wasn't falling apart. That past month had fallen away from us as if it were just a strange dream, a funny story to be told at supper.

I told them the story about Kareena, but left out the part about her overthrowing her father, running a rebel army, putting a hit out on her brother, and sending hit squads to kill sexual predators, of course. Instead Julia and I just recounted our overseeing the plastic surgery and forging of a new identity for a client who wanted a new life. She was a celebrity, and you could say that celebs were living and breathing demigods and demons of our material world, after all. Their lives became serialized modern myths and morality plays that we followed in the media.

Vivek was riveted by it all, as usual. My sister only shrugged, since she was quite used to my life being surreal. She just wiped drool off her baby's lips. My mother cooed about all the famous people I met on the job. She was especially tickled by the part about Julia and me posing as Kareena's managers as she made the rounds and finalized her contract to star on the variety show.

Later, while Julia and my mother were cooing over my niece with Vivek and Anji, my father and I commiserated in the garden.

"You've acted like a shaman as much as a babysitter," my father said. "You helped a woman become a goddess. That's part of your calling."

"Certainly makes for a good story to tell the grandkids," I said.

"This is looking at your situation from a certain mythical perspective," Dad said. "Or we could say you watched over a woman while she was in hiding and helped her assume a new identity to leave behind her old life."

"That's how I prefer to look at it, but I can't ignore the metaphysical angle given who I am and my relationship to the gods."

"You were doing what they asked all along," Dad said. "You seem less anxious about it all now. You used to be a bundle of nerves. Your mother and I wondered if we might have to get you sectioned."

"I thought I was headed for an insane asylum myself," I said.

"It happened to your uncle and that was how we lost him," Dad said. "He could never accept his unusual way of seeing the world. You seem to be almost at peace now. Not quite yet but I sense you're accepting it."

"I suppose I am. Better than going mad, really."

"You have no idea how relieved we are. And I think Julia has helped give you a sense of stability. You seem to calm each other down."

"Who's to say the gods didn't send her my way?" I said.

"Who indeed," Dad said, wistfully. "But what next for you? Your boss is in the middle of a scandal. Are you out of a job now?"

"Actually, I think that's resolved," I said. "The government is scrambling from all those files that got leaked. Roger has done a deal to get his charges dropped. They knew the files belonged to him, and he can help undo the damage by keeping more from leaking. In return, they'll say he was fitted up and was just the wrong man caught in the wrong place at the wrong time. All those people owed him a favor, now he's calling them in by force."

"He is a slippery man, your boss."

"I don't think he's going to be my boss for much longer," I said.

EIGHTEEN

"**D**idn't think we'd see this office again," I said as Julia and I walked into Golden Sentinels in Farringdon.

The place had been given a makeover. New computers, new workstations, but otherwise the same space we worked out of for the last few years.

"Wa-hey! Looks who's back!" Benjamin said.

Hugs all around. Everyone was home.

"So how was your workin' holiday, then?" Benjamin asked.

"Surprisingly profitable," Julia said.

"And we turned someone into a god," I said.

"Jolly good," Mark said. "You'll have to tell us all about it."

"Look, love," Julia said. "Ken and Clive tied the knot."

They held up their hands to display their wedding rings.

"When Roger got arrested, we went down the registry," Ken said. "Got Mark to witness. Bob's yer uncle."

"Congratulations," I said.

"Reckon we ought to be safe than sorry," Clive said. "If we had to go to court over Roger's fuckup, spouses can't testify against each other."

"That was practical, yes," Julia said.

"And we've got just the wedding gift for you," I said. "Fancy a sixty-five-inch telly?"

"That the one we bought you?" Ken asked.

"The same," Julia said. "We can re-gift it to you. It's nice and everything, but a bit too big for our tiny living room."

"Yeah, that's brilliant, love," Clive said. "We were thinkin' of buyin' the same model for our gaff. You'll be savin' us the trouble."

"Consider it done," Julia said. "You'll get it by tonight."

They gave us the thumbs-up. Ken and Clive were surprisingly easy to please.

"Ravi, can I have a word in private?" David said.

We went to the kitchen area.

"I'm sorry I got you tangled in all this, mate," David said.

"It's not your fault," I said. "You couldn't have seen all this coming."

"Roger was gearing up for this scheme for years. He hired me away from my old law firm because he wanted to use my contacts and my family's contacts to meet investors, then he did some deal to use the airstrip in Nigeria to fly the mercenaries out of."

"And you went along with it?"

"I just thought it was to give money and have the ear of the next leader of Gambia or Yemen or any of the weaker countries on the continent. Roger took a while to work out which country he wanted to have a hand in. I didn't think he was going to finance a whole bloody coup and take over a country through a proxy leader. That goes beyond the pale!"

"When did he settle on that plan?"

"A few months after you joined the firm," David said, and he saw my look. "It's not because of you, all right? He was just getting more and more confident in how much he thought he could get away with. He thought being a CIA asset and having friends in the government would give him cover."

"When you put it like that, it almost sounds like a rational plan, but nothing about the whole scheme was sane. It's a bit racist as well, since Roger came a cropper underestimating how savvy countries in Africa are getting now."

"You're telling me, mate. I was the one who had to write the contracts. Do you have any fucking idea how tricky it is to draft contracts that are about hiring a mercenary army, percentages of the revenue from the country's GDP and resources to be split between investors, and who gets what, and not use language that would be considered criminal?"

"Is that one reason you've been so stressed out?"

"Understatement of the year, mate. I tell you, once this mess is over, I'm out. I can't do this anymore."

"So where are you going?"

"I dunno, maybe go back to my old firm if they'll have me. My parents are a bit pissed off at me for getting involved in this whole scandal, not to mention I have to figure out a way to cover this up when I run for office in a few years."

"You're still planning on going into politics? Seriously, David?"

"It's been my plan since uni, mate. It's the only thing that would impress my parents. My brother and sister are both highflyers in business, and this is the only way to shut my family up. What's so fucking funny?"

I didn't realize I had started chuckling.

"Sorry, David. It just occurred to me that when you run for office, you're probably going to be hiring us to help you with all your dirty laundry."

David's face froze in horror. I think his whole life had just flashed before his eyes, or at least his entire career here at Golden Sentinels. David never meant anyone any harm. He was one of my best friends in university, and I wanted to reassure him somehow that things were going to be, well, if not all right, then at least steady without going horribly wrong. Unfortunately, all I could do was laugh at the absurdity of all this, and how we were both caught up in this cosmic joke. The gods were behind me laughing along. After his initial indignation, even David started laughing, because, after all, what was there left to do about all this?

"I hate to interrupt this touching moment," Julia said as she came up to us, "but Cheryl wants us to sit down for a debrief on everything that's been happening with Roger so we can get the story straight."

NINETEEN

"**R**oger was the one who ordered the guests dosed with the magic mushrooms," I said. "We've been assuming that he just wanted them in really compromising positions that he could use to blackmail them with later, but he was really after one target all along: Laird Collins."

"Same kind of play as taking out an entire airliner so nobody can figure out the real target was just one of the passengers on the plane," Marcie said.

"Roger must have been planning his revenge on Collins for over twenty years," Cheryl said. "He never stopped ranting privately about wanting to fuck Collins over like he used to fuck us over back when we were a small firm. I always thought he was being all mouth-and-trousers. Never thought he'd do this."

"Nobody did," Julia said. "That kind of thing is a bit beyond what we expect normal people would do."

"Except Roger has never been 'normal people,'" Olivia said.

"So what Ken and Clive uncovered in Nevada fits in Roger's grand plan," I said. "More than just revenge against Collins. He wanted to set up his own private military company, registered as an American business, and probably try to headhunt Collins's best people over to his own company."

"That's well out of fucking order," Clive said. "We're investigators. We don't go out and start fucking wars."

"This is not what we signed up at Golden Sentinels for," Ken said.

"Well, technically," Marcie said, "Roger would have kept his new PMC separate from Golden Sentinels."

"You're the one who ratted out Roger," I said. "It was your plan all along once you found out about the coup."

"I wrote a report," Marcie said. "As I always do, as part of my real job."

"You came up with that plan once you found out about the coup," I said. "Roger destroying Interzone would have thrown a huge wrench into your plans."

"It would have been kind of inconvenient," Marcie said. "The Company considers Interzone a reliable contractor and asset. The bigger issue was that Roger was going to mess with the geopolitical map that we spent years trying to establish a status quo with."

"I wouldn't have thought you lot cared that much," Mark said. "As long as the work got done properly. Roger was a trusted asset already with Golden Sentinels. Why would you have objected to him taking over Interzone's contracts?"

"Do I have to spell out it for you?" Marcie sighed. "Roger wanted way too much power than we would have been comfortable letting him have. Here he was with a nice private investigation agency we could outsource to, then he wanted to set up his own private mercenary army, and then he wanted to take over and rule an entire African country with rare minerals and resources that we were already trying to cultivate as an ally. We don't really need another tinpot despot on the global map, especially not one like Roger."

"Even if he was willing to play ball with you?" Benjamin said.

"We don't know that when an asset goes off the reservation," Marcie said.

"So if we step out of line, are you going to slap us on the wrist, too?" I asked.

"What are you looking at me like that for?" Marcie said. "My bosses read my report and assessed the situation, then told the British government that Roger was about to launch a coup against an African nation that was a US and British ally. The US informed them there were mercenaries about to board a plane headed their way from South Africa and got the local government to arrest them on the runway before they took off. British authorities made the call to arrest Roger and raid Golden Sentinels."

"You fucked us!" Benjamin said.

"Hey, I saved all your asses by warning you to get the fuck out of Dodge," Marcie said. "There was nothing I could do for Roger."

"You could have warned him, too," I said. "You wanted Roger to be punished because he overstepped his reach."

"Well, when an asset goes too far off the reservation," Marcie said, "we might have to remind them who's boss."

"And you can do that to us at a moment's notice," Mark said.

"Not you guys. You're my peeps. Roger, he always played all sides off each other. We put up with it as long as he didn't screw with us."

"Oh, of course," Mark said. "We're your assets. Part of your own precious network. We make you look good. Of course you want us around, as long as we don't step out of line like Roger did."

"Just don't go trying to take over what you think is a third world country," Marcie said. "They're a lot more savvy than you think nowadays."

"How many angles got played with Roger's arrest, Marcie?" I asked.

"Take a wild guess, Ravi," she said. "This is what you're good at."

Again, testing me like a teacher quizzing a student. And I couldn't help but answer. Habit.

"Roger was single-handedly trying to enact regime change and take over a country," I said. "His own private colonialist adventure."

"That's just the starting point," Marcie said, smiling.

"Africa is the Americans' gig, not his," I continued, "and conflicts with the US plans over there, whatever they are. They're already competing with China and Europe over Africa's resources. No way were you lot going to tolerate another player stepping in. So your bosses shop Roger to the British government, embarrassing rogue player detected, and the prime minister ends up owing the US a big favor."

"It's bad enough we have China investing in huge chunks of Africa," Marcie said. "The whole continent is a web of interlocking moving parts. One wrong move and the whole place could go up like a goddamn roman candle."

"So Britain can avoid a big political scandal," I said. "And the US gets to remind Britain that they're the ones in charge, they're the ones with the best intel. Thanks to sterling work by you, one of their best and brightest."

"I couldn't have done it without my network of assets," Marcie said.

"Did you know this all along?" I asked Cheryl.

"I've suspected for a long time," she said. "I'd been keeping records, doing my own investigation into what Roger had been up to."

"And you were working with Marcie on this?" I asked.

"I passed what I could uncover to Marcie. She went and confirmed the rest. When she said that Roger was going to have to be shopped, I didn't object. He's been going too far for too long."

Cheryl had been quietly watching Roger and holding back all these years. Given how little we knew of her past as an investigator and Roger's partner, I'd suspected she might have been the deadliest of everyone at Golden Sentinels. And she'd bided her time until she held all the cards in the end. Cheryl didn't set out to hold the winning hand. She'd planned to possess the entire deck.

"We're still in fuckin' limbo," Benjamin said.

"Not for much longer," Marcie said. "Just wait a bit."

"Hang on," I said. "Did Cheryl plot all this with you?"

"Dude," Marcie said. "Cheryl was the one who really had your back. When I gave her the list of guests at the party, she pieced together what Roger was planning since she kept all the minutes for when he first met them at Golden Sentinels. Her first priority was to keep you all out of the office when the cops came for him. You owe her."

"Well," Mark said, "she's the boss now."

"Fuck Roger," Benjamin said, sulking. "Fuck him in his greedy face."

Benjamin was taking this harder than the rest of us. He might have considered Golden Sentinels his home more than anyone else there. He'd helped build its technical infrastructure, tested all his computers and gadgets through the firm, after all.

"So what next?" I asked.

"Cheryl wants to get the firm up and running again," Marcie said. "That's going to be the first priority."

"Isn't the agency tainted now?" I asked. "We'd be hard-pressed to have any business after Roger's arrest and all the information we leaked."

"Nobody knows it was us," Olivia said.

"Oh, Ravi." Marcie smiled. "You're forgetting my specialty. I already have the PR offensive planned. We're rehabilitating the staff. Golden Sentinels may be dead, but it'll rise like a phoenix from the ashes under new management and a new coat of paint."

"Only Roger-free, I take it?" I said.

"That's the only change, and I'm sure nobody's going to object," Marcie said. "Cheryl still has the client list, and she's been talking to all of them, reassuring them they haven't been exposed by Roger. She's the one who's kept the real secrets safe all these years while Roger was playing at being a playa. The clients know she's the one who really kept the place running, and you guys were the lifeblood. Goodwill goes a long way. And I'll keep all your names out of the headlines. Roger will beat this rap and stay out of prison, but he won't be allowed anywhere near the agency from now on."

"Is he still going to be one of your assets?" I asked.

"He's gonna come crying to me, cap in hand, once he runs out of money paying his lawyers. He's going to lose his expensive house up in Roehampton, his wife is going to divorce him and take their annoying dog with her. He could still be useful. And we'll be keeping him on a much tighter leash."

"Roger won't be happy about that," Mark said.

"Some assets are easier to manage if we keep them hungry and desperate," Marcie said. "Roger was a naughty boy and needed to be gently whacked on the nose with a rolled-up newspaper."

"When he susses out you were the one who shopped him, he's going to want to get even," I said.

"Him and what army?" Marcie said, the smile not reaching her eyes.

TWENTY

"I'm surprised you're still here," I said. "I thought you'd be off to Hong Kong working for your father by now."

"I've done a lot of thinking in the last few months since I saw him," Olivia said. "And I thought, why should I go crawling back to him asking for a job when I can do far more interesting work here?"

"I always thought you were slumming it here," I said.

"Darling, my family's been dealing with money for generations," she said. "Even with my dad blacklisting me, I could have talked my way into a job in finance if I wanted to, hid in the shadows and moved money around. But I'm more than just a banker. I'm a hacker. I dig up people's secrets. I gather information. And I keep it for a rainy day. That's why Roger hired me all those years ago when no one in the daylight world would. I learned that information is worth more than money. It's information that moves all that money around. So I'm not slumming it here, Ravi. One day, I'll leave Golden Sentinels and strike out on my own, but I won't be working in a bank or finance. I've made my peace with that. I'll be dealing not in money but information. And my firm will be bigger than my dad's bank. This is where I need to be. This is where I get my power. You get your power from your gods. I get my power from information. Benjamin, for all his sarky, larky cheekiness and love of mischief, understands this. That's why we're together. Julia understands you and where she needs to be, and that's why she's with you."

"Did we just hear the secret origin of a supervillain here?" Mark said.

"If we did, she's *my* supervillain," Benjamin said, beaming with pride.

"You do love handling time bombs," Julia said.

So they were all back and they were staying, setting up Golden Sentinels again, installing new computers, restoring the database, and putting the security measures in place, good as new. The place had that New Private Detective Agency Smell.

"Golden Sentinels 3.0!" Benjamin said.

"Well done, children!" Roger strolled in, beaming. "Yes, releasing *all* the files was a bit much. I know that was Ravi's idea, but no matter. What matters is all that silliness is behind us, we can get back to work!"

He looked dapper in his tailored suit as always; the stress from the last time I saw him had vanished and the used car salesman charm had returned. The air in the office was different, though. The gods had gathered to see how he would react with us having none of his usual bullshit.

"What?" he said. "No smile for Daddy?"

You could have cut the tension in the air with a knife. He seemed oblivious, or pretended to be, keeping up that used car salesman grin of his.

"See? Didn't I tell you I'd make this right?" he said. "My friends came through, after all. You're lookin' at a free man. Throwing out all those files to the public did the trick, Ravi. I always trusted you to weaponize doin' the right thing, didn't I? Put the fear of God into the lot of 'em. We're home free."

We turned away and continued to restore our files and accounts on the computers.

"Right, Cheryl," Roger said. "There's just the formality of resuming leadership of the firm."

"Roger," Cheryl said. "Let's talk in your office."

Before long, Roger was shouting so loudly that we could hear him through the thick glass.

"But we agreed!" he cried. "You'd hand back half the firm when this blew over!"

"You agreed," Cheryl said. "I never said anything of the sort. I am not giving back ownership or control of Golden Sentinels to you. None of this lot trusts you anymore."

"Is this your revenge? Did you wait twenty-five years for this moment?"

"Did you really think you could waltz in here as if nothing happened after putting all of us in jeopardy?" she said.

"It was just an inconvenience!" he said. "I always put things right. You know me better than anyone."

"I know you too well. And this was the last straw."

"Look, I'm sorry, all right? I'm sorry we didn't get married. I'm sorry you lost the baby. I'm sorry you never met a bloke who treated you well."

"I never needed that. What I need is here and I'm holding on to it after you nearly destroyed it," she said.

"Who got you off the drugs, eh?" he pleaded. "Without me, you might have killed someone! You would never have found your place in the world! Look, Cheryl, everything turned out fine! Why do you have to punish me? Do you hate me that much?"

"I don't hate you," she said. "I don't love you anymore either. I just want you to go."

He stood there in shock. The gods stood outside the glass walls of his office and were filming him and Cheryl on their phones.

"Roger," she said. "You are going to say your good-byes, nice and smooth, and then you're going to walk out the door. If you don't, I will have Ken and Clive remove you. They have my permission to physically remove you all the way to the stairwell and to do with you as they please before sending you on your way."

"Very funny, love." Roger tried to laugh. "Pull the other one, eh?"

"As the head of Golden Sentinels, I'm asking you to leave."

Roger looked at her in disbelief. Had it all come to this after over thirty years? He and Cheryl were practically kids when they first met in the eighties and ended up together solving cases, ducking and diving, fucking and skiving. They nearly got married but didn't. She nearly had his baby but didn't. There was another life they could have had together but didn't. She suggested expanding and he scouted out Ken and Clive. He made contact with the Americans and they put Marcie in touch with him and she brought in lucrative contracts from the CIA, on condition that she became his handler. They needed a bigger office and she found this one. He hired David as the firm's legal counsel. She scouted Mark. He hired Olivia. David brought me in for an interview. Roger hired me while Cheryl was at first hesitant. I met Julia, who then came on her own for an interview with Roger. Now he was being cut loose.

Roger had been outplayed at last.

"We've all had enough," she said. "You nearly sank all of us this time. I've put up with your schemes and your bullshit for thirty years, and I founded this firm with you. It's as much my baby as yours. The difference is I don't hold my baby in the fire and snatch her back right before she starts to broil. We all took a vote here. It's over, Roger."

He was speechless, in shock.

"What am I supposed to do, then?" he said, sheepish.

"Don't you have friends to call and pitch another scheme to?" Cheryl said, already over him. "Or have you burned them all?"

Considering we'd released *all* his files, it would seem Roger was now without a pot to piss in. Those files had thrown up all the dirty little secrets Roger had been holding on to for decades. Everything from affairs, to secret love children, dodgy tax returns, financial records, recordings that many law enforcement agencies would love to hear, murders covered up, insurance scams from arranged accidents and property damage, illicit financial deals with sheiks, with Russian oligarchs, with bankers—all about Roger's friends and enemies alike. These were all on-the-record documentations. I'd had enough. We all had. Was he going to rage? Turn on his charm? Make another speech? There was a sense of the end here. He was all played out.

Roger walked out of his office, now Cheryl's. The color had drained from his face.

"This isn't the end," Roger said. "I've still got moves to make. You watch. I'll bounce back like I always did. It'll be like when I first started. Who's coming with me?"

We continued to work on our computers.

"Ravi?"

"I've got a backlog to restore here, Roger," I said.

"Come on, son. I brought you in here."

"I'm not going anywhere. In fact, once I finish helping with opening up the office, I'm quitting."

"Come on, you can't be serious. After all the work you did for the last three years? All that training, the knack you have for the job, and you want to just chuck it?" Roger said, almost pleading.

"I never liked getting one over on people," I said. "No matter how bad they were. I never liked burning down their lives, no matter how much they deserved it. That's what you don't get, Roger. I don't get my jollies from having power over people. It was a job and I didn't feel good doing it. It was never about having power for me."

"Ken? Clive?" Roger said. "How about it, lads? We can do things old-school again, without having all that technology, just stay on the streets with a phone, a contact list, and you can give a kicking to whoever you don't like."

"Nah, we're fine here," Ken said. He and Clive stood there like slabs of granite, immovable, and the hostility wafting off them made Roger back away from them.

"Mark?"

"Cheryl brought me in," Mark said. "I'm sticking with her, if you don't mind."

"Benjamin, my boy—?"

"Fuck off, Roger."

"Olivia? I'm your godfather—"

"And you nearly got me arrested," she said. "You're lucky I haven't told my father about that."

"Marcie! Surely you don't want me off on my own?"

"Roger honey, you went off the reservation with that coup attempt. The Company hates having to clean up after an asset. We're going to have to review our arrangement."

"This isn't the end," he said. "I built this firm and its branches from scratch!"

"With my help," Cheryl said.

"Well, I can start again!" Roger said. "I've done it before, I can do it again! Just you watch. Don't be surprised if you see a new firm on the map! And don't forget, I know all the secrets about this place! I know all your secrets!"

"And we know yours, Roger," Cheryl said. "Do you really want to play Mutually Assured Destruction with us?"

Roger stood there, deflated, trying to find a move, an angle, a play, but he was coming up blank. He looked around the office, as if saying good-bye. Then he turned towards the exit.

We pretended not to, but we watched Roger walk out, trying to hold his head high, but there was a sag in his shoulders, a weight in his step, the loss of nearly thirty years leaving a hole in his core. He was back at point zero, but with too many years. The gods waved him on as he went out the door, Kali dancing behind him in celebration of the types of chaos Roger was going to be getting into from now on, untethered as he was from Golden Sentinels and us. Lord Shiva waved his blessing. The show would go on. Cheryl turned her back at last. Ken and Clive went back to their desks and picked up the *Mirror* to look at the football results. Marcie got a call on her mobile from a client, about his latest crisis with his wife and his bit on the side. Benjamin went back to his work desk and started to take apart a drone. Olivia was back typing away on her computer. I saw Kwan Yin standing over Olivia. Everything did work out, after all. Kwan Yin looked over at my gods and nodded at them in greeting. They nodded back.

"That Roger," Cheryl said. "He knew from the start he would one day use you to burn his 'friends' if they sold him out. He always had a knack for reading people."

"Hard to believe he had me as part of his long game all along," I said. "I was his backup when none of you wanted to talk to him."

"What he always forgot," Cheryl said, "was that his own weapons could be used against him. You're not a double-edged sword, Ravi. You're a nuke, and anyone who uses you gets blown up, too."

"In the years I'd been working at the firm, I kept burning down people's lives on my cases. I never thought I'd end up burning down my boss."

"You're a weapon, Ravi," Cheryl said. "As all of us are here. You were just the most unpredictable one, and Roger's hubris was thinking he could control you."

"Karma's a bitch," Kali said, and giggled.

What a fucking year it had been. It was over. I was knackered.

"Are you thinking about leaving us, Ravi?"

I looked at Cheryl and the gang. She looked at me with neutral eyes. Everyone else was going about their own business. Mark had found his groove between working here and moving from squat to squat contributing to the anarchists he was in cahoots with. Ken and Clive were going to continue going after the people they thought deserved it. Benjamin was happy with his tech and causing mischief with Olivia. David would eventually leave the firm to run for office as an MP once the heat from all this coup mess blew over. Marcie was happy with her personal network of assets here. That left me and Julia. Julia wasn't passionate about the job, but it gave her something to do to take her mind off her addiction.

"Would you like time to think about it? If you want to be free of all this, I'll understand," Cheryl said.

Two years ago, I might have given my answer on the spot. No more racking up karmic debts with the lives I ruined, no more anxiety about the erosion of my soul, no more stress over the laws I was bending or outright breaking on a case. Now I wasn't so sure.

Suddenly, Roger poked his head through the door.

"Sorry to interrupt, children," he said. "But I forgot one last thing. You might want to check the news. Something's going viral, as they say."

Cheryl switched on the wide-screen TV.

". . . news conference this morning," the newsreader was saying. "Viewers might find the following footage disturbing."

The screen showed the president of the United States roaring like an overgrown infant, tearing off the last of his clothes and his underpants. His bum and his cock were blurred into a mass of pixels for the sake of whatever good taste was left there. He was bug-eyed and sweating like a sprinkler, wanking himself into a frenzy as Secret Service agents struggled to get him under control. "Oh my God! Oh my God!" some journalists were shouting as everyone in the room scrambled to avoid getting spattered by the president's fluids. The camera became increasingly wobbly as the president started flinging his feces and fluids at it and everyone. Then the Secret Service agents finally tackled him to the floor of the shit-stained White House press room and the camera cut out.

"The uncensored footage is on the Internet," Benjamin said, looking up from his computer.

We huddled and watched it several more times.

"Does his behavior look familiar?" Mark said.

"That's how Laird Collins and the guests were acting at the mansion party," Marcie said.

"After they were doused with the magic mushrooms," Julia said.

"How did Roger know this was going to happen?" I asked.

"And who could have gotten close enough to douse the president?" David asked.

"Wittingsley," I said under my breath.

Everyone heard me.

"How the hell did he pull that off?" David asked, blinking. "With all the vetting and security checks?"

"He's an expert at infiltration and guerrilla warfare," Ken said. "Old Tel would have found a way."

"Nice one," Clive chuckled.

"The White House has gone into press blackout," the newsreader on TV said, "and speculation is rife about the future of this presidency. After a year of turmoil and scandal, and now today's incident, many are questioning whether the president can stay in office—"

Cheryl switched off the TV.

"Come on, guys," Marcie said. "This isn't funny."

But she couldn't hide her smirk.

This had happened because I let him go those months ago when I had him cornered.

"Hang on," I said. "Why would he do this? Someone must have paid him. It's too much trouble unless he had assurances he would get away with it."

"Now, who would do that?" Marcie said.

"They're probably going to blame the Russians," Olivia said. "When in doubt, Americans like to default to that."

"Roger, did you—?"

I turned to the door, but he was gone. He just had to have the last word and make a grand exit.

We watched the footage again. We couldn't tear our eyes away. Maybe we were in shock. The days and weeks ahead were going to be full of headlines and pundits weighing in on this scandal, how the president could possibly survive the optics. This was uncharted territory. Chaos would be the key word in the media. A sense of things falling apart. One article would go on at length about the president turning the White House press room into a biohazard zone. The president's people would try to push the line that the video was faked using sophisticated software, but the witnesses would begin to publish their accounts, including the reporters who were there. They would all be gleefully writing about the president losing his shit in front of so many cameras and the state of his mental health. They wouldn't even know what he was doused with. We did, and from what we'd seen, there could be long-term mental health repercussions. "All part of the cycle of death and rebirth," as Kali would say.

I looked at Marcie. She saw me looking at her and just winked. I remembered her old lesson about the intelligence agencies fucking with presidents they didn't get along with, but this was off the charts. Had things gotten that bad with this one? This was chaos on a scale I could never have foreseen.

I heard a round of applause behind me. None of the others seemed to hear it. I turned around and saw the gods gathered on the office sofa, laughing and clapping.

"Well done, my son!" Kali cried.

Lord Shiva nodded at me in approval.

Ganesha pumped his fist in the air.

Bagalamukhi threw her head back and drank in all the secrets in the air.

Louise blew me a kiss.

I felt light inside, like I was ready to float out of my body.

"Julia," I said. "Fancy a holiday? Better yet, how about we go on a proper honeymoon finally?"

"Where?" she asked.

"Someplace warm, with a beach, preferably with no extradition treaty."

"I assume the gods are coming with us?"

"Almost certainly."

"Louise will be joining us," Julia said.

"Of course she is," I said. "What do you fancy? Bali? Phuket?"

"How long shall we be away?" she asked.

"As long as we want," I said. "Maybe forever."

EPILOGUE: THAT DAY BY THE BEACH

Julia and I lounged in our deck chairs, looking out at the sea.

We'd been there for over a month, with no contact with the firm, no phones, no going on the Internet. I shan't tell you where, in case we ever want to come back. We rented this modest little hut by the beach and spent our days taking walks in the sun, breathing in the air, then sitting down to record my account of the last three years in these books. Julia spent the evenings in our guesthouse typing it all up on her computer and uploading the files to a secure server on the cloud as additional backup. I let Julia name the journals. She called the first one "Her Nightly Embrace" after the case where we first met; the second one "Her Beautiful Monster," which seems to be what she calls me from time to time; and this, the third one, "Her Fugitive Heart," which . . . I'm not sure, but I think she was trying to tell me something there. When we weren't writing, we consummated our marriage, again and again and again. This was as close to bliss as we were going to get.

Julia sat on my lap as we lounged on the beach.

"What am I to you?" she asked.

"My wife. My better half," I said.

"What else?"

"My recording angel."

"Too right," she said, and glanced up at the road. "Looks like playtime's over."

We watched the woman in the light blue sundress get out of her rental car, take off her high heels, and walk up the beach towards us, her shoes in her hand. The office we rented the beach hut from had phoned earlier and told us that an American lady had called looking for us. We hadn't told anyone at the firm where we were going. My parents and sister knew, and we talked to them on the phone once a week, but I'd asked them not to tell anyone where we'd gone. Of course it would be Marcie Holder who tracked us down. She probably didn't even need to ask my family. I knew she would find us eventually.

"She really is a spy through-and-through, isn't she?" Julia said, waving at Marcie.

"I think it's her religion," I said. "For all her talk about serving King and Country, Marcie really worships at the altar of Espionage. It's a priesthood all in itself."

"Well, she's spent the last couple of years inducting us into it," Julia said.

Marcie finally reached us. We exchanged hugs and fixed her a margarita.

"Ready to come back to work?" Marcie asked. "Everybody misses you back in London."

"Did Cheryl send you?" Julia asked.

"I'm here on my own steam," Marcie said. "Cheryl wasn't going to force you. She knows the shit you went through and how you feel about it. As far as she's concerned, you don't owe her anything, and if you don't go back, that's cool. She's so—what's that term Benjamin likes so much?— Lawful Neutral about everything."

"Cheryl has always been very kind to us," Julia said.

"Oh, and everyone back in London says hello," Marcie said.

"I dunno, Marcie," I said. "I feel like I've had enough of all the dirty tricks, the blagging, the social engineering, the lies. We're tired of being a pawn in Roger's games, then in your games. I never liked causing all that chaos, unlike everyone else at Golden Sentinels."

"But you guys are so good at it," Marcie said. "So what are you going to do if you quit?"

"Maybe work in a bookshop," I said.

"Seriously?" Marcie laughed.

"Actually, we were thinking we might write books," Julia said. "Total escapism. Nothing to do with reality. Period romances with vampires. Bodice-rippers."

"Now I know you're shitting me," Marcie said. "Come on, kids. Think of all the fun we could be having again, this time without Roger making you do stuff you're going to feel guilty about."

"Marcie, you're just going to bring us work that makes us feel guilty," I said. "You sold Roger out. How can we trust you not to do that to us?"

"Because you're not going to go off the reservation and try to take over a fucking country. That already puts you in my good books."

Her smartphone buzzed. She looked at the text and tapped out a reply.

"Well," she said, "I'm not here to force you to do anything you don't want to do. And oh, a friend wanted to talk to you."

The video chat rang on her phone. She answered and handed it to us.

"Hey-hey-heeeey!"

I winced.

"Ariel," I said.

Her face beamed from the phone screen, chipper as ever.

"You guys still on vacay or you going back to work soon?"

"We haven't decided yet," Julia said.

"Maybe I can make you a better offer," Ariel said.

"Isn't your boss the one to make the offer?" I said. "I already turned him down. There is no bloody way I will ever work for him."

"You don't have to," Ariel said. "The offer comes from me."

"What are you talking about? Where's Collins?"

"Oh, you haven't heard? Laird Collins is on an indefinite leave of absence from Interzone. Has been for over a month."

"Where is he now?" Julia asked.

"In the loony bin," Ariel said. "And it wasn't completely voluntary."

"What the hell happened?" I asked.

"Turns out he never really got over those magic mushrooms all those months ago. He was getting more and more erratic, talking about seeing gods and trying to see them again."

Marcie and Julia both looked at me.

"I thought he would have recovered eventually," I said, a bit too defensively.

"Dude," Marcie said. "Some people never get over a bad trip. It can totally change their personality or create serious mental health issues."

"Mr. Collins was becoming increasingly unfit to lead the company," Ariel said with some relish. "He couldn't make any rational decisions on contracts, which was hurting the company's bottom line. He was saying some wacky things in board meetings, which got them worried. The last straw was when he was arrested running around his neighborhood naked calling for God and the gods to talk to him like before. His wife got him committed on a fifty-one-fifty, which is the rule for someone who might be a danger to other people or themselves. The board voted to remove him from the CEO position of Interzone."

"I suppose I should be sorry to hear that," I said.

I was not.

"You really did a number on him, Ravi," Ariel said.

"Me? I'd been trying to talk him out of that stuff. I was trying to stop him from going off the deep end at the mansion."

"Babe, your very existence did it for him," Ariel said. "He was convinced you held the secrets of the gods, and he wanted that, too. He kept trying to headhunt you because he wanted to have a shaman working for Interzone. When he got doused that weekend for the first time, he experienced what it must be like for you, talking to the gods all the time. Turns out not everyone's cut out to talk to the gods. It scared the shit out of him in a way that insurgents and suicide bombers never did. He blamed himself for being weak when he got to talk to the gods and wimped out, and he wanted a do-over. He was trying to figure out how you didn't go crazy from having the gods around you all the time."

"Did it ever occur to him that I was just insane?" I said.

"Are you kidding me? Babe, you're usually the sanest dude in the room. You have the entire Hindu pantheon hanging around you and you can just act like they're a bunch of annoying tourists hanging around in the background. Poor ol' Laird wanted that for himself, and that led to his downfall. When they arrested him, he tested positive for enough psychoactive drugs to fill a pharmacy. He was formally and officially diagnosed as psychotic and schizophrenic. Ergo, indefinite medical leave."

There was so much glee in Ariel's voice as she told us all that. Should I have felt happy? Relieved that a menace had been removed from society? There were plenty more people out there in the same line of business as Collins who were just as bad, if not worse. No, I felt no joy at this, only a nagging feeling that things weren't about to get any easier for me.

"So where does that leave you?" I asked.

"Me? You're looking at the new head of Interzone," Ariel said.

What the fuck?! What the actual fuck?!

"I'm wearing fancy dress suits now instead of khakis and camo."

I was screaming inside, but outwardly I was still calm. Barely. Once again, Ariel had snuck up on me when I least expected it.

"How did you manage that?" Julia asked, since my vocal cords had frozen.

"Well," Ariel said, "I do have a law degree, you know. On top of combat experience, I knew how to navigate the legal paperwork and political negotiations that Interzone had to deal with for our contracts. I've been working with our attorneys to keep the company going since Laird went whack-a-doo. Add that to the fact that the men in the field trust me, it wasn't hard to put my case to the board. My track record spoke for itself, including my title as liaison with other private contractors like Golden Sentinels, where we ran a whole bunch of successful operations together that earned the company a bundle. All that was thanks to me knowing you and us working together, Ravi. I totally owe my promotion to you."

Oh fuck. Oh fuck. Oh fuck.

"That's why the board voted me in," Ariel said. "We're going through a rebranding right now. Don't want people to remember us as the company where Laird Collins lost his marbles, so from here on, we'll be called Luminous."

"That's just bloody marvelous," I said.

"I know, right? Kali loves it."

"Congratulations," Julia said.

"Thanks. You wouldn't believe the other candidates Jarrod and I had to murder to bag me the top dog spot."

"I hope you're kidding," I said.

"You two kids have been a positive influence in my life," Ariel said. "It was Kali who brought us together, all the way back to the first time I met you on that plane from New York. It was like everything clicked for me right there."

"Considering you say Kali talks to you," I said, "how does this make you different from Laird Collins? Or me, for that matter?"

Ariel chuckled.

"For one thing, I don't believe in fulfilling God's mission to bring forth the Rapture, which is a huge relief for the board. I don't believe we're heading towards Apocalypse. I believe in continuity. Life goes on, and we just do our bit in that equation. And unlike you, I don't have any angst about being in touch with the goddess of death and rebirth. She's totally my jam."

On the beach, Rudra laughed, patted his stomach, and bellowed his fearful roar of righteous fury. Kali laughed and took a photo of him on her phone. I think I was having a bit of a nervous breakdown at that point, but I still held Marcie's phone in my hand. Julia's hand tightened on my shoulder to steady me.

"Sounds like you're going to be busy, what with so much work coming in," I said. "I guess we won't be seeing much of you from now on."

"Are you kidding, babe?" Ariel laughed. "I'm in a position to offer you and Julia a job."

I tried desperately not to wince.

"I'm not sure about having you as a boss," I said, croaking a bit.

"If you really are quitting Golden Sentinels, you can come work for me. Unlike Collins, I'm not going to convince you that there's any grand cosmic plan. I don't believe in any prophecies or the Second Coming. I'm not working to bring all that down."

"You just like the chaos," I said.

"You get me, Ravi. We're the same. We're both Kali's children. Destroyers of worlds. We bring the chaos. And now I get to pick where. So how about it? I promise all the chaos you can ever ask for, millions of dollars to be made, and we can have threesomes anytime we want. Or twosomes. Whichever you guys feel like. It'll be our own private Idaho here."

"Is that what you've been after all along?" I asked. "A space of your own aside from the war and mayhem you wage?"

"It's not separate, Ravi. It's *part* of the chaos. That's how I roll."

"It's not how I roll," I said.

"Oh, please. You're the master of making chaos. You just don't like to admit it. The gods just wind you up and off you go. It's your default mode. You can deny it all you want, but you are beyond natural at it. You can cause total fucking mayhem with just one word or gesture. We've all seen you do it, and you don't have any malice or evil intent as you do it. You're spinning the wheels of death and rebirth, burning away lies and crap like Kali's right hand. You do that from micro to macro. That's your function in the universe, babe. Get used to it."

"If that's true, then I should do nothing at all," I said. "Just retire someplace quiet where I do no harm."

"That's not gonna happen and you know it, Ravi," Ariel said. "Eventually you'll get bored and you'll do something, and the ripple effects take care of themselves. You might as well go where you're needed most."

"You're right," I said. "You're absolutely right. That's why I won't work for your company, whether it's called Interzone or Luminous or War Crimes 'R' Us or whatever the hell you call it. I don't do security or combat. I'm an investigator. I look for answers."

"I figured you'd say that," Ariel said. "That's why we're going to be part of each other's lives for a long time."

"I imagine you're going to be busy behind a desk now that you're the head suit of the company," I said, hoping this might be true.

"Maybe," Ariel said. "But if I get bored, I can just put on the camo and go out in the field with Jarrod and the boys to shoot some fools in the head."

"I was afraid you'd say that."

"Anyway, I just wanted to check in, say hi. Marcie figured your vacation was gonna be over soon, so I just wanted you to know I'm here and it's a whole new world."

"The more things change, the more things stay fucked, eh?" I said.

"Ain't that the truth?" Ariel chuckled.

"You're forgetting something about destroying and death," I said. "Kali is also about rebirth. Something new always has to come out of the mess you and I make. That's the other half of the equation that Kali represents."

"Yeah, but somebody's gotta be the one that breaks the eggs first, babe."

"Ariel, I want to be perfectly clear. I am not going to work for you. It's bad enough worrying about what kind of shit you're going to wreck. It would be even worse to be taking orders from you."

"Yeah, yeah. You protest too much. I'll be waiting. Oh, and your Cheryl might want to rename the agency, too. Rebranding is everything in a fresh start. Later, babe."

She hung up.

So that was it. Marcie's play. If Julia and I ever wanted to stay safe from Ariel and what she might drop us into, we were better off staying at Golden Sentinels under her and Cheryl's protection. It was bad enough before when Laird Collins wanted me for my soul. Now Ariel wanted me for my body as well. Marcie must have sussed this out all along. She didn't have to plot anything, merely let events unfold. I began to realize that underneath her cheerful PR agent façade, she took an insidiously Zen approach to tradecraft.

"You know you don't have to blackmail me into staying, right?" I said.

"That's just how all the chips landed," Marcie said. "I'm not going to force you to stay. Cheryl would be happy to have you since you two are good investigators. She won't force you either."

"Well," Julia said. "I think we've been on holiday long enough. I was starting to get bored anyway."

"Julia—" I said.

"You said it yourself, Ravi," she said. "What else is there for us to do? Go back to London and apply to work at the local bookshop?"

I glanced at the gods. They all gave me the thumbs-up. Even Louise winked at me.

"I think we should get some things clear." Julia turned to Marcie.

"Totally," Marcie said.

"As I see it," Julia said, "it's in your best interests to keep Ravi and me close and safe. We know far too much. And you need us as your off-the-books backup."

"I'm betting there's more you're about to ask for," Marcie said, her smile not wavering.

"Just one," I said. "Don't get us killed."

"Dude, I'm not going to send you into a situation like Vanessa van Hooten. You need to be used properly. Lookit, you managed to fuck up both the US and British governments without even getting near them. That's major chaos. You're a nuke. It means I keep you away from anything that causes you to blow up. I know that now."

I saw Louise standing over Julia, resplendent in a Versace one-piece swimsuit and sunglasses, her hair fabulous, backing up her younger sister. Every now and then, she glanced at Julia and smiled, beaming with sisterly pride. She looked over at me and winked.

"All right," Julia said. "We're not blackmailing you, just asking for assurances. Not from the Company, but from you. As a colleague and a friend. That you're not going to sell us down the river. We keep working, because it's what we do, and thanks to your training, we're bloody good at it. That includes not selling us out to the likes of Ariel at Interzone or any other entity that might pop up."

"You're my peeps," Marcie said. "I keep my peeps safe."

"Until you decide we're not your 'peeps' anymore," I said.

"Because if Golden Sentinels comes a cropper again," Julia said, "we go down and you go down with the rest of us."

"And don't I know it," Marcie said, sipping her margarita. "But hey, the firm is Cheryl's now. That's a safer pair of hands than Roger's ever were."

"We do make a good team," I said. "And I'm sure Cheryl has her insurance policies squared away even better than Roger ever did."

"I looked," Marcie said. "I don't know where she keeps them or what they are, and we know she's scarier than Roger. She trusts me even less than he did. Cheryl will never sell you guys out."

"So we're joined at the hip, then," Julia said.

I raised my glass.

"To Occam's razor," I said.

"To Occam's razor," Julia and Marcie said as we clinked our glasses together.

The formalities over, we sat and watched the sea. I watched the gods dance as they waited for what came next.

And that, dear reader, is my tale for the time being. Do you see why Julia and I needed to keep a record of everything now? If you're reading this, it means something might have happened that caused us to release it so that everyone would know. I hope we're still around. I hope I'm still working. And if I am, Julia and I will probably keep writing it all down.

The gods are watching. They're raising a glass to us and to you. We're riding on the wheel of karma that just spins and spins, and we continue to do what we do because that is all we are. And I have a feeling Julia and I might be filling up even more journals and hiding them away for insurance.

Wish us luck. I shudder to think what might lead to you discovering and reading all this.

But for now, we're going to sit here, drink our margaritas, watch the gods frolicking on the beach, and contemplate the forever-blue sky.

And wherever Julia wants to go, I will follow her fugitive heart.

ACKNOWLEDGMENTS

To the friends who provided advice, sounding boards, lessons and discussions, the same friends who kept me going through the entire trilogy:

To Michael Wilson and Minh-Hang Nguyen, whose lessons continue to inform the world of Ravi.

To Roz Kaveney, who grappled with her own writing issues as I did at the same time, across oceans.

To Richard Markstein, who kept me fed both mentally and literally.

To Alan Moore and our chats about gods and stories.

To Avra Scher, who kept me honest and whose suggestions always made things better.

ABOUT THE AUTHOR

Adi Tantimedh has a BA in English literature from Bennington College and an MFA in film and television production from New York University. He is of Chinese-Thai descent and came of age in Singapore and London. He has written radio plays and television scripts for the BBC and screenplays for various Hollywood companies as well as the graphic novels *JLA: Age of Wonder* for DC Comics and *La Muse* for Big Head Press, and a weekly column about pop culture for BleedingCool.com. He wrote *Zinky Boys Go Underground,* the first post–Cold War Russian gangster thriller, which won the BAFTA for Best Short Film. He is the author of the previous Ravi PI books, *Her Beautiful Monster* and *Her Nightly Embrace.*

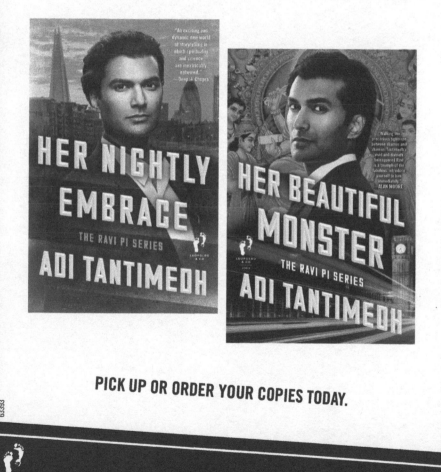